STARLITE PULP REVIEW #2

Pulp done right.

FEATURING:

Frank Bill ✦ Michael Bracken ✦ Alec Cizak ✦
'Doc' Clancy ✦ Eric Esquivel ✦ Gabriel Hart ✦
Eric B. Hunter ✦ Nolan Knight ✦ Veronica
Leigh ✦ Nevada McPherson ✦ Daniel Pyne ✦
Brian Townsley ✦ James Whelpley ✦ J. Wiltz

Starlite
Pulp

For information, contact : editor@starlitepulp.com

Site : www.starlitepulp.com   Instagram : @starlite_pulp

Youtube channel : youtube.com/@starlitepulp

Book and Cover design by Tristan and BT

ISBN: 979-8-218-19936-4

first edition: June 2023

"“The outcome of successful planning always looks like luck to saps.”

Dashiell Hammett

“The real angels in our midst always have tarnished wings”

James Lee Burke

“Yeah, when the train left the station/it had two lights on behind/the blue light was my baby/and the red light was my mind.”

Love in Vain, Robert Johnson

STARLITE PULP REVIEW #2

LINER NOTES

What you've got in your hands here is a collection of 14 stories, in various
sub genre's, all falling under the umbrella of 'pulp.' Our goal here at Starlite is to
put together collections of the very best pulp we can find—whether that means
Science Fiction, Noir/Crime, Horror, Adventure, or any other variation.
Problem is, so many submissions we receive don't fall into any individual
category—very few are simply 'noir,' for example (although that is probably the
most common). In this volume, we've put together an outstanding lineup of
writers, and we're proud to bring this pulp fiction to you.

The first story in here, 'Things are Different in Dallas,' (without
dropping any spoilers here) is an original take on a situation and scenario that
many of us know quite well. Its subject is, shall we say, a cultural touchstone.
Next is 'At Play with the Wasted Gods,' which takes the reader to a
postapocalyptic wasteland where men on horseback pass hollowed carcasses of
long-dead vehicles and scavenge for food and items to barter with—well, just
read it. It's something. Frank Bill brings us the third story, 'The Cruel Road to
Purgatory,' a meditation on the concepts of loss, forgiveness, and recovery. 'The

Starlite Pulp Review #2 2 Family Tree' by Review vet Michael Bracken is Southern Gothic at its finest. Veronica Leigh brings us 'Of Two Minds,' a 1930's crime story in rural Indiana, involving a female sheriff (a rarity in those times, certainly) and a difficult deputy. 'Made in the Shade' by Daniel Pyne takes us to Korea in 1952, and while it's difficult to pigeonhole, it's a damn good yarn. 'The Sick and the Well' takes a look at home-buying amid misrepresentation, mega-corporations, and the US Army. 'Misarriage' by Alec Cizak is a hostage negotiation tale that leads to a personal reflection, and 'Dalhart' by James Whelpley sees a prison guard with some difficult ethical decisions. 'Scattershot' by Nevada McPherson is a story about bounty hunters. Except it's really about freedom. We think. Would you rather be lucky or good? E.B. Hunter answers that for us in 'Luck.' 'The Gentleman and the Brat' and 'The Damn Fools' seem like war stories, but, again, can't really be confined to that box alone, as you'll see. 'Cracks in the Sidewalk' is a deeply New York tale...told by a lifetime Los Angeleno.

We don't ever start a volume with any kind of agenda, and this 2 nd Review is no exception to that, but we're pretty damn proud of this collection. We hope you enjoy reading it as much as we enjoyed putting it together. As always, feel free to contact us at editor@starlitepulp.com with any comments, and do us a favor and leave us some reviews out there! Until next time, here's to the blank page.

BT, Starlite Pulp, Spring 2023

THINGS ARE DIFFERENT IN DALLAS
BY J WILTZ

Today is the 12th of September, Jack. I suppose I should say Happy Anniversary. If you were still here, we would have given each other silk and linen today. I'm sure you would have read off a long letter from Klejman in that boyish, animated way of yours. That's one thing I'll still give you credit for. For all the ways you failed as a husband, you were always at your best on these days—any occasion you could turn into a performance, really. Herve' said it was because you were a Gemini; he said that *all* Gemini men are virile and brilliant. He might have been right about that. I think you could have charmed just about anyone—except for Nehru. It used to worry me sometimes that we were so mismatched. You'd be lighting up the room at some party or a convention, and I'd be fretting about candles and seating arrangements, or sitting alone in the car waiting to go home. You must have felt like you were living with a boring old lady.

But you never tried to change me, Jack. Somehow you even let your father and Judge Morrissey talk you into marrying me. I remember sitting across from you at Martin's Tavern in Georgetown, booth number three. You asked me to make an honest man of you, and of course I said I would, even though I knew your reputation. Ben Bradlee's father said you were a fearsome girler who had to make love every four hours or you'd start having headaches. Fishbait told me to stay far away. But what chance would any young woman have stood against you, Jack? You were so handsome and intelligent and clever and influential and all the other things which most men simply aren't. And of all the young girls you had falling down around your knees, I was the one you had chosen. I knew it would never be perfect between us—you said yourself that there were no loyalties in politics, only colleagues—but I was willing to accept that. I loved you enough not to expect perfection.

Still, you caught me off-guard when we landed in California after the honeymoon and you suggested I go on to Washington without you. You said it was nothing to be concerned about. You just needed some time alone to relax and collect your thoughts on the beach. "Things are different now," you said, "we're married" – though by then we both knew how little that bond really meant to you, didn't we? Lest we forget, I was engaged to be married when you first met me at the Bartletts. A few weeks later and I would have been the wife of a stockbroker—Mrs. John Husted, Jr.—but that didn't stop you from pursuing me.

So what could I do, Jack? I flew back to Washington and pretended you'd stayed behind to procure some sort of surprise gift for me. It seemed like something you might have done. I'm sure your many experiences with the fairer sex had taught you how much we love surprises—especially when they're expensive. As your wife, wasn't I entitled to think you might surprise *me*? Wasn't my heart entitled to break when you didn't?

And a year later, when the Addison's had you lying face-down in a hospital bed, paralyzed with infection, wasn't I at least a little entitled to wonder whether any of your honeymoon girls would have seen you through it the way I did? You know as well as I do, they would have betrayed you and left you helpless. But I was there every day, reading to you, teaching you how to paint, and writing the outlines for *Profiles in Courage*. Could any of your other girls have won a Pulitzer for you, Jack? Or translated all those books on Indochina? I wanted to ask you sometimes. I bit my tongue until it bled. And when you walked out of that hospital room and into the arms of countless one-night stands, I walked right behind you.

You said things would be different when the baby arrived. That was the great promise that carried us through to Chicago and the party convention where the whole world fell in love with you. I was by your side for all of it, the young senator's faithful and somewhat lovely wife. I watched all of them get lost in your charms. Poor Adlai, he became nothing more than a footnote in your grand biography. It was *you* they saw when they looked into the future. "Joe's boy will do great things for the party and the nation," they said. And naturally I shared their optimism, because I knew exactly how they felt about you. My American de Gaulle. How we all loved you.

And oh, how you must have loved yourself to abandon me as soon as the roles were reversed, when *I* was the one lying in the hospital, hemorrhaging and infected. I begged you not to go. "Please, Jack, not now. I can't be alone if it happens again." But you just kissed me and told me I'd be fine and left for Europe without me.

So, Arabella was born in Rhode Island while you were off sailing somewhere in France. She'd already been buried in Newport before you made your first call home. You told your father there was nothing you could do about it. "The child's passed away and Bobby's arranged the burial." There was nothing left to be done then, no reason to leave all those giggly young blondes in Cap d'Antibes. It was a tragedy, you said, but there was nothing you could do about it.

You can't imagine what that does to a woman, Jack. I sat in the darkness and prayed I'd never see you again. I hoped your boat would capsize or your plane would crash, and that you'd suffer for hours before you died. If I'd been able to speak with you, I would have asked you quite plainly what I had done. What sin had I committed that made you so willing to overlook my very existence?

Then I thought about what you had said—how things would be different when the baby arrived—and how I had failed to bring that moment to fruition. The baby *hadn't* come, or had come and gone, and you were no father. It was the second time I had failed to give you a family, Jack, and I understood it perfectly. You weren't there to hear it, but I told you through my tears that I was sorry and that I forgave you. It seemed to me that we had failed one another.

But love is patient. And a year later we had Caroline, the greatest of all our second chances. It was hopelessly naïve of me, but, just seeing you with her, so playful and exuberant, it really gave me hope that we had started over. When you told everyone at Hyannis Port about your plans to seek the presidency, I started to imagine you on your worst behavior. A whole year of campaigning away from home. Hotel rooms and front desk girls. Secret knocks and secret liaisons and Secret Service standing by on lookout. *But no*, I reassured myself, *things are different now. He wouldn't betray a daughter he adores and the wife who gave her to him for a few meaningless embraces.* And even if *we* weren't enough to break you of your old habits, there was always the election to consider. How could you possibly keep your dalliances in the dark with so many bright lights shining down on you? I knew better than to think about it too much. I just smiled and toasted you along with all the others. Then I spent the next year telling everyone who would listen that you could be trusted above all others to be the leader of the free world.

You repaid me with that receptionist, Pamela Turnure, and that other woman, Judith Campbell. I was told there were others as well. "This is your friend. Would you like to come up later and have a few drinks?" How many

New York nightclub performers were privy to *that* little line, Jack? I heard some of the lucky ones became regulars that you'd put up in houses and pay late night visits to. Such a rarity for you—those women you wanted to see more than once.

But the anonymous ones were always the easiest to forgive, out of sight and out of mind. I knew as much about them as they knew about me – at least until January. I would have given anything to see the looks on their faces when they found out their dashing new president did indeed have a First Lady, and a beautiful daughter, and a son on the way. "Ask not what your country can do for you," you implored them, "ask what *you* can do for your country."

And what about your First Lady, Jack? Did you ever ask what you could do for me, after all I had done for you? I came through a blizzard, pregnant, to stand by your side at the inauguration. Joseph Alsop started inviting you to his soirees again because of me. And when de Gaulle said you were incompetent after the Bay of Pigs, I was the one who propped you back up. It wasn't *your* name the people were chanting at the Porte d'Orleans. "Vive *Jacqueline!*" they said. I think it was even louder than the one-hundred-and-one-gun salute. "Vive Jacqueline!"

But I wasn't in Paris for my own glory, my love. I was there because you needed me – wife, protector, diplomat, and moderator, speaking for you in perfect French. I won the heart of France and handed it to you with Lacrasia gloves. No easy task for one of your others, I'm sure, but I was the one you were once smart enough to choose. And for you, my dearest one, I could have done anything. It was a victory you had to concede. You told the press at the Palais de Chaillot that you were nothing more than the man who had accompanied me to Paris. Vive Jacqueline. They really loved me.

And right there for a minute, Jack, didn't you love me too? When Malraux brought the *Mona Lisa* to the National Gallery because he thought so highly of me. Or when we re-furnished the White House and stripped out that awful pink and green Eisenhower bathroom, laughing the whole time about the way we were turning the place into a palace. Or that night when I told Khrushchev not to bother me with his propaganda: "Oh, Mr. Chairman, don't bore me with statistics." Didn't we all have a great laugh about that? Weren't you proud to call this chic young debutante your wife? Even the Soviets found me enchanting, Jack—just like Nehru and Ayub Khan and those beautiful women who sprinkled me with rosewater in India.

But you preferred Mary Meyer. That was my reward for international diplomacy. Betty Spalding told me it happened in the playroom with our children's toys scattered all around the floor. I wish that had surprised me. But by then I knew nothing was sacred for you. I just thought, *how appropriate. Spending time in the nursery with one of his little playthings.* A woman in love learns to look the other way, Jack. I'd become an idealist without illusions, as you liked to say. I might have gone on like that forever if it weren't for your birthday party. That was the bridge too far.

You probably wouldn't even remember this now, but I told you I'd be riding Ninbrano in the Loudoun Horse Show that weekend. And I could tell from the way you looked at me that you were so ashamed. You said, "Do you really think that's a good idea? An elegant woman riding in a horse show? Does the thought of that not embarrass you?" You tried to make it seem as if you were concerned about *my* wellbeing—as if there was any sort of shame or bad public relations in riding a majestic animal.

But what did you do just as soon as I was gone, Jack? You let that neurotic blonde sing "Happy Birthday" to you in front of everyone at Madison Square Garden. That childish parody of seduction. I've seen and heard it too many times now: "Ha-ppy birth-day, Mis-ter Pre-si-dent..." The audience laughed and cheered. They thought they were watching a movie star playing a role for her commander-in-chief. But you and I know the truth, don't we? She was a mistress openly flirting with a married man, and you were blushing and giggling about it like a little schoolboy. I couldn't let that stand, Jack. Your affairs had caused me enough pain behind closed doors, but this one was on full public display. And you were embarrassed that I was riding a horse.

That woman was dead eight weeks later. I've always been good at putting things together on short notice. The newspapers said it looked like an accident or a suicide – too many barbiturates at one time. I hear she was lying naked on her bed with a phone in her hand. Do you know what I said to her as she was dying, Jack? I said it was a shame she wasn't invited to *my* birthday party the week before. She would have seen you at your best if she'd been there.

Maybe she could have sung her little song for me.

Sometimes I wondered if you knew. When we lost Patrick, you knelt by my side in the hospital, weeping and begging for my forgiveness as if I were the Blessed Mother. You told me things would be different from then on, that you'd finally be the friend and husband I deserved. And I could swear I detected fear in you, Jack. I could see it in your face when I was drawing targets on your forehead from behind my veil at the memorial service. I could hear it in your voice when you were telling Caroline and John-John where their little brother had gone and how he would always watch over them from Heaven. You told them you would do the same one day, but hopefully not for a long, long time. I always loved watching you with them, Jack. I gave you three more months because of it.

And then November. I'm not really sure where to start about that. It's become a sort-of cottage industry here. People study it like one of those modern paintings, trying to decipher what it all means. You'll hear one person say that Oswald was a patsy—it was the CIA that did it, or the FBI, or Sam Giancana. Then another will say no, Johnson did it so he could be president and take us to Vietnam. I've heard it was Castro down in Havana with his big cigars. It was the Russians, a lone gunman, a magical bullet, a man with a black umbrella, the South. You know how Americans are, Jack. The country wouldn't exist without a deep distrust of authority. Let the people think they've been lied to and they'll churn out conspiracies forever.

But the last place they'll look for answers is in the woman sitting next to you, screaming, "Oh, my husband! My poor adulterous bastard husband!" I wore your blood on my clothes like a trophy, and the only thing they noticed was that they were pink Chanel and had a pillbox hat. I gave you the most elaborate victory party of a funeral, and all they saw was sweet little John-John saluting his father's casket.

So where does this leave us, Jack? I'd like to think there was a peace made between us in November. I felt it as soon as the bullets ripped through you and tore away your thoughts of all the others. Mary Meyer and Judith Campbell and Pamela Turnure. Your hotel girls and Inga Arvad and all those honeymoon blondes in California. The girls in El Morocco and the whores of Cap d'Antibes and even your little birthday girl. They were all gone—blown away—so that for one brief shining moment, I had your undivided attention.

And with my brownish-black hair dipping down into your dying eyes, I spoke to you without words. *Hell hath no fury, Jack. I thought you would have learned that from one girl or another by now. Now I see that it had to be me. Go ahead and close your eyes now, my love. Rest easy knowing that I've held up my end of the bargain: I've made an honest man of you. You told me time and time again that things would be different, and now I've made it true.*

Things are different in Dallas.

AT PLAY WITH THE WASTED GODS
BY BRIAN TOWNSLEY

He rode above them like loss was tended to and fettered only by those mired in the mud of the Earth herself, their shadows pooled about the stems of the mare's forelegs as the semblance of affliction. Each to each their breath hollowed the day.

The beggared masses holding out hands scabrous and empty, rising up and rising down as the day entire. His boots rode heavily in their spurs, the clink and shuffle of harness a music to the unlearned. When a ramshackle bearded miscreant laid his foul hand upon the flank of the beast, the man atop reared his gunbutt and spoke forth a violent diction of carved walnut that caved the man's face sending teeth into the crowd like coin. As if its equal.

*

Heading towards Dixon the two travelers fell upon a man attempting what may be described as mischief with a soiled bedsheet and an Oak. It was hooked upon a limb and there fastened weakly with the tether itself the man. The two riders sat their horses on the sloped earth and watched as the man failed upon his given task.

"Dumbass caint even hang hisself," one said.

"Reckon we oughta help 'im," said the other, who chuckled then through teeth brown where there were teeth at all.

But their help was unwanted and as they rode forth the man hurried his preparations knowing the sheet unworthy of such an action given the particulars and his attempt upon their arrival reeked of childish vagrancy. His face wore the look of one unable to hang even himself.

They sat on their horses and one pointed forth.

"See you're having a time with that," he said. He caverned something solid from a molar and spit. "I ain't never seen such a thing. We figger'ed we might help. We've, uhhh, got some experience with that kinda endeavor."

The first man laughed at this as if it were the first dirty joke told.

"I don't need no help," the man blurted, all terror and impotence, fidgeting with the bedsheet in the hopes that this current approximation of a knot might be the necessary equation.

"Well," the second man said, unsaddling and pulling his rifle clean from its leather scabbard. "If you don't need no help, I should kill you for your damn incompetence," he said. "Aint never seen no man work so hard to kill hisself. It's like you aint got no fuckin brain atall." He spat into the grass as if to illustrate some point.

The man with the bedsheet wound about him froze then, unsure then or now of another action. The wind drove westward effortless and with it hints of lavender and faroff wildfire.

The first man chucked his horse closer until he circled the man with the bedsheet and thereupon seized the knot attached to the branch and wound it about the pommel of his saddle. There is no look quite like a man who has failed to kill himself yet does not desire assistance in the same matter from another. This man wore it now, all panic and confusion and idiocy.

"You clean?" The second man asked, as he walked towards the man in the bedsheet and the tree. He looked at the man closely. The suicide man had on a pair of cutoff dungarees and nothing else. His hair was red, or ginger as they referred to it in these parts, and his skin a milky translucent thick with herds of freckles.

"Beg pardon?" The victim asked.

"You heard me, boy," the second man said, and pulled the knife from his belt then. It looked a blade larger than a thigh itself when pulled free.

The man astride the horse jerked the sheet then as a fulcrum from the branch it lay upon and pulled. The bedsheet lifted the man from his feet and he kicking asunder in the appeal for gravity. And seconds ago, the hope to be free from it.

"Now Eugene, that aint polite atall," the second man said, ambling towards the jerking man in slow strides, and smirked like a child. "Now, I done asked you a question, boy," turning his attention to the bucking figure in his foreground, limbs flung without gravity and alien to their possessor. "Is you clean?" He asked, and waited a moment for the answer that did not come and stuck his knife then to the hilt in the man's sternum, the tip run clear through his back and the tiny birthmarks there. Tributaries of blood pooling on the below.

The stuck man's eyes widened and then faltered. "I'mma take that as a yes. Fucker," said the second man, his wrist at rest upon the sunken leather handle of the knife. Then he split the belly of the man southward to the groin with a two-handed effort and pulled the knife out briefly amongst the chorus of innards sung vertical and after parting the spilled intestine like curtain grabbed the man's balls and rived them clean from the body. There was a single cry given skyward, and then a sharp intake of breath that gave birth to silence for the dead. The hatted man looked at the knife then in his hand and smeared the remains on his pants and resheathed it. His right hand held the man's ballsac and amongst the bloodied chutney he pulled from it two testicles by their aborted stems and tossed the remainder to the earth like so much afterbirth. One larger than the other and that a rounded polyp that would fetch a good price. He raised them then to the horsed man and smiled an infernal blackened almost toothless celebration.

When he rehorsed he pulled free the jar from its bearings and placed the testes among their collected brethren in the whiskey sauce. The second hunter tossed the sheet over the man in a sort of halfhearted burial for the damned.

Before they rode off the second man unhorsed and walked again to the incompetent corpse and unsheeted the body like he hadn't done it to begin with. He looked skyward as if some message there sent and bent then and began skinning the man whole.

*

They squatted that evening under the stars. Firelit. They each had words to say but kept them inward and thus their silence in common. The oak behind them hung a shadow not unlike a man's from a branch like some drapery in the wind, bending and floating in weightless accordance.

The wood popped and split in the firelight, embers and smoke rising like souls of the fallen to some halfbreed god. The second of them spit free a cork from a bottle of whiskey and drank until it ran down his chin in rivulets dammed and manipulated by his beard. The first, Eugene, held forth a pan over the fire and strips of meat therein humming in rebirth. The men would grab from the pan as the meat was ready and they tossed the strips from hand to hand to minimize the heat before testing the lean and gamey flesh on their lips. The stars above them shone like pinholes in some aged and rotting cloth.

"What you gon' do with that there suit," the first man asked, finally, nodding between bites at the skin flapping in the breeze.

"I'mma sell that there mansuit. Whatchoo think?" The second man shook his head as he finished speaking, so inane did he consider the question.

"They aint gonna be nary a taker. I mean, I sure as shit hope there is. But I don't see it, me," the man responded. "Now them balls we got jarred in the whiskey, and them pickled ones too, now that's a different tale altogether." He nodded to confirm the truth of this for his own audience.

"You got any smoke?" The second man asked, ignoring altogether the comments on the worth of their stash.

"Naw. No chew, no smoke. Aint got a thing but my balls at this point," he said, and reached down and shook them once complete in their sac for good measure.

"Well, shit," the second man said. "I been having dreams bout that adjectival bitch again. That's how I know she gone' buy that suit. Aint nary a doubt in my head."

"Huh," Eugene answered, and shook his head at the thought of it. "Aint seen her in a time. Guess she got her fill of teeth," and he laughed at his own joke if no other arrived. "Come to speak on it, I was wonderin why you's skinnin that boy back there."

The second man heard this and did not respond. When he had finished the last of his meat he lay back until he was flush with the earth and spoke: "We'll be in Dixon tomorra. This the way this shit gon' unfold. I'mma meet up with Tannie and we'll discuss. We'll—negotiate." He used the word like it had more than its four syllables. "She can use that skin, trust me you. Tole me last time I's there myself. Wiccans and medicine ingredients or some shit. Anyway, then we're gonna have us a time. Think about the whore you want, you. Shit, you can probably buy that three-titted bitch this time. If my suit sells." He paused amidst the night and its brilliant silence interspersed with brief choruses of crickets chirping. "I'mma sleep now," he finished.

Neither man said anything for a time. The moon shone full like a drunkard's face and the shooting stars shone like an airshow from some past or present unthinkable now as history condemned.

*

Dixon appeared on the horizon amid horizontal waves of fallacy. Neither of them would have believed it there at all if they did not know that it was exactly as shown. The midday sun was unmerciful in its glory. The flag of skin hung limp from a staff on the saddle of the second man, still seeing opportunity for drying where none was allowed. The blacktop they rode on besmirched with the carcasses of rusted out automobiles longsince rendered impotent. Remnants of longago flags tattered and hung from the windows of some.

The highway descended to the town and its ornamental lampposts hung now with corpses at various states of decay. The leg of somebody now legless stuck footfirst onto a sharpened stick as if a pogo game had gone wrong. The men ignored such warnings, as they were welcome and they knew it and the town knew it and anybody crosswise would know it soon enough. A man in rags sat on the hood of a Firebird, its painted visage barely recognizable amidst the years of rot. He laughed periodically at nothing, the bellylaugh of one unable to discern reality or too mired in it to react otherwise.

They rode to the cantina and unhorsed and tied their steeds to the post. Each gave the man tending the horses a coin which he accepted openhanded, his other hand armed and privy to the instructions his eyes might communicate. The duty of watching horses was a privileged one against the hungry delegation of human ruin about this town. Any town. The men unsaddled their bundles and unhooked jars and wares and weapons until the mounts themselves naked besides harness.

Before departing inward the man spoke. "That you, Theory?"

The second man stopped. Looked for the first time upon the horse valet. "I know you, chief?"

The valet kicked his boot into the dirt and shook his head. "A time ago," he said. "Name's Williams. We rode an RV westward some. Had some trouble with the natives if you recall. Long time ago, I reckon."

Theory looked down in recollection. "RV have writin on it?"

"Yessir. Hell I believe it said The Chosen Man, or One, or somesuch altogether bullshit."

"Well shit yes, I remember that. It did say that. The Chosen One, spraypainted on the side a' that bitch like an adjectival advert. We hooked the hitch upto a team a horses and rode that trailer out to Vegas. You ever been to Vegas?" Theory asked Eugene, looking sideways.

Eug shook his head no and spit.

"What happened after Vegas?" Theory asked the valet.

"I got into some trouble," the valet answered, and kicked at the ground again. One of the horses whinnied and pulled the reigns sharply. A man in rags was approaching. His face was obscured by a hood but the hands and forearms that dangled as he stumbled forward belonged to man alone. The valet turned his attention there and raised his .45. "Boy, you best get the fuck outta my space," he said to the citizen. The man paused and extended his hands towards the horses in a gesture of longing and exhaled something akin to an old testament sigh. All longing and instinct. The valet shot once, directly into the hood covering the man's face, and said citizen fell earthward tumbling over and landing bent about one of his legs awkwardly, as if some new stretch imagined and now practiced. Yoga for the dead. They all looked at the figure once, his revealed face scabrous and boilmarked and now with a dime-sized hole in the forehead.

"Trouble, you said?" Theory asked.

The valet looked up and picked up the conversation again: "Yup. Y'know. With Sinatra. Big black fucker got it in his head I was out to take one of his women."

Theory leaned back and laughed at the thought. It was an uncommon occurrence, and came out more hack than laugh. "Well," he said, as he had finished, "were you?"

"Yup," the valet said, and laughed then as well. "Y'know—he got like fifty. Figgered he wouldn't care...anyway, Tannie brought me here. Helped me out. Tendin horses beats the Zero, man."

Theory nodded to that, knowing truth where truth sat. "Well." He put his hand on the man's shoulder. "You take care of them horses now. And I'll keep you in mind. Can always use a shooter on some jobs." Theory nodded to Eugene and together they walked into the saloon and left the horse valet to tend his thoughts.

Tannie was behind the bar and she smiled at them upon their arrival. The bar itself had one time been a postmodern meat market, the tabletops a brushed stainless steel and the bar itself the same. The lamps that hung above the men and their table were globes, many of them altogether removed or in some manner broken. Two of them complete as eggs by Theory's count. The floor had been a gunmetal gray tile once but was now caked in sawdust and bootprints and time forgotten.

The men reciprocated what passed for smiles in return to Tannie's and set their booty on the bar. The gathered therein took notice from whatever card game or narrative their mind was set and thus one eye now on the pair and their jars erect and sacks slumped upon the wooden bar. The barkeep ambled over in a sort of onesided shuffle so voluminous an effort seemed required. Had they dispatched the eight foremost philosophers of the land they could not reason nor classify the girth of the woman before them save the commonly held perception that she was nothing short of the bastard daughter of the gods of war and gluttony. But that was tomfoolery and each man in his own heart knew that such a pairing could never birth a creature so cunning. Tannie was wider than she was tall and yet stood above any man in the place. She was thought to be immortal and the terrorizer of dreams. Many in the room would testify to such given anonymity.

"You two look like something that belongs out there, you," Tannie said, and nodded at the leprous masses walking the streets out the window. Her voice thrown about the room like hollowpoint molasses.

"Been workin," Theory said. "Since you won't get the hell out my head."

Tannie shrugged, all feigned innocence. "I need somet'ing," she said, "I know who to go to—I go to Theory. This is wrong?" She pinched the man's soiled bearded cheek then with a hand no smaller than a horseflank.

Theory pulled his cheek away and thrust a hand into the leather bag sorrowed on the bar and from it produced a suit of skin. Tannie grabbed it immediately and held it by the shoulders for inspection. All eyes in the bar now on the cored manskin. She turned it to the back and then ran her finger over the dried maroon caked to the underside like those things best left to the imagination. "This," she said, and nodded, "this is fine work, Theory. You think I don't know who to go to?" She waited for an answer and then laughed at her own victory. Finally she lay the suit down softly on the bar like a child.

"What else ya got for me, you?" She asked. Her hair was hidden in a white bandanna the size of a bath towel and halfmoon earrings dangled from her lobes. She smiled after the question and dimples cratered her cinnamon-colored cheeks.

Theory put forward the two jars of testicles, one pickled the other whiskeysoaked. Tannie picked up the pickled first, brought it close to her eyes and slowly spun the thing clockwise. Two small cucumbers and an egg swirled about the lifegivers. "Ok," she said, and put the jar down. "I can sell this," she said with a single nod. "Nothing too impressive, I might add, but I'll take it." Her accent made it sound like some other word entire. "And the other?" Theory handed her the other jar and she repeated her curiosity. "The small ones?" She asked with eyes wide, and looked at each of the two men, like a pendulum.

"Toddlers," Eugene answered. "They's three sets in all."

"No," Tannie answered, as if the number three somehow unattainable.

"Yup. All clean."

Tannie placed the jar upon the marble and looked at the ground. She said nothing for a time and the bar itself seemed to hold its breath in anticipation. Theory reached for the skinsuit, some semblance of holding onto one's own should things go awry. As if Tannie had seen this she raised her head then and smiled at them. It was a smile born of fable and sinister youth.

"This, she motioned to the bartop and its articles, that you have brought me is lacking in quantity, no? But the quality, ahhh, there you have few equals." She fingered the skin on the bar and shuddered quietly, inhaling like the want of an addict.

Theory spoke: "You know how this gon' go now, Tannie. Until we set the adjectival price and bleed the deal you caint be fondlin all over my shit. You see what we got, and it here's a good lot. Them whiskeyballs there themselves'll fetcha somethin lengthy." Theory spoke in a measured tone, firm yet careful—fully aware that angering Tannie in her own bar could very well lead to neither Eugene or he leaving at all. Like a sober man questioning the wasted gods.

Tannie's expression was one of amusement.

Outside, the dark fell like a shout. The beggared masses stared in the windows and the light there.

"What'cha askin for, puppet?" She asked, and licked her finger after she had worked loose a clotted chunk of dry matter from the skin.

Theory looked skyward though no sky was there to be seen. The wooden ceilingboards were a poor substitute but a decision made nonetheless. "I want four things," he said. "One, I want to know why this skin. Two, Eugene gets whatever the hell he wants here tonight. Three, I get a bath, a clean room, a supper worth a damn and a bottle of whiskey. And four, you get the fuck outta my head." He glared at her despite the danger.

"Such willfulness," she said, and shook her head in some semblance of coy appreciation. "I'll gives this one here, and she pointed a sausage finger at Eugene, whatever he like. And you, my little butcher, get the cleanest room in the house. No disturbances!" She shook her finger in his face to show him her understanding. "And any bottle a whiskey ya like, you. Food, no problem," and she shook her hand dismissively at the idea. "As for your head, puppet, I will do what I can." Then her voice lowered: "But you aint gettin no answer as to the skin, boy. That is for Tannie and her sisters only. I like you, Theory, but you just a bullet aimed in the direction I want." She waved her hand twice as a flourish. "You take that, or you get that skin outta my bar yourself." She smiled and the night hid in her dimples.

Theory knew that everyone in the bar had heard the terms, and should he choose to walk from the bar with such a deal he and Eugene would be set upon by every man armed before they reached the archway. Set upon like the wretched souls waiting outside for a chance more than fate. For just as she could not take what did not yet belong, the negotiated deal was now possession to any man in ownership of said items. Theory looked about the room and the men there holding cards and bottles up as if otherwise entertained. He knew he wouldn't make the door. He was also sure that he and Eugene could clean half the population, if pushed. But what he really wanted was some reading, and a night's sleep.

He slapped the bar once. "Ok," he said. "I'll take that bitch of a deal." Eugene clapped his hands once and raised them in a sort of victory salute. Theory turned his back to the bar and knuckled his hat off his forehead. "Shiiit," he said, and exhaled like some gamble had been won to which he alone were privy.

*

The third floor room he was given was ornamented in longago maroon paint
that was peeling and cracked. The blackened hardwood was worn smooth and
forded in footfalls. The room was given two windows, one south and one east,
wholly paned despite the expectation. The lamp on the nightstand was held
together with black electrical tape and provided a single bulb in a flickering
delineation of light. It was, however, by Theory's way of thinking, better than a
fire on the flatlands or his back against a tree. He still kept near fully clothed
and his gun beside him but figured somewhere aslant and without genesis that
he was safe as houses under this roof. It was a gift of a night from the
bloodborne chaos that ruled his life. Time was he'd have been with three
whores downstairs with a lampshade on his head shootin bullets into the wall
while barebacking a midget. That time, however, was now Eugene's, and
Theory stretched wide the knuckles of his hand and the wrinkled scars of age
that crisscrossed the skin there. He opened the bottle and spit the cork onto the
floor. It smelled of apple and coriander and burned the nostrils like an epiphany.

He reached into his knapsack and there a leather strap strangling three
thin hardbound volumes like a schoolboy would have carried. Once. Very few
boys these days, and schools a rumor at best. He loosened the bindings and set
the three books onto the bed. He felt almost giddy with possibility. These had
been a perk from a smash and grab some months back and he had been unable to
set upon them since for fear of other eyes about. There was a collection of short
stories by a man named Pynchon, a collection of pulp fiction, and a book of

poems by a man who called himself Simic. Relics from this world, entirely unconnected to his own. He ran his calloused hands over them and settled upon the third tome, a 20th century compendium of poems known once for their ironic wit and droll musings. He threw it on the pillow and kicked loose his boots and took a draught from the bottle enough to drown a child. Then he lay back on the bed and broke the seal of the binding, the spine creaking in a glee of its own.

When Theory was a child his father had prepared him for this world. He learned to fight with weapon and without, he learned strategy playing moldy board games with makeshift pieces, he learned to ride, and he learned the power of words. His father had learned from his father and his father a teacher himself. Reading was in the blood, he would explain if asked. He knew few others with the ability. Sinatra, of course, and his librarian. Tannie, certainly. Most knew basic words, the kind written on walls or signs. The Gods, or so they were referred—it was rumored they had warehouses of the things. But theory doubted it. Which made these books here more of a payment than Tannie could possibly match. Priceless in their own way, and thus a burden in themselves. Especially because if anybody in the building knew that he had them he would have to leave a trail of bodies to keep them.

*

Later, he was contemplating the worth of a poem about a world war from well more than a century ago when the light went out. It did not flicker, or hang in the desperate attempt at life but simply was not as before it was. Theory sat up and by feel alone placed the book atop the others, began to wrap them again in the leather noose. He could hear the breath from his nose as if a horse as he re-booted, slipped his coat on, and hatted himself.

All about the room silent as the deaf. Theory slid to the side of the bed opposite the door and drug with him the books and his semiautomatic as if his children. He waited, and in return the bottomless night brought forth more silence. He leaned his head against the mattress in his frustration at the omnipotence of time. The ash we will become. Seconds breathed and became minutes, and Theory began to curse himself for his paranoia.

He stared at the window south and the stars given skyward, those symbols and stories passed down from mud to concrete of fathers and sons, creation and destruction at once naked and blasphemous. Now, only light. The handle on the door creaked upon its bearings and in rolled a sphere thrice until it stopped near the foot of the bed. The door closed as quickly as it had opened and the night still again as it is wont to be.

Theory counted to ten and stayed behind the bed. Nothing exploded in the blackness, no doors opened, no guns spoke. He crawled on hands and knees, keeping the gun at the ready and dragging the books, to the rolling object. It was, of course, Eugene's head—his eyes were still open and gazing lazily at the wall though the incision at the neck smelled still of burnt steel. Theory lay the leather strap of books down and picked Eugene up by his hair to examine if anything foreign had been placed in the neck and it was then he heard the boots upon the staircase. It was the sound of the inevitability of order. There were at least two of them, perhaps more, and with this knowledge he laid Eugene's head down and picked the strap of books up. The room was black except for the starlight and he discerned upon the windows and with that jumped feet first through the south panes and whatever lay below. It had proved a guess but whatever gods were left granted him an awning above the first floor entrance and so his fall was hearty but not without some level of grace. He landed upon his back as if shat out the machinery of birth and at once saw a man of uniform tending the front door. He fired quickly and the man's brainpan exited the rear of his helmet like projectile vomit.

Williams the horse tender appeared then from the corner of the saloon riding a mare with Theory's horse in tow bucking like anything with spirit given orders until he saw his leader and thus whinnied and bent foreleg for accomodation. Theory sat upon his horse then and pressed his hat down on his head and nodded at Williams, spit out a 'Fuck!' for good measure and, pistol in one hand, books in the other, wondered at the absurdity of security and his own foolishness one to the next. He shot once at the night sky for no reason he could defend and rode west as if all of the devils themselves followed. And perhaps they did.

They rode hard until their horses refused and sat then under a night sky slotted with shooting stars like music and wished for the arrival of a new day while questioning the desire for such a thing as if madness were melody and

tragedy a thing unlearned.

THE CRUEL ROAD TO PURGATORY
BY FRANK BILL

A single headlight ignited the dark. T-boned Tharp's Chevy Silverado with the splash of driver's side glass. Hood and grill tore, crunched about the steel frame. Bulldozed Jezebel and Tharp into a tumble from the back-road-blacktop until it combusted into a mess of timber. Explosion of powder burn from air bags marring flesh. Unmoving, their outlines lay with the sound of sizzling liquid from all things mechanical beneath the hood of each vehicle.

Time stalled and faded....

Suspended upside down, rush of fluid to the face and brain, sounds were hallucinatory. Creak of a door. Heft of weight against the ground. Lungs flexing for air. Feet crumpling for distance. The violining of crickets, owls and cars far beyond the country roads.

Awake, Jezebel was awake, how long she'd been out, her mind rushing for pieces of the puzzle she found herself in. A mild breeze scattered the sound of leaves across bare roots and dirt. Eyes batted. Breathing sped to a rhythmic beat of blood circulating through her frame. A pant of panic. Hanging upside down. The warmth of the dead and her wet hand patting his shape, grabbing at his thigh. Pulling at faded Levi's. Fingers dug into a muscular forearm, loose as a night crawler and soaked with self.

Trickle of lights strobed in the night with the pat of booted feet. Mumbled speech came undeciphered. Jezebel's mind was in the same condition as the truck, a wreck.

Hand reached, touched Jezebel's thigh through shattered glass. Startled her. She hung in shock. Strapped in. A male voice spoke from outside the Chevy to her, "Mam? Mam? Keep still. EMS is on its way."

Twist of her neck. Pain. Ache of adrenaline. Jezebel reached once more. Squeezed the thick forearm. Her face wet. Warmed from a bump or gash, she called out to him, "Cooper? Coop?" His nickname, what everyone called him.

No reaction. No reflex to either pronunciation.

From outside the Chevy the male voice spoke once more, "Mam? Stay still, please. You been in a accident. Mam?" Tharp Cooper's face, her husband, a hauler of stone for the Harrison County Quarry, she couldn't find it. Couldn't find his complexion. If she could see it. Look into his emerald eyes, she'd know everything was going to be okay.

It wasn't.

Aftermath was, the memory of loss wrung her of worth. Haunted her most on nights when her blonde mane, straight shoulder length, natural, not dyed but bound up in her do-rag hanky, bumped to the grunt and thrust of chemical stained skin that weighted and perforated her 125 pound frame. Longing to feel something other than blunt and dead inside.

Eyes clamped. Mind drifting, reliving each and every detail of the wreck while her heart tormented for something she'd never get back. Something tossed, melted and mangled. Rectangled in an overpriced box some six feet into the soil where souls deviated to heaven or hell, if you held that type of faith.

She did not. Had lost hers somewhere between Maker's, Jack or Jim. Bringing the clarity of life into focus after that night. He was inanimate. Gone, no more.

Now, heated breath stained by copious amounts of coffee. Fingertips smudged by smoke, running about her neck, started towards her scarred cheek. "No fingerin' my goddamn face, Arvin." Jezebel exhaled.

Arvin, the weighted sack of puss and wrinkles that never got the wet from his ole lady, Doris, since their daughter, Meme, died in a car accident. Missed nearly six months of work at the chemical plant. Near drank himself to death, so the rumor mill went. Had her buried not twenty feet from the kitchen window of his house in Doris's flower garden so he could wake up every damn morning, see her with a fresh cup of Folger's and Old Forrester.

He was the only thing available, getting coffee in the break room when she had that urge that came on like a matrix of caffeine and ephedrine rimming one's bloodstream.

Like Jezebel, Arvin wanted to feel something, 'cause loss did that to a person. Handicapped their senses to feel, to live life.

The factory was full of them. Stories of the defunct and ruined. Misfits and bad luck turned to suicide or murder, it was a never-ending laundry list of men and women who'd not wanted college. Just wanted to earn a good wage with benefits and retirement. Found the harsh realities of living. Jezebel fit right in, being a single mothered widow.

The grunt came deep and bulbous. A contraction of stiff-shaking. The heft of mass that rolled to the passenger's seat tremoring. Dickie work pants handcuffed about the ankles of mossy shins coated with a sweaty crust. His cock flaccid, shrunk as quick as the seed he'd dropped into the shriveled latex that he could barely remove with a shaking grip. Winded, he tossed the deflated balloon of goo out the truck's window to the lot's heated pavement. Wet beaded and trickled from crevices of loose skin about his bulldog face. Oreo colored locks glistened within the lamp's quartz lighting where they sat in the back corner of the parking lot.

Four nights a week, Jezebel parked here out of eyeshot to foreman's, knowing she'd get that urge to feel something. The other three she was off work. Usually drinking at a local dive in town cashing in on the drink specials.

Pants pulled and belt buckled below the slops of his veined-belly, Arvin glanced to Jezebel, removed a Skoal tin from his pocket, pinched a chew of shaved hair-like tobacco into his lip. Jezebel was thirty-three, though her complexion appeared closer to forty-three, no longer shiny, the booze and smokes had tarnished that after the loss.

Though leaned back, her custard skin, breasts half covered by her unbuttoned work shirt that lay over her nipples, she was still shapely in lean curves of frame, eyes stenciled by black like that of a cat and Kentucky blue. Arvin told her, "If I's twenty years younger, I'd marry you. No way in hell I'd see you in a sweat hive factory, offerin' yur wares on lunch breaks tuh creased sleeves of men like myself."

Hooking her lacy bra, fingers following the button holes of her work shirt, sleeves rolled to the elbows, Jezebel reached for her boy cut panties, pulled them from the floor. One slim leg at a time through the openings, she slid them up her pale legs that were pickled by bruise. Then slid her Dickie work pants on. "Just needed to feel somethin', you know? Somethin' other than numb. You's my only choice."

Jezebel reached for the box of Camels in her shirt pocket, hazed the tobacco to an orange glow. Sucked smoke into her lungs. Exhaled from the side of her thin lips.

Arvin eyed Jezebel. "What's yur story? You know mine. Losin' my daughter. You, you lost someone too, didn't yuh? Cause it don't make sense. You could have yurself a good young stud, with a good income. Leave all this crud and heat fur it steals yur damnsoul."

Jezebel tugged hard on the cigarette, rolled her eyes. A year ago she'd dated a mid-twenties pugilist hiding behind good looks and a needle of HGH he fed his tissue. Thought he'd give her face a swell one evening when his roid-rage reared its extension of horn points while she was doing dishes. Snapped in mid-conversation over a what she was gonna cook for supper. She wanted baked chicken. He wanted grilled steak. Balled a fist into her locks from behind. She squeezed an eight-inch butcher's blade from the sink. He pulled. She turned. Stabbed till she scraped bone. Broke it half off in his hip. Dropped his ass squalling. Told the SOB she'd four more inches of steel to break off if he wanted to try it again. He lay wetting the kitchen tile whimpering like an ass beat pup. Jezebel dialed 911. County cops showed up with the EMS. And her cop brother in-law told her, "I warned you he was a damn repeat beater to the females."

Since her husband's death, Jezebel'd had her fill of swarthy men. Enough of their shit to fill several septic tanks and she said, "Arvin, I's young enough to be yur goddamned daughter, kinda sick when you think about it that way. Daddy fucks his siblin'. Then wants to console her. Get personal. Know her deep dark secrets. All you need to know is I don't need a man. One I had was my life. Now he's gone. And so is that life."

*

From the silver tap, golden liquid fell and bubbled into the iced glass with a half-inch of foam. Went down just as crisp as it did that night eight years ago when Javi was nothing more than a man who'd found citizenship after he married an American girl. Baby on the way. Working for his brother, Carlos, as a roofer. It was a Friday night, they'd stayed at the site afterwards, had a few too many. Driving home to the rental he and his pregnant wife lived in was a blur from one side of the road to the next. Carlos and he were still drinking, gunning the gas, missing the STOP sign on a country road and everything combusted into darkness.

He woke in a hospital bed. Wife waiting by his side along with the county cops outside the room. Little memory of what happened. Until much later. Was begged to keep quiet.

He did. Took a plea bargain. Ten years manslaughter. Drunken driving. Was released in eight for good behavior. To survive behind cement walls with bars of steel and razor wire, tattoos and blacks, whites, Hispanics and everything in-between, he had to either be a bitch or earn up with his kind. Fell in with the Kings. Kept his chin to chest. Lifted seven days a week. Read books. Went in at five foot eight inches and 180 pounds. Came out the same height but now weighed 225. And he wasn't obese.

Did things behind those walls to prove his worth. Shanked, beat and choked inmates that needed violated. Made a name for himself by taking out a major ruler. Got drugs from one drain, toilet, air duct, asshole or throat. Worked with the guards who took payments. He did it clean. Neat. Now he was out. Wanted to celebrate his freedom.

When glass touched his lips. The hops came iced, skunky and bitter. Sinking within his jaws. Down his throat. His eyes watered at the taste of his sovereignty. Glutting it down, the lady behind the counter asked, "Want another?"

Waiting on his brother, Carlos, who stepped off to the right of the bar. Stepped down the hallway that led the bathroom to relieve his bladder, Javi told the tender, "Keep them coming." Fixed his brown eyes on the female. Maroonish-red mien. Skinny. Not bony. Just toned and tanned. The place was an authentic Mexican restaurant with a bar at the center, a brick wall at eye level, booths and tables sat outside of the bar, the eatery for family, for men, women and minors. Before Javi had gotten sent away, the building had been a Subway sandwich shop. Now it was a place where most of the locals in town hung out, eating and catching drink specials, that's how Carlos explained it when they parked between the white lines.

To the left of the bar was a hallway that went to the kitchen, a dark-haired young man kept peeking from the hall to the bar, eye-fucking Javi. He'd a webbed net over his head, a white apron. What the fuck, Javi thought. Then a man with a young boy bumped him. Javi glanced to his right at the man, the boy stood a few steps away, his two hands balled up into bones and skin. Javi swelled himself up. Nodded ,"I know you?"

The man looked at him, unblinking. A head of buzzed hair. Thick shouldered. Carved from hardwood, he looked through Javi, shaking his head. "No excuse for whut you done. Shouldn't be allowed to breathe let alone walk the streets of this town."

Over the man's shoulder, the boy's eyes bubbled. But his tongue was silent. The female spoke to the man, "No one under twenty-one is allowed in the bar area." The man eyed her hard. She sensed a territorial dispute. Slid the fresh beer to Javi. Treaded to the hallway and back into the kitchen.

Sizing him up, Javi believed the man looked military. Was in shape. Hard. Javi told the man, "Got no beefs with you, best move on before feelings stray."

Lifting the beer to his lips, he took a deep slug. Swallowed. "Just having a few drinks before I visit my daughter."

Sarcastic, the man told Javi, "Sad, first stop ain't tuh see your seed, it's fur the same shit that got you locked up. Your gonna fuck up I got my eye on you, this time you won't wake up in a hospital bed. System won't cut you a deal. I won't give'em the chance. You'll get buried. And I'll be navigating the shovel."

Javi held the beer just below his mouth, eyes stalled with anger, getting threatened by this stranger. Javi twisted a glare from hell and raised his speech, "You know who I am? Who I am affiliated with? Do you know-"

Before Javi could say *The Kings*, Conrad's hands were moving, he'd cut Javi's legs off with his own, jammed him to the stool. Javi wobbled. Was off center. The man's right hand controlled Javi's left. Clamped and pressed the glass into Javi's mouth while his left palmed the rear of Javi's head. Placed pressure between jaw, skin and teeth. Pressed hard as if trying to guillotine his lower jaw from his upper. The man's name was Conrad. He kept his elbow tucked into his chest. Didn't give Javi leverage to use those slabs of meat he called arms that lumped outside of his wife beater.

Conrad told Javi, "You removed something that can never be replaced." Conrad listened to Javi slur motherfuckers at him with brew seaming from the corners of his mouth. Told him, "Heed my words. I'm gonna release you. Hope you come at me cause I'll leave you in a pool of your own feces all over this

Goddamned floor and won't be nothin' your brother or any of your gangbanger buddies can do about it."

Conrad released Javi. Beer foamed down his pumped chest as he coughed, Conrad and the boy turned from him. Walked out of the bar area and to the exit door.

From the hallway of the bathroom Carlos stepped. "Shit's going on? I go take a piss and you're already stirring trouble."

"Wasn't me bro, was that fuckin' gringo motherfucker with the kid." Javi pointed out the window to the side lot.

Carlos looked out the glass, caught the image of Conrad walking away, amongst the parked vehicles, "Shit, should've known better than to bring you here, everybody in town comes to this place."

"I'm a free man. I did time I should never have done."

Carlos shooshed Javi, then said, "Yes, brother you did. But some are still doing theirs."

*

The phone rang, Jezebel's eyes opened, her room blacked out by window blinds, a fan oscillating air over shadows, she fumbled her grip, knocked the cordless from the nightstand to the floor. A voice repeated her name, "Jezebel? Jezebel? You there? Jezebel?"

Nights made you groggy. But the factory made you discerning. Depressed. Hateful with its heat, loud and ancient metal machines that were manual operation, laborious and would breakdown nightly, were never replaced, just fixed long enough to make it through another twelve-hour haze. Jezebel despised it. Every inch of its humidity, its filth. The white hats with their starched button-ups, donut bellies rimming over creased dress slacks and college degrees of 'I'm better than you smiles.'

Rolling to her stomach, reaching to the floor, clothes lay piled. She grabbed the phone. Turned onto her back. Looked to the pictures hung from walls and arched on dressers. Dusty and old. She reached to her nightstand once more for her smokes. Pulled a fresh one from her pack. Found her lighter. Lit her cigarette. Talked into the phone, "Time is it?" she mumbled.

"3:30."

"The hell you want? It's my first damn day off."

"He's out. Motherfucker's free. Two years early for good fuckin' behavior."

Release of air dropped from her lungs with a room of quiet. She didn't need to ask who. She already knew. Those first few months she imagined removing his appearance for thought a thousand different ways. Pistol between his eyes, to the rear of his skull, the left temple, the right temple. She'd imagined hogtying him behind her truck, resurfacing the back roads with the pieces that created his being. She thought of spreading his appendages wide, staking him flat in one of her father's hay fields and bush hogging his ass. Fertilizing the field with his hindsight. But time changes a person's perspective.

"What you want me to do 'bout it?"

"Whut we always said we'd do."

"You been keepin' tabs all these damn years?"

"Intel. Fucker was at El Nopal restaurant, drinking with his brother in the bar."

"Intel? You ain't overseas no more fightin' the Taliban." She huffed. "Just let things be."

Jezebel hung up the phone. Hung up on Conrad. Her 'I'll stomp your ass and ask questions later brother-in-law.'

Eight years. It'd already been infinity.

Cigarette smoke irritated her vision. She bent to her left. Opened the hickory honed nightstand. Pulled a leather holstered XD-9 Springfield Armory 9mm pistol from it. Conrad had given it to her after the accident. 'Personal protection or redemption,' he said. 'Its your choice.' Took her out to shoot it. Let her get a feel for it's cold heft. Precision recoil. She'd once contemplated this day. What she'd do. How she'd handle it. Back then, she was younger, naïve, never considered consequences for her son, Guy. To lose one parent was tough, but missing both would be a cruel road to purgatory for each of them. Selfish on her part.

When the insurance money had ran low, and social security wasn't enough, she'd no other option but to work. She'd drank and pill popped anxiety prescriptions, numbed herself to a state of blank pages that could be pulled and piled into a drawer, where they'd never be touched again. She'd sit for hours staring at nothing but silence. Went to widowed-wives-counseling until she'd attained to a rubbery chicken bone divested of its meat. She'd contemplated stripping, but it didn't offer benefits. She'd not wanted her son to deal with those types of rumors from other parents as Guy aged. Listening to other sons and daughters run their motor mouths when they discovered such facts from their creators.

Laboring in a factory meant she was viewed as a hardworking single mother, a widow. It meant retirement, a pension if she lived that long. If anything happened to her, Guy would be left with his uncle, Conrad. He was a good man. Tough as nails. He'd been an Army Ranger. Got called back for Afghanistan. Did his tour of duty. Came back home to his day job as a county cop, but losing his baby brother crushed him.

Guy was six when she came to her parent's home that night after the accident, a mess of crusted fluid, abrasions, tears, swells, shock and a relict. He was fourteen now, and she could hear him in the dining room.

Placing the pistol back into the nightstand, cigarette dangling from her mouth, Jezebel came from her bed, toes of chipped polish maneuvered across the floor with a slight limp, a repercussion from the accident. Crack of door. Inferno of daylight, down the hardwood hall she half walked half hobbled, family photos, dusty and crooked hung as she entered into the area where Guy sat, medium length hair pushed over his ears, black as spades, he'd an athletic build like his father. Had wrestled from grade school and into junior high. Five-six and one hundred and sixty pounds of rage sipping a glass of ice water and reading the paper like Tharp once did.

"What you got planned for today?" Jezebel asked.

"Its evening, days done gone. Done been out with Conrad." Guy said with sarcasm.

"Whut'd you all do?"

"Hung out at the station, went to lunch."

"Where'd you eat?"

"What do you care?"

"I care, but I worked fifty hours this week. Sweatin' my ass off and dealin' with aged and disposable fucks every night so you can have—"

Cutting her off, Guy says, "I seen him."

Angered, pulling the smoke from her lips, Jezebel jerked and indexed ash into a thick glass tray on the table. Blew smoke from her lips with a suspicious glance, "Seen who?"

Guy pressed his index finger into the newspaper that lay on the table spread open. "The man who killed my father."

Jezebel thought of Conrad, the son of a bitch. What did he think he was doing to her son?

"You seen him at El Nopal's, with Conrad?"

"Yeah, uncle Conrad pointed him out, give him a talkin' too in front of everybody. He's a free man." Finger still mashed to the newspaper, "Made the front page of the paper with his picture and father's picture, was sentenced to ten years, released early for good behavior. Shouldn't even be allowed to breath."

"Cut that talk from your tongue."

"It's true. Look at him. Tell me I's wrong. Damn *Latin* thug."

"Know who you sound like, your uncle. What he did is done. Cain't never be undone."

Guy stood from the table, angered by her response. "Your a zombie. A drunk. I found another pint of Maker's in the garbage this morning."

Pulling hard on the cigarette, Jezebel winked one eye, ran her left through her lengths of bed head, she was trembling. Pulled her smoke from her lips, pointed at him with her cigarette between index and middle finger ashing the air, "What I put into my body is my business, it helps me sleep. Quiets the memories."

"Helps you forget? You ain't the only one that lost somethin'. Ever think its good to remember him?" Guy paused, then told Jezebel, "I'm done talkin' to you. Goin' to the garage to lift weights."

There was a distance that had formed between them. Those first years were rough not having a father around, but Conrad helped. Got Guy into wrestling. Took him to practice, bought him an Olympic weight set when he turned ten. Showed him how to lift. Took him hunting. Fishing. Camping and target practicing from time to time. Guy was heavily influenced by his uncle Conrad's short fused ways. Then Guy was gone for a year overseas. Jezebel got tested as a mother when Conrad was over there.

She failed miserably.

Stone-still, with his back to Jezebel, wide shoulders butterflied out, Guy stared back down at the table, at the front page of newspaper. A jarring shutter rippled his frame. Jezebel stepped forward, stood beside Guy, wanted to reach around him, hold him, but couldn't. She glanced down to the black and white paper, the aged photo of the man's profile that held the face of her husband's killer.

She needed to face what she once conceived to be a monster but first Jezebel needed a drink.

*

The empty shot glass pierced the table with hints of live mariachi music from the other side of the brick wall that separated the restaurant from the bar area, his mind seered with disgust from the gringo bitch not allowing Javi to see his daughter, let him take her out to eat, get to know her.

He'd been a free man now for two fucking days. His brother had dropped him off at El Nopal. Javi wanted to be alone, Carlos left him his cell phone to call when he was ready to come home. A guest room at Carlos's home, full of his books, clean bed, satellite television. Peace and quiet out in the country. Carlos had done well for himself. Owned a construction and real estate business. Last thing Javi wanted to do was sit in that room like he'd sat in his cell, viewing pictures of his daughter, Lita, just as he'd done for the past eight years watching her grow.

His wife, Anita had divorced him while he was inside. Started dating. Got engaged. She couldn't do it anymore. Couldn't wait for his release. Didn't blame her. But she'd no right, not letting him see his daughter. Saying she wasn't ready. His daughter was almost eight, old enough to make that decision. As if enough hadn't been taken already. Men always conducting what you could and couldn't do. Governing you with rules. Having lock downs. Rummaging through your bunk. Looking for weapons or contraband. But he'd made the decision. Couldn't remember much about that night, except he knew he wasn't the one navigating the wheel. It had been Carlos and Carlos begged him. Knowing he'd never make it inside. He was too soft. Carlos got him the best lawyer. Spared no expense. With no priors, Javi got a deal. Ten years if he pled guilty with the possibility of early parole. He got out in eight.

"You want another?" A young man asked with a fishnet over his cold dark reams of hair, white cooking apron over his upper body, it was the same eyes that'd been peaking on him just days ago.

Snapping out of his haze, Javi looked up. "'Nother what?"

"Another shot of tequila?"

"Sure and give me a beer." Javi said.

"Draft or bottle?" The young man asked.

Goddamn, Javi thought, one fucking question after the next, nothing was simple on the outside and he said, "Draft."

"Which one?" He asked.

Too many choices. You didn't have that inside. Think long and you were wrong. Maybe dead. "What you got?"

"Miller. Bud. Coors. Tecate. Dos Equis."

The world had become complicated while he rotted in that cell. Earned a rep and he told him, "Dos Equis."

"Lime?"

Gotta be shittin' me, Javi thought, questioned him with, "Lime?"

"Would you like a slice of lime in your brew?"

For god sakes, "Yes."

The young man turned to the tiled bar that sat six feet behind him, the colors of yellow, tan and brown stucco decorated the molding and shapes of the area where a female sat lone amongst the empty wooden stools, flat screen TV to her left on the corner, another one back behind the bar up on the wall. She glanced his way every now and again, acted if maybe she'd approach him, then turned her back to Javi. Her hair blonde hiding her complexion, hanging below her shoulders, streaked with dark the shade of rye. The young man snapped his fingers to the blue shirted staunch of man opposite the female, standing behind the bar, "Dos Equis with lime and a shot of our best tequila." The young man yelled.

Screeching the bar stool, white legs streaked across Javi's eyes, the female stepped to the tile, she wore a military green hippie kind of skirt, flip flops, her toes broken chips of hot pink polish, she walked to a hall that led to the bathroom. The young man slid into the red vinyl seat on the other side of Javi's table. Javi eyed the female. That's what he needed. Hadn't had anything other than one of rosy palms and her ten sisters in eight years while fingering through the sticky pages of cock books stacked in his cell.

Eager the young man held out his hand to shake Javi's, "Names *Dog*."

Javi looked at the young man oddly. Something wasn't right. This kid wanted something. An approval or some shit. Other than the female, Javi, the bartender and *Dog*, the bar area was empty. Small kernels of chatter wisped from the dining area outside thebar, Javi took his shake. Firm. Sweaty. He nodded. "I'm—"

Javi glanced back to the squeak of the bathroom door, locked eyes with the female. She was familiar. Froze for a moment. Pushed locks from her face.

Smiled. Sat back at the bar. Raised her attention to the tender, "Another Margarita, on the rocks." The tender asked, "With Patron?"

"With Patron." She said.

"—Javi. I know who you are. Who you're affiliated with. What you did," the young man paused, glanced around, finished with, "inside. You're the man who took down Mastodon." Dog said.

Everything one did inside had to count. It was a power struggle. No wasted movements, wet towels were best, made it tighter to choke, cut the circulation for air. Either for raping, so no one could hear you scream or for killing. Soap was a hammer used to tenderize the soft slabs of meat in the shower. Soap could gag a man that didn't wanna quiet.

Mastodon had been major muscle for a Louisville gang. Moved meth and cocaine on the street. Inside he was feared more than he was respected. Punked most newbies. Javi'd been warned. Javi wasn't a punk. Two men corralled for Mastodon in the shower. Javi held his soaked towel. Mastodon came, six-five, two fifty, shaved head, kill shot eyes, a torso of grub worm shank and knife scars, his pigment was the consistency of diesel exhaust. Before he could lay fingers or organ to Javi, he took a soapy bar to his temple, one man roared, took a foot stomp with a bar to the eye, the other slipped on the extra bar Javi drove a heel into his nose, then from his mouth to his throat. Mastodon got a channel lock clamp with one hand, the other fisted his face once, Javi spun, swung the soap-loaded towel into the temple. The thigh. Ribs. Back to the temple. Bastard's sight went retard. Javi smothered the big bastar's chest with teeth bites, bear hugged him to the tile, working his way to the nose between his teeth until bone met cartilage, on the floor he spit red skin. Maneuvered Mastodon on his back, the towel around his neck with one man tugging to get Javi off of him. Pounding the back of his skull. But his fists were small. Teeth grinded. Punches were weak. Jerking Javi free, a parting followed with a pop. Water ran red over the tile. Weighted and limp, the frame of Mastodon was body bag ready. This was six weeks into Javi's ten year sentence. He was looked at by other inmates not as a threat but as a new piece of respect.

Javi released his shake. "Did what I had to, to survive. Out here—"

A short mushroom stubbed man came to the table with a frosted 32oz mug of dark beer, a halved lime and shot of tequila. Laid it on the Formica. Walked away. Javi finished with, "—I got a chance to start over."

Dog shook his head, "Start over? What you going to do, earn coin as a roofer for your brother's construction company like before?" Dog looked around the bar area, raised his lip, "Shit *Holmes*, your rep, you could be a king pin in the Midwest. In this town." He tells Javi thrusting his index finger into the tabletop.

Taking the shot first, Javi washes it down with the beer. "How the hell you know who I am, what I did?"

"We're part of the same armada Javi, anyone whose part of the *Kings* knows who and what the fuck Javi Torrez means. You don't need any more shunning by the white skins bro, that ain't no life."

Javi swigged his beer, "Being a roofer is a life without a target on my back. They's always someone bigger, stronger and more methodical waiting than the next, knowing they turn is coming, being a banger is one without much mileage but plenty of mythology and praise, you're too young to grasp that knowledge, but—"

Dog cut him off. "—don't give me that too young *bullshit* Javi. Once a *King*, always a fuckin' *King*."

Javi shook his head, "What are you eighteen? You're a boy, impressionable. These are not the times of Pancho Villa or Hector Leyva, you're in America, can afford to live free. That all I want. Can't afford to go back. Got a daughter. Wanna see her grow up. Go to school. Get married. Simple pleasures."

Dog released a huff of wind, gave a dead eyed stare, "I'm twenty one. And *The Kings* saved me. I bleed and die for them, no questions asked. You're indebted to do the same. remember that."

Javi carved a stare into the Dog that was just as hard as the one he offered. He was dangerous. Had no boundaries. Javi could see this. Pulled a wad of bills from his pocket, compliments of his brother. Dog waved a hand, "Its on the house. Free."

Javi shook his head. Laid a wrinkled bill on the table, "Nothin' in life is free." He stood up from the booth.

Dog raised his tone, "I ain't done talking. Got a line of men at your disposal. Waiting to be led."

Javi told Dog, "I am done." He turned away. Left the half full mug of beer. Walked towards the bar. Behind him, Dog shouted, "Don't turn you shun me."

Javi ignored Dog's words, sat down at the bar. Looked to the female, "Can I buy—"

Her eyes met his. He recognized her. She was familiar, and scarred with melancholy.

*

Fumed, the young man that'd been talking with Javi followed the tiled hall next to the bar that led back to the kitchen, as Jezebel told Javi, "There was a time when I wanted to kill you."

She was tired of recalling all of it. She just wanted to forget. To heal. She thought of the pistol in her purse. She came hoping to see him as she'd done the past two evenings. Waited till closing. Needed to face him. Know if he was the monster she'd once made him out to be. She wanted closure.

"I can't blame you." Javi told her.

Then this evening, he walked in. Sat alone. Quiet. Ordered tequila. He was bigger than before. Rounded. Bulky from the penitentiary. Wanting to approach him, she couldn't, not with the young man at his table.

"Tharp was my everything. Still is. I was a train wreck those first few years. Now I'm just an accident, can't never be fixed. Work in a tin walled hell of heat, grit and fumes with men and women who've their own downfalls of loss, booze and drugs. Hate the work, I'm providing for a son who despises his mother."

She sipped her margarita. He sipped his beer. He seemed agitated.

"Your son, what is his age?"

"Fourteen."

"Fourteen, ah, if I could go back." He said fumbling with the sweat beads on his mug.

Through the bar, to the left the young man kept glancing in on Javi and Jezebel. Javi was fuming, making eye contact with the young man.

They ordered another round.

"You married, kids?" Jezebel asked.

"My wife divorced me while I was inside. Missed the birth of our daughter. She won't let me see her. I want to start over, work for my brother. Live simple. But˗ " Javi paused, contemplated what was coming, "˗but I don't think it will be allowed." Javi went quiet. Wanted to tell her, it wasn't he who'd taken her husband, Tharp Cooper, from her, but Carlos. His soft as whipping cream brother.

But he couldn't. He was blood.

Buzzed, that's what Jezebel was. Not drunk. She was on her way to quieting those thoughts and inner voices of severity. Sorrow. Melancholy. She was getting that feeling. That craving. Closed her eyes. Her view of this monster was now distorted. It no longer held weight. Value. Opening them she questioned, "Why won't it be allowed? You done your time."

"There are choices I made inside to survive that will haunt me. Things that cannot be undone."

"Do those choices have to do with you and the young man who sat at your table?"

"Ah, you're attentive. Yes. Yes they do."

Jezebel hesitated, tried to place her words in order, then said, "I forgive you. Never realized it until now." Jezebel took a sip of her drink, told him, "I came hoping to lay eyes on you. Face you, offer my peace." Or the other piece.

With a scuffed suspicion Javi looked up and asked, "How'd you know I'd be here?"

"My brother in-law told me you'd been here after your release, hoped you'd come back. Its where most of the locals come for food and drinks."

Javi's right eye pinched, "Your bother in-law, he's military looking with an attitude?"

"Yeah, and built like a brick shithouse."

"Yes, a brick shit house. It makes sense now." Javi said, he was fidgeting.

"What makes sense?"

"What the man said to me, telling me I shouldn't be allowed to breathe or walk the streets of this town." Javi glanced to the hallway that led to the kitchen, Dog stood with two other men, attired in hair nets and white aprons tainted with food, each was needled by a tear of ink below their left eye. Flexing his fists and arms, Javi pressed his chin into his chest. Reached and finished his beer. Excused himself.

"Everything okay?" Jezebel asked.

Scratching the ceramic with his bar stool, Javi told her, "Things will never be okay for me." Javi paused then walked away. He wanted to say he was sorry for her loss but it made little difference now. Walking to the restroom. Moments passed. The young man and the two men from the kitchen passed behind Jezebel carting butcher knives as she stayed seated. Treaded the same path as Javi and entered the bathroom behind him.

Uncertain of what had just transpired, Jezebel felt somewhat at peace, withdrew cash from the leather folds of her purse, glanced at the pistol that lay within, she fanned out two twenties on the bar. Buzzed, she thought about forgiveness. Second chances. Choices. Stepped to the hallway. Glanced at the Men's restroom. Entered with the pistol pulled from her purse, viewed the knives in the men's hands, pressed the pistol into the rear of Dog's skull. Eyed the other cooks training blades on Javi, and with her heart rushing, she says, "Everyone deserves a second chance." And she tugged the trigger.

FAMILY TREE
BY MICHAEL BRACKEN

"Marie!" the six-year-old's grandmother called from the porch of their crumbling Greek Revival style plantation home. "You leave that tree be and get back over here."

The southern live oak at the far corner of the expansive but unkempt front yard had grown old long before the first Badeaux established Belle Marie in southeast Texas. Seventy feet tall, with a trunk twenty-three feet around and a limb spread approaching eighty-five feet, the oak had massive lower limbs that swept toward the ground before curving upward. Clumps of ball moss and resurrection fern clung to the thick dark bark among the stiff leathery leaves, and drapes of Spanish moss hung from the tree like so much dirty laundry.

"Yes, *Grand-mère*," Marie said as she turned and shuffled back to the house where she lived with her grandmother.

Belle Marie, a thriving cotton plantation in the years preceding the Civil

War, had begun a slow slide into oblivion upon the emancipation of the Badeaux family's slaves. After the stock market collapsed on Black Tuesday, taking the last of the family's money with it, the remaining Badeauxes—Marie's grandparents, her mother Amiée, and her uncle René—had stopped maintaining appearances and had let nature regain control of the grounds surrounding the plantation home, the barn, and the family cemetery behind them both. The once-white plantation house was now more the color of dirt, with graying black shutters that closed against the storms that blasted up from the coast and across the bayou.

As soon as Marie reached the porch, her grandmother brushed aside the girl's wavy black hair and grabbed her ear. "What have I told you about that tree, *ma chère?*"

"Stay away."

"That's right. That tree killed your *grand-père*. You stay away from it."

As her grandmother dragged her inside, Marie glanced back at the young man leaning against the southern live oak and wondered why her grandmother did not chase him from their yard.

*

Marie's grandmother took the family's black 1940 Ford pickup truck into town once each week, visiting the grocery store, the dry goods store, and the full-service Sinclair station with the green brontosaurus painted on the side. Marie was fascinated by the dinosaur, but her grandmother insisted it was just make-believe. Her grandmother insisted a lot of things were make-believe, but that didn't stop her from praying each night to a God that Marie had never seen.

In town during a weekly shopping trip when she was ten, Marie wore a frilly knee-length skirt they had found packed in a trunk in the attic. Marie's grandmother had worn it as a child, long before the Badeaux family's descent into landed poverty.

As she walked behind her grandmother through the grocery store, Marie spun around, causing the skirt's hem to rise. She noticed a man following them, not too closely and not too obviously, and she saw that he smiled a bit each time she spun. She stopped and looked at him.

Marie's grandmother turned, saw the man staring at Marie, and glared until he turned and walked away. Then she grabbed Marie's shoulders and through gritted teeth said, "You don't want to be like your *maman*."

*

Amiée hid in the brush and watched as Leviticus Fontaine bathed in the river. The quadroon from Blacktown was near the same age as her brother René, a year older than her sixteen, with skin the color of honey and tightly curled black hair cropped close to his scalp.

Lining the edge of the bayou, in a cluster of houses known as Blacktown, descendants of Belle Marie's slaves and those from other once-thriving plantations of southeast Texas eked out a meager existence. Amiée had never been allowed to play with the children from Blacktown, and all she knew of coloreds were the few she saw when shopping with her mother. They had their own water fountains and restrooms, and she wondered what made them special.

When Leviticus rose from the thigh-deep water and turned toward her, Amiée gasped. He looked nothing like her father and brother. The sound gave away her presence, and the young man stared into the brush along the shore until he located the white girl staring at him.

"You can come out now," he said. "You seen everything anyhow."

Leviticus splashed out of the water and reached for his clothes as Amiée crawled from the bushes.

He gestured in the direction of Belle Marie's plantation home. "You from the big house?"

Amiée nodded.

"I seen you before."

"I ain't never seen you."

"Moses tell us keep our own company," he said. "He sell shine to ever'body but tell us keep our own company."

Amiée reached out and touched the young man's chest. Unlike her brother's, the quadroon's chest was as devoid of hair as her own.

"You cain't be touching me like that." Leviticus stepped back. He hurriedly pulled on his pants and his shirt. "I got to go."

As he turned, she called after him, demanding that he meet her again the following day.

"I cain't," Leviticus said, but he did.

They met often after that, their relationship a secret from her family.

*

Marie often asked about her father, receiving a similar response each time.

"Casualty of war," Marie's grandmother said. She sat in her rocking chair by the fire holding Uncle René's dog tags, the ball chain of which she moved through her gnarled fingers like rosary beads while she prayed for his return. She wouldn't believe he was dead until she had something to bury. "He joined up before we even knew your *maman* was with child."

"Just like Uncle René?"

"Just like," her grandmother said.

"Then why don't we have any of my father's medals?" Marie asked once when she was twelve. "We have Uncle René's."

"His people have them," her grandmother said.

"Who are his people? Do I know them?"

Her grandmother knew but she did not say.

*

René and his father had been duck hunting in the bayou without success, and he trailed several steps behind the older man as they threaded their way through the outbuildings of Belle Marie, the buttstock of his shotgun tucked under his right arm, the pivot of the open action in the crook of his elbow, and the empty double-barrel safely pointed groundward. As the elder Badeaux continued toward the plantation house, René heard a sound and turned.

The barn door stood ajar, leaving a gap of only a few inches, and René peered inside. When he saw what was happening in the hay, he pressed a shotshell into each of his shotgun's two chambers and snapped the gun closed. Then he pushed open the door, stepped inside, and raised the butt to his shoulder. "Get off'n my sister."

Leviticus Fontaine removed himself from Amiée and rolled to the side. "I didn't mean no disrespect, Mr. Badeaux," he pleaded. "Your sister'n me, we just—"

Amiée used her hands to cover herself from her brother's disapproving gaze.

"What I tell you?" René demanded of his sister.

Leviticus rose to his feet and reached for his trousers. "I just be going now."

"You ain't going nowhere, boy." René squeezed the shotgun's triggers, peppering the quadroon's chest with birdshot and stippling his sister with blood.

Amiée screamed.

She took the dying boy's head in her lap, no longer concerned with covering herself, and glared at her brother. "Why'd you go and shoot Levi for? He'd ain't done nothing you ain't done yourownself."

Their father, who came running upon hearing the shotgun's roar, slammed into the barn and took everything in at a glance. He grabbed Amiée's arm and pulled her to her feet. "Get on up to the house and get yourself cleaned up."

*

That night, René crept into his sister's bedroom and finished what Leviticus had started. Amiée was too numb from the day's events to protest, and when René finally left her bed, she curled into a ball and hugged her knees. On his way out, René paused at the doorway long enough to tell her what they had done with her young lover's body.

After collecting the boy's clothing and a length of rope, René and his father dragged Leviticus from the barn, around the plantation house, and across the lawn to the southern live oak. Over many decades, the oak's trunk had grown hollow, and generations of Badeaux boys had hidden inside while playing their childhood games. Seven feet from the ground, the trunk split into several heavy branches, and René climbed up into the split. His father tied the rope around the quadroon's torso, under the arms. René caught the end of the rope when his father tossed it to him, and he braced himself while his father lifted Leviticus as high as he could. Together they maneuvered the barely breathing boy into the tree before dropping him, his clothing, and the rope into the tree's hollow trunk, where he died several hours later.

Three days after René shot Leviticus the Japanese attacked Pearl Harbor. The next day, the entire family gathered around the radio and listened as President Franklin D. Roosevelt declared December 7, 1941, "a date that will live in infamy."

Within the hour, the United States declared war against Japan, and before the week ended, René hitchhiked to the nearest city to enlist.

*

When Marie was a baby, she remained home with her grandfather when her grandmother went shopping in town. That changed with his passing, and she accompanied her grandmother every week until she reached her early teens. After she could care for herself, she often remained home alone.

One afternoon while her grandmother was in town, Marie sat on her bed in the second-floor room that had once been her mother's and stared across the expanse of the plantation home's front lawn at the southern live oak. Years had passed since she had last seen the young man leaning against the tree and she wondered where he had gone.

She also wondered if her mother had ever sat in her room, staring at the tree that dominated the yard, and what she thought about if she did. Marie knew nothing about her family history beyond the few stories her grandmother shared, so she believed her mother died during childbirth, just as she believed her father died during the war, but Amiée had survived Marie's arrival. When Amiée realized that her just-birthed child was a girl, she rose from the bed and took from the nightstand the knife her mother used to cut the umbilical cord, intending to kill the baby. Her mother pulled baby Marie to safety, so Amiée turned the knife on herself and sliced upward along the length of her forearm. Marie's grandmother screamed for help, and by the time her grandfather reached the second-floor bedroom, Amiée had collapsed. By then, she was beyond help.

Marie knew nothing of her mother and did not remember her

grandfather, either. She was barely able to roll over on her own the afternoon her grandmother returned home from shopping and found her grandfather in a heap beneath the southern live oak, with her on a blanket only a few feet away. He had been struck in the head so hard that dark bits of bark, threads of Spanish moss, and slivers of his shattered skull clung to the blood coagulating in the greasy black hair surrounding a gaping scalp wound.

Marie's grandmother buried him in the family cemetery behind the barn, next to Marie's mother and the empty plot where Uncle René would have been buried had the Army returned anything more than his dog tags and posthumous medals.

With her grandfather dead, Marie and her grandmother were alone in a home they could neither repair nor afford to pay someone else to repair, and the degradation of Belle Marie continued apace.

Marie finally turned away from the window.

*

Neither sixteen-year-old Marie nor her grandmother saw the disheveled man who limped down the road from town and up Belle Marie's front drive until he reached the plantation home's porch. He didn't bother knocking and walked directly inside. When no one greeted him, he shouted, "Where'n hell is ever'body?"

Marie and her grandmother, in the kitchen preparing dinner, heard the man's voice. Marie followed her grandmother into the parlor where the stranger stood.

"*Maman?*" he asked.

"René?" Marie's grandmother gasped in return, her eyes wide with surprise. "You're dead. The gov'ment sent me a letter told me you died in the war."

"They was wrong, *Maman*," Uncle René said. "I ain't died in no damn war."

"Then where you been, son?"

"Tryin' to get home." He slapped his left leg, the knee shattered by friendly fire and fused into place. "Where's daddy?"

"Out back to the cemetery."

"And Amiée?"

"She's with him."

"That's too bad," René said. "I been missing her something powerful. She's the reason I come home."

"I prayed hard for your return," Marie's grandmother said, "but I didn't expect it like this. I was just praying to bury you next to your daddy and the rest of the family."

"You ain't got to do that, *Maman*. Not anytime soon." Uncle Rene eyed the dark-haired teenaged girl standing behind his mother. "Who're you?"

Marie didn't answer, but her grandmother did. "Aimee's little girl."

She reached back, took Marie's hand, and pulled her around to stand in front. "This here's your Uncle René. He come home from the war."

"You a ghost?"

"Good as," he said with a twisted smile. "I come back from the dead, ain't I?"

"We was fixin' to eat supper," Marie's grandmother said. "Come on back'n join us. You can tell us ever'thing."

A few minutes later they sat at the kitchen table picking at vegetable stew.

"You look just like your *maman*," René said as he leered at Marie across the table. "She was near about your age the last time I saw her."

*

Uncle René contributed little, not even cutting firewood, and spent much of his time resting. He claimed the war, long over by then, had exhausted him.

Three mornings after his return, Uncle René disappeared into the bayou in search of Moses Fontaine's still. While he was away, Marie's grandmother prepared for her weekly trip into town.

"Come with me," her grandmother said. "You can see the dinosaur."

Marie laughed. "I'm not a child anymore, *Grand-mère.* That thing is old and faded and—"

"I'll buy you a cold Dr Pepper at the lunch counter."

"I don't want to go," Marie said. She looked up at the darkening clouds. "There's a storm coming, *Grand-mère*, and I don't want to be out in it."

Only three months earlier, Hurricane Ella, having weakened to a tropical storm with forty-five-mile-per-hour winds, made landfall near Corpus Christi, and forecasters talked of another storm of similar strength rising from the Gulf to strike southeast Texas.

"We'll be home before it blows in."

Marie crossed her arms under her breasts and glared at her grandmother.

They argued, but Marie remained obstinate.

Finally, her grandmother gave in. Before climbing into the pickup truck, she said, "You lock up tight. You don't want to be like your *maman.*"

Marie had heard her grandmother's cautionary advice so often she no longer paid attention. She watched her grandmother drive away, and then she stared up at the darkening sky as storm clouds chased one another inland from the coast.

With the house to herself, Marie tuned in a radio station broadcasting out of southwest Louisiana that played devil music from Jerry Lee Lewis and Elvis Presley. As she danced around the parlor, she paused to finger her uncle's medals and noticed that his dog tags were missing.

Before long the rain began, so she closed the shutters against the storm and waited in the darkness for her grandmother or her uncle to return, but neither did before she put herself to bed.

Marie squeezed her eyes closed. A loose shutter flapped against the house somewhere downstairs as the wind blowing in from the Gulf grew stronger, keeping her awake as she huddled under a thick pair of handmade quilts. She wore an ankle-length, pastel pink and blue nightdress that had belonged to her mother, the loose material wrapped around her legs.

When Marie heard a noise not caused by the storm raging outside, she opened her eyes and saw her Uncle René silhouetted in the open doorway of her bedroom. She shivered, but not from cold, and she tried to remain as still as possible.

Soaking wet, he wore a yellowed cotton undershirt beneath suspenders that held up loose-fitting green chinos and the boots in which he had returned

home. His dog tags hung around his neck, the ball chain, polished to a shine by

her grandmother's gnarled fingers, glinted in reflected light. He had been

drinking shine purchased that morning from Moses Fontaine and had the glint of

desire in his dark eyes.

He entered Marie's room and tore the quilts from atop her.

She screamed for her grandmother.

"She cain't hear you little girl. She ain't come back from town."

Marie rolled away from her uncle, onto the floor. She scrambled to her

feet and rushed into the hall. At the top of the stairs, she stumbled over the hem

of her nightdress and tumbled partway down the stairs before she caught herself

on the railing. She sat up as her uncle reached the top of the stairs. When she

saw him, she grabbed bunches of the flannel nightdress and pulled the hem to

her knees before hurrying the rest of the way down to the foyer.

There was nowhere in the house she could hide where her uncle could

not find her. Without thinking, Marie pulled open the front door and had it torn

from her grasp by the wind. Barefoot, she ran into the night—across the porch,

down the steps, and across the expansive front lawn toward the road, toward

town, toward her grandmother, if she were returning.

Broken limbs and thorns and moss and tree trash swept across the yard

by the storm caused her to stumble repeatedly. Despite his limp, her uncle was not far behind.

As they reached the southern live oak, he caught a handful of her nightdress. The fabric tore as Marie struggled to free herself, and she fell backward, landing beneath the tree.

Her uncle reached down, ripped the front of her nightdress completely open, and stood on the hem. Marie tried to scramble backward, using her feet and elbows to propel herself, but she had little traction, could not untangle her arms from her nightdress, and made no progress.

She watched wide-eyed with fear as her uncle slipped his suspenders from his shoulders and dropped his pants to his ankles. As he straightened, one heavy branch of the southern live oak, a branch far too heavy to be so affected by the gale-force wind, swung around behind René and slammed into the back of his head, sending him sprawling into the dirt and mud at Marie's feet. He had been struck so hard that bits of bark, threads of Spanish moss, and slivers of his shattered skull clung to the blood oozing from a gaping scalp wound.

Marie looked up to see a familiar honey-skinned young man with tightly curled black hair cropped close to his scalp leaning against the southern live oak. He smiled at her and she hesitantly smiled in return. Then a pair of headlights washed over them as her grandmother's pickup truck turned into the driveway. Marie blinked and the man was gone.

The pickup slid to a stop. Marie's grandmother ran across the yard to where Marie lay shivering and her uncle lay dead from a blow to the back of his head.

Marie's grandmother looked at her dead son and at her granddaughter's torn nightdress, and she knew what had been about to happen.

She knew. She had always known. And she had done nothing.

"Get a shovel," she said. "We got a place already reserved for your Uncle René."

OF TWO MINDS

BY VERONICA LEIGH

October 1932

Ouabache, Indiana

Sheriff Claire Williams was humming to Al Bowlly's "Hang Out the Stars in Indiana" as it played on the radio. She directed her Ford Model A down the winding country road, which divided the densely packed woods. With only golden moonglow and the car's headlights to illuminate her path, the blackness of the night had dropped its shroud over the valley. When her husband Reginald was alive, he did all of the driving and she relied on him to convey her to and fro. There was a time when being out at night unnerved her. Especially in autumn. Indiana in the autumn was thoroughly ghoulish. The thin veil between the natural world and the supernatural lifted once the sun went down.

Here I am, out on my own. I've come so far. She straightened proudly in the driver's seat, relishing in the freedom she possessed. A day didn't go by when she didn't miss Reginald. He was her husband, her true love. But on his death, she inherited his position of sheriff through *Widow's Succession* and independence was bestowed upon her. Her only regret was that she didn't have this liberty when he was alive. *What would Reginald think of me now? On my own, working, driving, solving crimes, only accountable to God.* Her recent successes fed her confidence.

Her ponderings were abruptly interrupted when a blur of brown streaked from the woods. She pumped the brake and the car came to a screeching halt. For a second, she believed it to be a deer, but on focusing her gaze, she was taken aback to find a woman standing in the middle of the road.

Claire pressed a hand to her chest, her finger tips grazing the sheriff's badge pinned to her coat.

The woman's quivering form—skin and frock—was streaked in red-brown stripes, like a zebra. *Blood or mud?* It was too far away to make out. The lady opened her mouth and began to scream, fanning her arms up and down frantically.

Claire shifted the Model A into park and turned off the engine, before scrambling out of the car and hesitantly approached the hysterical woman. "Ma'am? Are you all right?" With the car off, the light had been killed, but her eyes adjusted quickly. Her nostrils flared, detecting the foul stench of blood on the woman's body. "My God, what happened?"

"He—he's trying to kill me." The woman grasped Claire's shoulders and whimpered like a wounded animal. "P-please help me! I don't want to die."

Claire began to tremble, not from her own fear, but due to the fact that this woman was hanging on her, and shaking. *Who is "he?"* Naturally her mind went to a violent husband. The first murder she had to solve involved a violent husband and father. Her home town of Ouabache was small and everyone knew each other, and knew of those who lived out on the outskirts. Yet Claire didn't recognize this woman. Nothing about her, not her face, clothing, or demeanor was familiar. It was as though she had appeared out of nowhere. *Like a ghost.* The valley was riddled with folk tales and ghost stories, but in October the imagination came alive and lately there had been numerous reports of spirits in and out of the woods.

Claire cupped the woman's elbows, convincing herself this person was real. "You're safe now." She assured the woman, and figured once she got the lady to the sheriff's office, she'd be able to make sense of everything. "I'm Sheriff Williams, I'll protect you. Who are you?"

"Amy Dubois." The woman supplied.

Dubois. The only Dubois she knew was Isom Dubois, a widower who lived on the affluent east side of Ouabache. He worked as a postman, kept to himself for the most part, never attending social functions, with exception for church on Sundays. This Amy Dubois must be some relation from out of town, since Dubois wasn't a common name and no one else in town bore it. *Perhaps this Amy Dubois is the ghost of a deceased relative and that is why she appeared out of nowhere.*

Claire blinked, shaking her head at herself. She really did read too many gothic romances. "Come with me, Miss Dubois." She wriggled out of Amy's hold and claimed the woman's icy hand. "We'll figure this out." She coaxed the woman towards the Model A and on opening the passenger door, she urged the woman inside.

Claire headed around to the other side, drawing in a breath to calm herself. However, when she climbed back into the driver's seat and turned on the car, the Model A vibrated. Not from its own power, but from Amy Dubois who still quivering. She drove them back to the sheriff's office, finding assurance that Amy was flesh and blood as she didn't vanish as quickly as she had appeared.

*

The entrance of the sheriff's office was dimly lit, but Claire's heart stuttered on observing that Amy Dubois' condition was far worse than she initially realized. *Dear God in heaven!* No wonder Amy reminded her of a ghoul, she had a chalky complexion and her mouth was not defined, fading into the rest of her skin. Her wide greenish eyes were sunken in and her black hair hung listlessly about her hunched shoulders. The homespun dress she wore was from decades earlier, and would have even stood out in old fashion Ouabache. From closer inspection, some of the zebra-like streaking was purplish and Claire suspected it was bruising from being grabbed.

Deputy Frank was in the corner of the office, whittling, crafting a small bird when she led Amy into the room. "Deputy Frank, we have a visitor." Claire announced.

The deputy barely cast a glance at Amy, but it was enough to capture his attention. He shot to his feet, dropping his creation. "Amy Dubois?" The name came out in a faint rasp. The color drained from his face; he looked as though he had seen a ghost.

"You know Miss Dubois?" Claire arched one of her brows, her interest more than piqued.

When Claire had become sheriff and began to work with Deputy Frank, she soon decided she didn't like him. His disrespect to her, his good ol' boy ways, his shifty behavior was a thorn in her side. He might wear a deputy's badge, but she truly believed him to be on the wrong side of the law. Unfortunately, her feelings on the matter were not justification to sack him.

"Y-yes, I mean I d-did. We went to school together." The rims of Deputy Frank's ears reddened. He stumbled around his desk and gingerly approached their guest. "Amy, do you remember me? My name is Joseph Frank, but everyone called me—"

"Frankie!" Amy gasped and her formerly dull eyes started to sparkle like twin emeralds. "I missed you." She lifted her delicate hand and pressed it to his cheek. Then she flung herself into the deputy's arms and buried her face into his shoulder, sobbing against him.

Deputy Frank tenderly petted her hair, murmuring in her ear.

Claire was gaping at the couple, more astonished by the bond between Amy Dubois and Deputy Frank than by everything else that transpired. Never before had she witnessed the deputy's gentle side.

Watching them from the corner of her eye, Claire slipped behind her desk. In a hushed tone, she telephoned the local doctor Jed Loving, inviting him over. In the past crimes she solved, he functioned primarily as a coroner, but was able to offer information about Ouabache's residents and its history. Tonight, he would offer his medical expertise. She bided her time until the doctor arrived and was in consultation with Amy, before quirking her finger and wriggling it at the deputy to follow her into the back, where there was a small kitchen.

The deputy dragged his feet and didn't conceal his expression of reluctance to obey her order. Claire waited a minute and felt a wave of impatience when he offered up no explanation in regards to his past connection.

"Deputy, why were you astonished to see Miss Dubois?" Claire inquired, folding her arms.

Deputy Frank's frown deepened. "Because she died twenty years ago, when she was fifteen. We all went to her funeral. It was a tragedy." He sniffed and blinked rapidly. If she didn't know better, she would think he was fighting to rein in his emotions.

"You loved her." Claire concluded.

"I did. I still do." He tugged at his collar, to loosen it. "I asked her to marry me and she accepted. Then she was gone."

For once she felt a twinge of sympathy for Deputy Frank. The ill-fated romance the man described must have taken place when he was a young, impressionable man. It was before life had stolen his true love and beaten the hope out of him. Perhaps Amy's supposed death was what sent him down the dark path he was currently on. He had lost his way.

What is lost can be found.

Claire clasped her hands together in front of her. "Miss Dubois trusts you. I'll ask the questions and you will be her friend. If she needs your support, you'll help her." She had tried to sound compassionate, for she could well understand losing her true love.

Deputy Frank eyed her and outwardly bristled. His upper lip curled into a slight sneer. "Of course, sheriff." He stepped away and headed back into the office.

Claire lingered, reviewing the peculiar events of the evening. She was on a leisurely drive in the country when Amy Dubois staggered out in front of her car. On bringing the woman to the sheriff's station, she discovered that Amy and Deputy Frank once loved each other, and that Amy was thought to be dead. The olive branch she attempted to offer the deputy was rebuffed. *He was fine until I informed him I intended to question Amy.* Could he be involved in Amy's alleged death and twenty-year absence? Her past distrust of the deputy might be clouding her judgment, but her instincts in solving crimes often proved correct.

Claire moved back into the office and noted how the striped bruising on Amy's arms were thin. *A small pair of hands made those flesh wounds.* She glanced at the deputy, studying him. He was a small, wiry man, only a couple inches taller than Amy and his hands were also small.

He did it. *I don't know how, but he did it.* Her mouth twisted into a purse. She would figure it out though.

*

Claire gestured for Jed to follow her outside and the doctor did as bidden, trailing her out onto the sidewalk in front of the sheriff station. They left Amy Dubois in the deputy's care, and Claire had to admit, Deputy Frank played the part of devoted lover perfectly. He served her tea and spoke to her gently. *If I didn't know better, I'd find it touching.* She thought with a roll of her eyes.

Main Street greeted them with an eerie quiet. The majority of the residents in the tiny town of Ouabache retired for the night once the sun went down. There were a few who worked at night, moonshiners included, but the latter tended to give the area a wide berth. A stray cat or dog wandered around, but they were overshadowed by the blackbirds that plagued the valley this time of year. The dreaded horde arrived in October and stayed through the winter, until spring, leaving their droppings everywhere. The infernal cawing grated on her last nerve.

Claire and Jed carefully stood under the overhang of the building, to avoid the blackbirds' grotesque deposits. "Well?" she prompted impatiently.

"Where to begin?" Jed sighed and shrugged. He withdrew a tin of chaw from his pocket, unscrewed it and took a pinch, then poked it in his mouth. The tin was returned to his trouser pocket and his right cheek poked out. "Miss Dubois has been recently attacked, she's been hit in the eye, the mouth, scratched, and there's bruising on her upper arms from being grabbed. Then there is the condition of her health; Miss Dubois is malnourished and dehydrated. Her paleness leads me to believe she hasn't stirred outdoors in ages. From all she has been through, she is troubled." He gave her a sideways glance. "But I suppose that is to be expected from someone who died."

"Is her father Isom Dubois?"

"Yes. The man was broken when his daughter died." Jed cast a glance towards the front door, as if Amy was standing there. "And though it's been years, I do believe this woman is Amy Dubois."

"I'm concerned about the deputy's connection to Miss Dubois. He has been involved in shady dealings in the past." Claire shifted and watched through the window, able to see the deputy and Amy's interactions. Deputy Frank's present kindness didn't fool her. He could not be trusted. "What are your thoughts?"

"Sheriff," The doctor drawled, and instantly she knew she wouldn't appreciate his opinion. "I think your dislike of him is now distracting you from the situation at hand."

Claire frowned, but couldn't deny he had a point. She was fixated on the deputy and was convinced of his guilt in harming Amy Dubois and that he was likely involved with other wrongdoings in the valley. *I don't think I'll ever be able to trust him.* Since she couldn't bring him to justice for that, she was determined to catch him on another crime.

"You don't want to mistakenly pin this on the deputy and come to find out it was someone else." Jed advised.

"There is something about all of this that doesn't feel right." She insisted, and sharply turned on her heel and went back inside. The doctor was right though. There was no place for personal vendettas when another human life was at stake.

Claire retrieved her desk chair and drew it close to where Amy and Deputy Frank were, and sat down. She hoped the informality of this interview would put the lady at ease. But the second she took a seat, Amy Dubois began to whine and rocked back and forth in her seat.

Deputy Frank sent Claire a harsh look while cradling Amy's limp hand in his own.

Claire disregarded the deputy. This was about Amy, not him. "Miss Dubois, Deputy Frank believed you died years ago." She had instructed the deputy to be a friend to the lady, but she understood that she had to do the same. Especially if she were to gain Amy's trust. "Can you tell me your whereabouts and who harmed you?"

"My daddy put me in the attic." Amy lowered her head, and she suddenly was smaller than what she was. Her tone also took on a girlish lilt, which made her seem younger than her years. "He wasn't kind to me."

"Why would he put you in the attic?"

"I told him I was going to marry Frankie. Daddy forbade me, but my heart was set on it. So, he put me in the attic and said I couldn't come out until I changed my mind. I never did."

Deputy Frank drew Amy's hand close to his mouth and reverently kissed her knuckles.

Claire longed to make a face, but kept her expression placid. *This seems too farfetched to be true.* Did Amy truly expect her to believe that her father kept her hidden away for twenty years and no one in Ouabache knew about it? And that he tricked everyone into believing that she died? While she didn't know Isom Dubois well, she couldn't believe him capable of such horrors. When she first found Amy on that country road, hysterical and bloodied...well, up until this moment, it never occurred to her to doubt Amy. After all, Jed confirmed that she had been abused and she hadn't been outdoors in ages. *Or perhaps this is an elaborate ruse concocted by the deputy to undermine my authority.*

Ever since she obtained the office of sheriff, Deputy Frank shirked his duties, neglected to inform her of occurrences in Ouabache, behaved in an unprofessional manner, and participated in a crime. If he could trick her, make a fool of her, he would and he might be able to displace her as sheriff. He could have enlisted this woman in his scheme and would reward her later. *Jed might think she is Amy, but is she really?*

Claire leaned back in her chair and carefully scrutinized Amy, watching for any little tick that might betray her. "How did you escape, Miss Dubois?"

Amy withdrew from the deputy and shivered. "I don't know what possessed me, but tonight when Daddy brought me my supper, I pushed him and ran out of the attic and the house. He caught up with me in the woods, and attacked me. I got away." She lifted and dropped her slim shoulders. "I'm sorry, the next thing I remember was running out in front of your car."

"Amy, Sheriff Williams is good at her job." Deputy Frank declared. "We will find out the truth."

Claire couldn't believe her ears, and stared at him in disbelief. Never before had the deputy praised her for her successes. It didn't feel natural. *This is a ploy; it has to be.* Nothing made sense. Not the encounter on the country road, the story Amy offered up, or Deputy Frank's actions. Jed was wrong, the deputy was up to something and he couldn't be trusted.

Claire demurely nodded. "Yes, I promise, you will have justice." She could play their game. Countless times she had to plaster on a smile and humor the good ol' boys of Ouabache to perform her job as sheriff. This was no different. She'd play along, they would be none the wiser, and then she would prove that the deputy had ulterior motives. "And you are safe here, no one will hurt you again."

Amy mouthed the words, "thank you," and dissolved into tears. Deputy Frank slid his arm around her and held her close.

Claire fumbled with her wedding band, twisting it around her ring finger. They'd pay a call on Isom Dubois tomorrow morning. It was too late now, or else she'd go. However, he should be able to shed light on his daughter's death or confess to holding her captive, whichever was the truth.

*

Claire pulled the Model A up in front of Isom Dubois' house. A smile tugged at the corners of her mouth, but she maintained her somber expression. Deputy Frank was in the passenger seat, arms crossed and fuming. *I'll drive.* He announced when they left Amy in Jed's care and headed for the car. She marveled at his gall, that the deputy thought she would hand over her keys and let him take the lead. His thin frame was rigid with rage when she refused and he had to endure the torture having a woman drive him to interrogate a witness.

Deputy Frank sprang from the car seconds after she climbed out. Claire hastened up to the Dubois property, taking it in. It was a normal, two story, grayed trimmed, well-kept, clean place. Nothing remarkable, nothing that screamed sinister. *No one would guess a woman was locked away in the attic. If it indeed happened.* She squinted and noticed the shutters on the attic window did appear to be nailed shut.

Claire took charge and knocked on the front door, wincing at the shrill screech the hinges made when the door creaked open. "Hello?" She glanced at the deputy stationed at her side and when he shook his head in confusion, "Mr. Dubois, it is Sheriff Williams and Deputy Frank. Are you home?" Her voice echoed throughout the house but she received no answer. They had been able to secure a warrant to search the property, but she felt uneasy entering without permission of the owner. "Mr. Dubois?"

"To hell with this." Deputy Frank dashed forward into the foyer, then he mounted the stairs to the second story.

The attic. Claire followed, regretting wearing her dress shoes when a pair of boots would have been more sensible. She drew up her skirt a fraction and ran the best she could. Listening to the deputy's heavy footfalls, she followed the noise to a thin ladder in the master bedroom's closet, which had been let down and led to the attic. Careful not to turn her ankle on the thin rungs, she climbed up and found Deputy Frank standing in the center of the upper room.

Claire straightened to her full height and let out a small gasp. There was a bed shoved off to the side, the linens were dingey and someone had decorated the walls with clusters of lines, tallying the number of days they had been locked away. A tray of food and drink had been knocked to the floor, supporting Amy's story.

"It's true." Claire shivered, partly from the autumnal chill of the early morn, and partly from how creepy this was. Mr. Dubois had locked up his poor daughter. "How Mr. Rochester of Mr. Dubois." The deputy's silence claimed her attention and she turned to him. "What is it?"

Deputy Frank reached out and touched one of the walls, stroking the place Amy had marked. "I've passed by this place thousands of times and she was right here." Gone was the cocky man she had become acquainted with in the past few months. Guilt was etched in his features.

"The one behind this won't go unpunished." Claire assured him and it dawned on her that an apology was necessary. Jed was right, she allowed her dislike of the deputy to distract her. Rather than focusing on solving this crime, she focused on finding a way to blame this on the deputy. While she would never care for him, he and Amy deserved better treatment. "I'm sorry, I doubted you and I doubted Amy."

Deputy Frank opened his mouth to speak, paused and inhaled. "Do you smell smoke?" He asked, holding up a finger.

Claire sniffed and could make out a faint smokey scent bleeding through the walls of the house. They shimmied down the attic ladder and back down the stairs, but rather than go out the way they came in, she hurried through the house and left out the back door. Deputy Frank was on her heels.

The gray headed Mr. Dubois was a hundred feet off, tossing pieces of lady's clothing into a small heap. Flames flickered, crackling like a demon as she neared. A lazy stream of smoke rose, lifting into the sky. While Indiana was prone to rain in October, the drought changed that and left everything dry and crispy. Setting a fire and burning things was dangerous.

"Mr. Dubois, stop!" Claire shouted and brought her hand up against Mr. Dubois' boney chest, guiding him back. "Step away from the fire!"

She was relieved when he complied. Considering he locked away his own daughter, there was no telling what he was capable of. The Mr. Dubois she knew from church was mild mannered, hardworking, and devout. But obviously that Mr. Dubois didn't exist. It had been a façade. *This is the real Isom Dubois.*

Deputy Frank fetched a bucket of water from the house and doused the flames. Once the steam rolled off and the contents cooled, Claire made out remnants of Amy's clothing, shoes, and a hat. She peered into Mr. Dubois' face and noted traces of shame behind his bushy beard. The longer she observed him, the pieces of the puzzle fit. He was a small man, with small hands, His fingers would likely match up to the flesh wounds on Amy's arms.

"Well, Mr. Dubois, we have a miracle on our hands." Claire clasped her hands together. She was unable to resist sarcasm, feeling the man was more than deserving of it. "Your daughter who died twenty years ago is alive and at the sheriff's office. Here I thought only Jesus could be resurrected from the grave."

Mr. Dubois lowered his head, but he still said nothing.

Deputy Frank addressed the older gentleman. "Would it have been so terrible if Amy had married me?"

"You think that's why I did it?" Mr. Dubois scoffed, shaking his head. He likely would have laughed if he hadn't been caught in the act of destroying evidence. "No, I didn't like you and I wanted only the best for Amy. But I hid her away because she is of the devil."

Claire was too astonished to form a reply. Her hair stood up on the back of her neck. She had expected a variety of excuses, including disapproval of Amy's love for the deputy. However, claiming Amy was of the devil wasn't one of them.

"If I hadn't, she would have wreaked havoc on mankind." He raised up his opened hand. "All you have to do is look at her-"

"Shut up, shut the hell up!" Deputy Frank threw down the bucket and had balled his fists, ready to beat the man.

Claire stepped in between them. "That's a confession if I've ever heard one." She signaled to the deputy, who produced a pair of handcuffs. Allowing Deputy Frank to do the honors and subdue him, she announced, "Mr. Dubois, you are under arrest for the imprisonment and abuse of your daughter, which is a gross understatement of what you have done."

Mr. Dubois briefly closed his eyes and shook his head. "God have mercy on your souls." When his eyelids lifted, he looked to the heavens, as if expecting the Almighty to cast down a bolt of lightning.

Claire led the men back to the car, satisfied that they arrested the one who caused Amy Dubois such pain. Yet so much had been taken from Amy: time, freedom, and love. Freedom and love, she could regain. But twenty years could never be returned to her.

*

Claire was greeted with an unsettling silence as she and the deputy guided the restrained Mr. Dubois through the front door of the sheriff station. A quick glimpse around the room informed her that there had been a tussle. Chairs were overturned, her desk drawers had been dumped out, and papers were strewn on the floor.

Amy and Jed were nowhere in sight.

A low, rumbling moan reached her ears and following the sound, she traced it to the small kitchen. Jed was sprawled out on his belly, a gash on the back of his head. There was a broken lamp lying beside him.

"Jed!" Claire crouched down beside him, and with some encouragement she rolled him over and helped him into an upright position. "Are you all right? What happened?"

The movement elicited a long, exaggerated groan from Jed. "I'm fine. Thankfully, I have a hard noggin." He swiped his hand at his wound and examining his blood-stained fingers, he shrugged, "I don't rightly know. Miss Dubois hit me, and she was speaking in a man's voice."

Claire was skeptical, wondering if the doctor might be a little tipsy. *I've found him intoxicated before.* But he was sober when she left him and he wouldn't have imbibed when he was supposed to watch after Amy. Or perhaps he was hit harder than what he thought. Taking his hands, she pulled him to his feet and let him lean on her as they made their way back to the front.

Deputy Frank and Mr. Dubois stood there awkwardly, the former not offering help in assisting the doctor into a chair. Claire rolled her eyes; if it didn't directly involve Amy, the deputy was of no use.

"It was the devil in her." The latter clucked his tongue. "I told you, she's possessed and that's why I had to lock her away."

Claire passed one of her hankies to Jed, to sop up the blood. "You claim that Amy is not herself." Though she initially dismissed Mr. Dubois claim, that Amy was of the devil, this time she chose to listen and play devil's advocate. "Is she someone else?" She edged closer to the man.

"She's the devil." Mr. Dubois hissed. "She's possessed by seven demons, like Mary Magdalene."

"Stop saying that." Deputy Frank commanded, swatting the man on the side of the head.

"Deputy, none of that!" Claire gasped, but collected her composure and detached Mr. Dubois from Deputy Frank. She led him out of the office and down to the jail. "Sir, are you speaking the truth?"

"What do I have to gain by lying about my girl being possessed?" Mr. Dubois asked. "Who would believe me?"

Claire handed the man off to the jailer and eyed him between the bars of his cell. He was convinced his daughter was of the devil and possessed, enough to lock her in an attic. However, she met Amy, sat down with her, and though she was abused and troubled and Claire briefly thought the woman was scheming with the deputy, there wasn't any taint of evil in her. *Dear God, could Amy Dubois be possessed?* Hoosiers were prone to believe in ghosts, spirits, and demons, especially during the autumn. Superstition was carved in their bones. As a Christian, she believed in good and evil, in God and the devil. Demons were real in the Bible and perhaps they were real in this scenario too.

She rejoined Jed and Deputy Frank at the office, perplexed by the latest occurrences in this case. Just when she thought she had it figured out, there was another twist.

"Sheriff," Deputy Frank drawled, "Don't tell me you are taking the word of a man who imprisoned his own daughter. Amy wouldn't harm a fly."

"I don't trust Mr. Dubois and I don't know that I believe Amy is possessed." Claire looked to the doctor and knew he was not wrong. She motioned towards him. "But Jed has no reason to lie; if he says Amy hit him and was not herself, then that is what happened. And now she's out there, on her own."

Jed continued to apply pressure to his head and managed to get to his feet. He was wobbly, but determined, "Then you need to find Miss Dubois before she harms herself or someone else." He said.

Claire nodded and prayed she wouldn't make another mistake.

Amy's life depended on it.

*

"Amy is not demon possessed." Deputy Frank stated as he and Claire crept through the woods from where Amy had emerged the previous night.

By instinct alone, Claire believed that Amy would return to the woods or the road she had been discovered on. *Dear Lord, let her be nearby.* Otherwise, she didn't know where to search. The likelihood of Amy returning to the home she was imprisoned in was slim. Whatever friendships she had in her youth had long since faded. Her only connections were to her father and Deputy Frank. Jed volunteered to remain at the sheriff's office, in case Amy turned up there, and to doctor his head wound. He also spread the word throughout Ouabache for the locals to keep watch. Claire had considered sending out a search party, but thought better of it. If Amy assaulted Jed, she could easily assault another innocent.

Thankfully the morning's clouds had parted and the sun was bright. They'd have a better chance of locating Amy in the daytime than at night. She might have been lucky enough to find Amy the first time at night, but she doubted it would happen again like that.

"Deputy," Claire made certain to keep up with his quick stride, and was grateful she was wearing the new pair of boots she recently purchased. They fit better than her husband's and they suited trekking through muck and mire than her regular pair of shoes. "Anyone locked up for twenty years is bound to have some demons."

An unnatural howl pierced the air, causing her to stop in her tracks. The deputy didn't notice it, too fixated on his hunt. Claire grasped his elbow, drawing him back. She pressed a finger to her lips. The howl sounded again. It wasn't a wolf's or a coyote's cry, nor was it akin to any other animal's holler.

Deputy Frank's sharp eyes widened and his face blanched.

The howls were from the west. *It's Amy.* She didn't know why or how Amy could be making such a noise, but it had to be her.

Claire rushed in that direction, hopping over fallen limbs and wild brush. The deputy trailed her, huffing and puffing. The trees of the woods receded and they met an open field. Amy was in the center of it, shrieking in a tone that should have belonged to someone else.

"There she is." She pointed; her arm extended.

Whilst Amy was a long way off, Claire watched in horror as the woman started screaming and slapping herself. It wasn't Deputy Frank or Mr. Dubois who had violently harmed Amy. *She did it to herself.* There was a jug of what looked to be petrol at her feet. Amy grabbed the jug and tipping it upside down, she dumped the contents on herself.

Deputy Frank broke out into a frantic run. "Amy, stop!" He shouted.

Claire followed and didn't stop until they were within a few feet of Amy. "Miss Dubois, what are you doing?"

Amy tossed the jug aside and turned to them. "You found me. Please, he's going to kill me." She tremored all over, reeking of petrol. The fumes made Claire's eyes water, but the woman's behavior took her attention off of that. Suddenly, Amy's expression altered and she gnashed her teeth. A deep guttural voice escaped from her. "SHUT UP! QUIT WHINING! DO IT!"

Claire flinched at Amy's demonic groans and wished she could flee, but this was her job. She couldn't abandon Amy now.

"No, please don't hurt me." Amy whimpered, pleading with whatever it was that possessed her.

Amy produced a cigarette lighter and with the scrape of her delicate thumb, she flicked it open and a flame appeared.

"Amy, please don't!" Deputy Frank begged. He craned his neck back and seemed to be called up heavenwards. "Oh, God, don't let her do it!"

Amy, trapped in her own world, didn't react to her beloved's request.

Clare waved her hand in front of the woman's face, claiming her attention. "Amy, we know you are there and you can hear us." She spoke in a clear tone and kept her face placid in hopes of calming Amy. "Put the lighter down and we'll help you."

"I love you, Amy!" Deputy Frank declared. "I will take care of you!"

Rage contorted Amy's features. "NO, I'M SENDING HER TO HELL." She growled, and then a second later, she resumed her normal way of speech. "Maybe I should, I'll be free." She tilted her head in contemplation.

Claire's thoughts raced as she tried to come up with something, anything to prevent the woman from killing herself. "No, God does not make mistakes." She advanced a couple of paces, her eyes clamped on the lighter in the tremoring woman's hand. "You have a soul, you have a purpose here, Deputy Frank loves you dearly."

"SHUT UP!" The masculine voice hissed. "NO ONE COULD EVER LOVE HER!"

Amy brought the lighter closer to her body.

Oh God! Claire had only a few seconds before it would be too late. Otherwise, Amy would be swallowed up in flames. She moved quickly but precisely, and batted the lighter out of Amy's hand. The lighter somersaulted onto the ground, several feet away.

Deputy Frank was next to act. He threw himself at Amy, wrapping his arms around her. The other voice screamed and she struggled to wrench herself free. Despite his slight build, he was strong enough to maintain his grasp until Claire snapped the handcuffs on Amy's wrists.

Claire backed away, exhaling the breath that she was holding. *Dear God, thank you.*

*

Claire sipped her tea, relishing in the strong liquid that soothed her throat and warmed her insides. She set the cup down on her desk and listened to the harmonious hymn the deputy was playing. *Leaning on the Everlasting Arms.* Deputy Frank had retrieved his guitar from his home and toting it in, he spoke briefly to her:

"Thank you for saving Amy."

"You'll have to let me know if I can do anything more for her." Claire replied.

The deputy and Amy were in the corner of the office, he serenading her with a variety of hymns. It reminded Claire of the story in the Bible, where young David played music on his lyre to chase away the unholy spirits that plagued King Saul. Deputy Frank's music seemed to do the same; Amy was calm and humming along.

She had hated that she'd have to put Amy in a cell at the jail later, considering all the woman had been through. But she had no other choice, until she could figure out what could be done. The deputy would likely accompany her, so Amy wouldn't be alone. Mr. Dubois would be in a neighboring cell, but she could well envision him keeping to himself, saying nary a word to his daughter. The man was as confusing as Amy was. Perhaps more so.

Jed chose that moment to wander into the room, and pulling up a chair, he sat on the other side of the desk. "A penny for your thoughts?" He plunked down his own cup of tea.

"I wonder if Miss Dubois' demon came before her father locked her up or afterward." Claire said.

"Surely you don't believe Miss Dubois is possessed." Jed harrumphed.

Heat rose to her cheeks. "I'm a Christian and I believe there is good and evil in this world." She leveled her gaze at him. "How would you explain it, doctor?"

"For centuries men and women have suffered various maladies and demons have been blamed for it." Jed took a lengthy drink and put the cup back down. "I think Miss Dubois has two personalities warring inside of her, and one is trying to dominate the other. She needs treatment."

Claire didn't argue with him. He knew more about the human mind and body than she did. Even so, she never heard of such a thing before. Two personalities trapped inside of a person? Whatever it was – two personalities or a demon – it was what Mr. Dubois had referred to when he excused himself for locking Amy away.

"In a sanitarium?" She arched a brow and laced her fingers together, laying her hands on the surface of the desk. "They're not kind to the patients in places like that. God help her."

Jed nodded in agreement. Amy would suffer no matter where she was. Left to her own devices, she would harm herself. Her father preferred her to be trapped in an attic and forgotten. A sanitarium would offer her "treatment" at the hands of harsh nurses and orderlies, the medicines and procedures worse than the malady.

"I was wrong to suspect that Deputy Frank was behind this." Claire stated. She had apologized to the deputy but guilt festered down deep. Amy's life was at stake and she had been pettily caught up on personal dislike.

"Even a bad man can love another." Jed shrugged and picked up his cup once more, nursing on the brew. "And a sheriff can't be right all the time. The previous sheriff wasn't, you won't be."

Claire managed a strained smile. She truly was grateful for Jed's advice and support. He often believed in her when no one else did. *Deputy Frank deserves a second chance, I suppose.* The deputy was shady and his behavior offended her at times, and while she had suspected he had been involved in crimes, she didn't have definitive proof. Though she would like to have a different deputy, for better or for worse, he was hers.

In time, she would learn to trust him.

MADE IN THE SHADE
BY DANIEL PYNE

Well, he was heartbroken, Fleming. That was the gist of it. Twenty-four-years-old and aching. Broken-hearted, downcast, slump-shouldered, roguishly underfed, he looked and wallowed in the part of shattered man and yet, he hoped, came across as still somehow soulful, resolute. So far, Korea had played out in a breathless, fluttery blur, an incomprehensible cascade of coming attractions, where the film kept skipping sprockets.

Not to mention how he had nearly died.

Which would have made for a much shorter story, for sure.

Seoul, Korea. Autumn of '52. Ground zero of the coldest war, two brash young shadow warriors in long woolen civilian greatcoats made their way down a great hallway lined with hundreds of stacked dining chairs, dusted plaster white. Lazy grey exhaust from a rank Tiparillo vised between exposed molars stung the vodka-red eyes of the fellow American walking with Fleming.

Were they best friends? To be determined. In-country pals, for sure – Andy Dowler had already proven to be a worthy wingman when it came to that ~ but a war zone distorts, and Fleming hadn't really known the other man long enough to be confident about the long-term prospects of their acquaintance.

They had time, right?

First, though, there was the imminent ass-kicking both planned to deliver soon. On each other.

War is hell.

Three weeks into his first Agency posting, barely settled, sleep-deprived from the crazy firefights courtesy of allied mop-up skirmishes around the city, Fleming had been paired by the Seoul station chief with Dowler, whose heavy six o'clock shadow at least helped foster the illusion that he was, at twenty-one, a grizzled veteran. In point of fact he had only been in-country six months longer. Small, square and muscular, Dowler was to be the senior man on a routine brush-contact operation, and he clearly took quite seriously his mentor's role in all things Fleming from the getgo.

Dead of a hot night, mired in a sulfurous humid fog from recent KPA shelling, they had made their way across fallow farmland on the city's edge to the sallow lights of a half-collapsed grain warehouse. A double-agent was bringing them stolen Chinese battle plans for yet another shock-attack by communist troops to try and re-capture Seoul.

Fleming, still vague on the local topography, had felt utterly dependent on "the senior man" as they trekked to and entered the cavernous make-shift bazaar, where massive canvas panels had been strung up over its blown-open end. It was stifling inside, the air almost dead. A rumbling diesel generator kept carnival string lights barely alive, pulsing bright and dim like some live thing breathing, while bats whistled back and forth in the steel rafters. The ruined warehouse was crowded with a warren of make-shift kiosks offering black market goods. Smoldering grills and hot pots reeked of kimchi and mystery meat; in one far corner were tables of local men playing Go and gambling with dice. Fleming could have counted the other western Anglo faces like his and Dowler's on one hand with a couple fingers left over.

A maze of blankets and sheets hid an open-air brothel. Heavily painted women smoked and stared listlessly from folding chairs, waiting, patient, eyes dead, limbs slack, like sprinters between heats.

With no more than a word that got lost in the dull rumble of generator and crowd, Dowler had stopped abruptly in a ribbon of shadow, his face obscured, his eyes tiny pricks of reflected light, and he had pointed to a bulgogi grill where the fiery fat of marinated beef ribs flares in fits and spasms above a steel drum filled with incandescent charcoal. Fleming had leaned closer, smelled his colleague's souring flop sweat and cologne, and understood that his partner wanted him to make the exchange because Dowler was worried he'd be recognized here.

Eager to prove himself, Fleming had taken the grimy envelope, fat with cash, and tucked it away in his coat pocket. He didn't know what the asset would look like but had assumed that the man would find him. He was afraid to ask questions. They'd spent some time on live drops in training. He assumed from Dowler's lack of explanation that he should know.

Idle dark eyes had followed him as he zig-zagged through the narrow aisles. Feeling foolish and exposed, he had fingered the handgun in his other pocket, slipped off the safety, the way he'd been taught, and kept his finger loose on the trigger guard, so he couldn't accidentally shoot himself in the leg.

A thermal caught the smoke from the barbecue and he was enveloped by greasy black fumes. His eyes stung. He felt more than saw the slender shape detach from a huddle of men watching the shirtless grill-master work; in the time it took Fleming to glance back at Dowler for some signal that this was their contact, the shadow had intercepted him. Dowler had vanished. Fleming's heart began to race. He had a glimpse of a salmon-hued face ashen with untreated frostbite, felt the money being lifted from his pocket and getting replaced by something squarer and heavier.

An amateur's startled reflex caused Fleming to bark, "Hey!" The face swiveled back to him, but kept moving away, showing only irritation and alarm.

Or was it abject fear?

And in the instant before the warehouse exploded with small arms discharge, Fleming realized: *there are no cool customers in real life war— everyone is scared.*

He was caught in a crossfire. He couldn't see who had started shooting, or why. Nothing could have prepared him for that moment; it was terrifying and banal, total chaos, happening with such immediacy that even afterward, he couldn't put it in any proper order. The guns sounded small and hollow, like the cap guns he'd played with as a kid. Was this so much different? He felt counterfeit; a child playing spygames. Then the courier fell in an awkward tumble, limp, shabby coat flying up to cover him like a coroner's shroud, and there were screams and shouts and clatter of kiosks collapsing and a cyclone of movement carried Fleming away from ground zero where, as things cleared, there were three more bodies stretched prone on the concrete floor.

Very real, and very dead.

A civilian police whistle shrieked. The exits became jammed. Someone seized Fleming's arm, he tugged frantic to free himself, and when he whirled to confront his assailant, he realized it was Dowler.

"We gotta go."

Fleming swallowed a lump of panic. "What just happened?"

"Beats me." Digging into Fleming's pocket, Dowler felt for the swapped-out packet and had shoved it back down even deeper. "Don't lose that. We gotta go."

Jostled off-balance, Fleming's free hand had flown from his other pocket, and his pistol had clattered away. *Rookie mistake. Swell. Stupid.* He had never felt so ill-prepared for anything.

They zagged back toward the furling sheets of the make-shift brothel and fought their way directly through them. Dowler had seemed certain there would be an exit in the warehouse wall on the far side of the maze. Fleming wondered if he'd been there before. More gunfire and shouting. The painted women and their clients were already in a panic, tugging on clothes and rushing to get out. Dowler shouted at them in English, waved his own gun and Fleming again felt the stab of failure for having lost his.

The sheeted walls were collapsing ~ someone had cut the line that held them. Dowler tumbled over a draped lump that cried out. Fleming yanked the sheet away and exposed a small boy, huddled up against a pilfered US Army cot.

"Holy moly." Grimacing, Dowler clutched his knee and began moving again, then looked at Fleming, rooted where he stood, held by the haunted eyes of the boy, no more than four-years-old, skin and bones, weeping, scared, snot-smeared.

"No, leave him," Dowler had growled. "He's not your problem."

And Fleming had thought: *then who is?* Without even bothering to disentangle the boy from the sheet, he picked the bundle up and stumbled after Dowler. A steel door in front of them was swinging open and closed as people pushed through; Dowler held it for Fleming, and they stumbled out into the night where a one-legged crone spotted the Americans and began to scream, making a beeline toward Fleming. She winged out crutches to try and beat him across the shoulders. He hunched to shield his bundle and ward off her blows.

The boy squirmed out, shed his sheet, and ran to bear-hug the old woman's one

quaking leg.

"What did I do?"

"It's her fucking son," Dowler had told him. "She thinks you're trying

to steal him."

A few more locals had joined in the melee, hurling anything they could

get their hands on and swinging walking sticks that the Americans managed to

dodge. Fleming got all turned around again, and for the second time Dowler had

to grab him and pull him away.

"What're you, some Red Cross chick?" Dowler had hissed.

"Huh?"

"Saving the little children. Lady Fleming. Nurse chicklet. And look

what it got you."

"I was just trying to help," Fleming blurted, breathless.

"We can't save everybody."

"Or anybody. Evidently," Fleming had snapped.

That had made Dowler laugh, a clear release of tension, his gallows roar

booming across the fleeing market crowds, then he and Fleming sprinted out

across the field toward the scattered lights of Seoul. There was no troop carrier

parked where they'd been assured it would wait for them.

Fleming's head was spinning, but in a good way. Exhausted,

exhilarated, awash in the spike-rush of abject fear and escape, he was already hashing back over the night's events to put them in a better order, one that seemed even braver, and deliberate.

Dowler, a thin brown cigarette cupped in one hand while he held a match flame to it with the other, looked suitably bemused. "Another day at the office, Chick," Dowler had cracked wise, blowing out a lungful. "Ho dee ho." The lit end of his smoke glowed and sparked.

Chick? Fleming had flinched, said nothing, hoping that by ignoring it, the nickname wouldn't stick.

It took them two hours to hoof it back to their make-shift home base in a former toy factory they shared with an allied military hospital, where another depressing letter from Fleming's ex-wife was there waiting for him, along with the section's relentlessly upbeat Korean intelligence attaché, who'd been up late organizing a charity boxing match on which, he bragged humbly, lively wagering had already begun.

"Who's fighting?" Fleming had wondered.

"You and him," the Korean agent had said, impatient, as if the answer should have been obvious.

Because it was. And here they were.

*

"You know what your deal is, Chick?" Dowler drawled as they walked, and it wasn't a question. His restive eyes, set deep and wide, tended to dance, playful, when he was about to wind you up.

"Here it comes."

"You're a cocky son of a bitch. No matter how hard you cry the blues."

Fleming bristled. "Hey, seriously ~ could you not call me Chick?"

"Which is why I don't fret about you," Dowler continued his thought, ignoring the request, but added a sardonic, "seriously" to show that he'd heard it.

Shooting the breeze like salary men on a free-time lark, they could have been in Bakersfield, Des Moines or Minnetonka. Well, except for the occasional incoming enemy sorties, the unforgiving cold, the sandbags piled halfway up glassless window frames, the high lathe walls cracked like eggshells. That latest airmail letter from Fleming's ex bulged, taunting him, from his pocket. There was no point in reading it again. The words wouldn't change.

"But back to my original point," Dowler prattled on, "didja ever think, ever really consider, that maybe your ex *is* bonking everybody?"

Fleming shot him what he hoped was his iciest look.

"Word to the bird, daddy-O. Word to the bird."

Fleming took a deep breath and decided this was probably Dowler's attempt at pre-brawl psyops; wages of war. There was the sudden boom of a stray PRK shell dropping somewhere outside, pretty close, and the building trembled and both men flinched, but nothing came down from the walls except dust.

It left them quiet, grimy canvas high tops scuffing through the dusty ruins of what must have been Seoul's grandest international hotel before the insults of urban ground war, advance and retreat. Fleming only knew the city in its ruined aftermath. Rumor was that Vice President Nixon had stayed here when he was a congressman.

Dowler shuffled sideways, feigned a jab and mussed Fleming's hair. "Hey. Chin up, sport. What difference should it make? You gonna go ape every time she looks at a guy? It's done, leave it behind."

"There's the girls to think about."

"Why? Are the little ankle-biters boning everybody too?"

"Whoa." Fleming scowled, anger flaring hot. "That's out of line."

"You think?"

"Andy, they're eighteen-months-old."

Dowler gave a deadpan side-glance.

"I think you should stop right there."

Typically, Dowler ~ emphatically single and currently romancing a WAC cryptographer who, he swore on his mother's grave (though his mother was still alive) had more playable positions than the Chicago Bears ~ didn't, moreover couldn't, stop himself: "I mean, women. I don't know what else to tell you."

Wrung out, and feeling his spike of anger ease, Fleming tried to end the discussion with a dry, "Yeah, you do. You're the World Book Encyclopedia of useless unwanted advice."

Boots slapping on ruined carpet weeping tiny pyroclastic clouds of ash, they strolled through a carved double doorway into a vaulted lobby filled with crumbled plaster and concrete through which a swept path snaked. Charred timbers crisscrossed the last of the gaping roof overhead. Torn tar paper fluttered in the cruel wind. A frosted long black marble check-in counter was incongruously intact, but everything else had been rendered stone-age rock pile by all the bombing, bombing, bombing, friend and foe.

"Puts a whole new light on things, though," Fleming confessed, unable to let it go either. "Aw, what's the use? I've still got a thing for her, Andy. I always will."

Dowler glanced sidelong. "So?"

The lobby elevators, shafts sheared off, cars gutted, featured rusty cables sprouting insanely like antennae, into a slate grey February sky. Dowler and Fleming could see their breath.

"I'm ..." Fleming couldn't believe he was going to say this out loud, "... heartbroken." Pathetic. "Okay? Completely gutted. How do you get 'cocky' out of that?"

"I see the deeper meanings," Dowler said.

Oh.

*

They marched under a high sculpted archway and into a beautiful bombed-out

ballroom where a milky light filtered through fractured clerestory windows.

Sarcastic cheers rose from chapped-faced grunts crowding a makeshift boxing

ring on the other side of the vast, warped and splintered parquet floor, as Eighth

Army soldiers clocked Dowler and Fleming's arrival.

Dowler spat out the stub of his smoke and stepped on it. "But okay, fine,

you wanna hang around, love your girl ～ who,
I'm sorry if the truth hurts, was no cheerleader before, so it can't come as too

much of a shock if she ain't no cheerleader now."

Soldiers split to let them through to the ring.

"You guys are so late." Resplendent as always in a dove grey suit and

tie, flower in the lapel, right sleeve pinned up on account of the arm he'd lost at

the Imjin River, Pou Min-ho (all the Americans called him "Boo" and he didn't

seem to mind) intercepted them with two pairs of red stuffed pillows that passed

for boxing gloves, and the two Yanks shrugged off their overcoats, revealing gym

shorts, pale legs, the khaki high tops and dank sleeveless t-shirts.

Fleming watched the one-armed Korean shove two gloves over Dowler's

chubby hands, while the senior man continued his lecture, "Assuming that half

of what you imagine is happening with her is actually happening ～ which Dollars

to donuts, it's not, except in that tiny little battlefield you call a head ～" he took

a breath, "～ I don't know how much value there is in continuing to play around in that sandbox. Although I admit, I did enjoy when you got convinced she was giving blow jobs to some Puerto Rican waiter behind the counter at Waffle House."

Fleming felt his face flush. "I only said 'taking an unusual interest in.' And okay, maybe that was an overreaction, but ~"

"No, no." Dowler clipped Fleming's next complaint right off. "Go right ahead and suffer, Chick, cuz it's not like a.) There's other fish in the sea. And b.) There's not more important things to worry about."

"Fish in the sea. That's all you got?"

"Please," Boo said to them. "Combatants. Concentrate on the task before you."

They stopped talking and moved apart. Pou Min-ho helped slip the gloves on Fleming. He laced them tight while a frenzy of last-minute wagering blew up between some of the Second D and X Corps. Then the two friends ducked through the ropes and into the ring to beat each other silly.

"What other things?" Fleming asked as a razor-burned staff sergeant with an unfortunate hairline checked their gloves and murmured instructions they wouldn't heed in a thick Cajun accent they couldn't understand even if they had tried.

"What?"

"Other things."

Dowler tilted and rolled his neck. "Oh, I don't know. The A-bomb. The H-bomb." He made as if to think about it. "Or. Not to split hairs. A million crazy-ass Commies amassed across the thirty-eighth parallel with all their evil red intentions?"

Dowler wasn't wrong, but Fleming let his eyes get hooded and gave his best dismissive Bogart shrug. "Big deal," he said, backed into his corner.

Dowler smiled and nodded, as if to say: *there, that's more like it, the Fleming I know and love.* He thumbed his nose with his glove like Marciano, and some grunt found a bell to ring and started the match.

Ding.

*

It wasn't like Fleming had set out to be a spook. Events had just conspired to make it happen. If anyone had asked before Uncle Sam conscripted him (back in '46, long after the end of world war redux) to shore up the rapidly demobilizing and war-weary ranks ~ if anyone had asked what Chess Fleming intended to do with his life they would have been answered by a freshly-turned eighteen-year-old's dead-eyed heck-if-I-know stare.

No, infantry was what he had expected, and craved, with a teenager's zeal for adventure (the feckless, romantic, exotic kind you would see on the silver screen) and blind confidence in his own immortality, plus just enough Midwestern patriotism to leave him at the mercy of the relentless chain of command. Luckily for Fleming, he had a talent with words and puzzles and tested into Army intelligence, where an adjutant general everyone called Spooky behind his back had learned of Fleming's nearly encyclopedic knowledge of movies and effected an immediate transfer and deployment to Okinawa so that he could curate Saturday Night Flicks and lift the troops' morale. The closest Fleming thought he'd get to spycraft was the clandestine backdoor contact he had made in Metro Goldwyn Mayer's distribution department, allowing him to screen bootleg first run features before they were even released in the States, much to General Spooky's pride and delight.

War might be hell, keeping the peace was hellacious, Fleming had thought miserably at the time; a tedious, thankless, unspectacular grind.

And now he was fighting his friend.

Wham wham wham.

Sweat poured off them as, fierce and graceless, they pounded each other stupid. Fleming, pale white body he usually kept covered up practically luminous, was the better fighter; he'd done some PAL boxing back home, growing up.

But Dowler had no quit in him.

Ding.

Round one, stand-off. G.I.'s jackal-howled.

The staff sergeant stepped between them and the fighters staggered to opposite corners, where Fleming sagged heavily on the ropes and spit blood and his mouthpiece out into a bucket held by Boo.

"I'm getting killed."

"Yes. Good. Do not take him out too soon, Chester. The spread will look like a fix. Perhaps two more rounds, then ~ pow."

Fleming frowned. "Take him out? I'm not taking him out."

"You are Tri-State Golden Glover."

"Glove. Ten years ago, Boo. When I weighed, like, seventy-two pounds soaking wet."

"No one knows this. You are the lower dog, due to your peaceful nature."

"Underdog."

"Pow." Boo was already walking away, across the ring to where Dowler was heaving to catch his breath.

Fleming called after the Korean agent loudly, annoyed: "I thought this was for charity, Boo. The Blind Orphan's Fund. You said this was for charity." And then the phrase Boo had tossed off all casual settled on him: "Wait. What spread?"

Boo didn't answer from Dowler's corner. But the senior man had heard Fleming over the din of soldiers' between-round bantering. "There's a spread?"

"I have good money on you to win, Andrew," Fleming heard Boo tell him.

Dowler hacked, spit in a bucket, "Oh, sweet Jesus." His face was already pinked and getting puffy. He looked deadpan across the ring and Fleming fashioned a loopy grin he hoped would disarm. Fleming knew Dowler thought he was still just a raw recruit.

Boo murmured something Fleming couldn't quite hear, but as Dowler stood the Korean raised his volume above the din of the enlisted men, exhorting both boxers: "Don't lead with your face. Invoke your God for strength. You will prevail. I am confident. *Hannulee moonuh jyudo sossanal goomungee itda.*"

Dowler said, "You know we don't speak the lingua, Boo."

Boo turned to him and said, "Means there is a hole to escape through even when the sky collapses on us. This proverb has provided hope and faith through many difficult times."

"A hole in the sky."

"Yes."

"He's my friend," Fleming heard Dowler protest.

"And so, you owe him your best effort." Boo fished a mouthguard out of Dowler's bucket and jammed it between Dowler's teeth. "Fulfill your own prophecy. Believe there will be a way and you will find a way." He looked across at Fleming.

"You're a wing nut," Fleming told him, over the surge of anticipation from the crowd.

"Thank you."

Ding.

*

It was only after arriving in Japan that Fleming had discovered General Spooky ran a special branch of the old OSS, which was slowly revealing itself to be unequal to the thunderheads of cold war massing over the horizon.

But nobody had seen Korea coming. All eyes were on the red menace, Stalin and Mao.

Well, not quite *all* eyes ~ Fleming's had been focused more locally; honorably discharged in '48 and back in the home of the brave, grateful beneficiary of the G.I. Bill, indulging himself in fuzzy studies at Hannover College where, after two years in the company of men, he became blindsided by a fetching eighteen-year-old with legs that caused coronaries and a complexity that rocked his world.

Anna had ambushed his dreams; he had listened to hers and didn't judge them. They sparked like crossed load lines, despite her avowed wariness of older men. Even knowing she had a steady boyfriend at the time, Fleming proved undaunted. He wooed, they wed, war flared on the Korean peninsula, but Fleming had already done his soldier's turn. Twins were born the same month he got his degree. Time to settle down and raise a family, live some version of the new American dream. Anna's Arizona-based father had even proffered a career-ladder opportunity in actuarial accounting.

Looking back on it, he was never able to explain to himself why he'd turned down the good, quiet life that had been unfurled before him and instead accepted the invitation from recently retired General Spooky to join a newly reconstituted civilian spy agency, Central Intelligence, determined to bulldoze the commies out of Asia.

His fresh family was in Okinawa by August, but the mission was Korea, so he became husband in absentia, much to Anna's dismay. Sure enough, just shy of Christmas Fleming's lonely and beleaguered wife had flown back to San Francisco with their baby girls and filed for divorce.

"What's the point of being together if you're always gone?" she had said. "I'm stuck alone with rug rats in a country where I don't speak the language and my husband is like a thousand miles away." When he tried to bring up the company's support network, she spat, "Yeah: a bunch of blue-hair expat wives who will never be my friends."

A temporary stateside transfer enabled Fleming to rejoin her in Cow Hollow, where for a few tender months they tried to salvage the marriage while he rode a desk at Moffett Field. It hadn't worked. Nothing stuck. The fate of the free world hung in precarious balance across the Pacific and here he was changing diapers and suffering his wife's lingering post-partum blues. Having already been denied his opportunity to save the planet from the Fascists, Fleming was hell-bent now to do his small part to keep the flames of freedom burning.

For Pete's sake, what part of "a man's sacred duty to God and country" didn't she get?

All of it, thank you very much.

Things got ugly. He grew paranoid, convinced without evidence that while he burned midnight oil vetting intercepted Chinese radio traffic transcriptions, his wife was catting around the city, sowing those wild oats he'd denied her by tying her down, sleeping with everybody and his uncle ~ then petulantly refusing to deny it.

Fleming's mom, distraught, urged patience. "You're babies with babies. You'll grow into this, you'll see."

He didn't. He became the poster boy for callow youth.

Lobbying Spooky for a field agent posting in Seoul (newly re-liberated for the fourth time via Operation Ripper) had been his reckless last-ditch attempt to call Anna's bluff ~ she hadn't blinked. They split. Korea proved a wilderness of mirrors, and the General had been forced to resign the day Fleming landed. All that tethered him to a rational world were Anna's sporadic terse reminders to pay his child support and alimony on time.

Then Kinpo. Whatever romantic illusions Fleming had clung to that his new posting would provide a noble justification for his rash decision got shattered in the senseless melee of the midnight market. He'd left his wife and babies for a fruitless, wildering cold war St. Vitus' Dance that, if he had ever bothered to reflect upon it, could only have ended in deadlock, with both sides collapsed from exhaustion.

*

At the bell, Dowler launched himself out into the ring where Fleming's stolid Jake LaMotta footwork and methodical left jab were waiting. Bam-bam.

Muscle memory, the exquisite ache. Bam-bam. Fleming lost himself in familiar rhythms, forgot that someone he knew and had grown fond of was who he was hitting. Well. Bam-bam. Fight to win, right?

Dowler eased some blows with his arms, and tried to counterpunch, shoulders low, round, head tilting sideways, feet shuffling, sliding, bobbing, drawing on his clearly improvised, street fighter's skills. Fleming didn't know whether to hold back or hold forth.

Mumbling through his mouthpiece Dowler taunted, "I can do this all day."

Fleming doubted it and slipped a right uppercut through that landed. Dowler's whole body went liquid. He sunk down on his knees, but bounced right back up again, relentless, wobbly and defiant, cackling, "all day," and giving a shoulder fake that didn't fool anybody, followed by a naïve roundhouse that opened him up for another vicious uppercut from Fleming.

This time Dowler went down on his ass, eyes glassy. Fleming knew he wouldn't stay there. Mulish, Dowler got himself upright, gloves up, a deep gash over one eye.

Suddenly Fleming felt trapped. No way out. How had they gotten here? A hundred soldiers howled for blood. He studied Dowler. "You okay?"

Dowler answered with a wild, weary swing that missed and carried him right into Fleming's somewhat apologetic counter. It purpled his nose.

"You wanna stop? We can stop."

Dowler looked pissed, now. "Take a hike with that."

It was hopeless. Everything was hopeless. You try to do the right thing, and somehow it always goes wrong. Dowler lunged in for a bear-hug, blood from his cut greasing Fleming's shoulder, and Fleming let him rest, intending to twist, shrug the shorter man off and end this pointless exercise so he could go back to the station comm closet and put through another shortwave call to his unhappy ex-wife.

Or was that just another futile act?

Somehow Dowler managed to square himself while his gloves clamped Fleming's ribs. They were face-to-face; Dowler looked spent, done, his whole body bruised and shaking. Feeling rotten about what was coming, Fleming made the effort to meet his friend's crazy doomed gaze before punching him out, whereupon—

Crack.

—Dowler cheerfully head-butted Fleming as hard as he could in the spirit of mutual destruction.

Cartoon stars and pinwheel fireworks.

"Ain't that a bite?" Dowler hissed, but he was already tilting, legs giving way.

Fleming's world skewed sideways. Thoughts clouded. He felt himself falling. The crowd hushed, held its breath. Both boxers went down.

And out.

But the last thing Fleming remembered seeing before the concussion overtook him was Dowler's toothy, blood-limned grin; another pyric victory in the age of the A-bomb, because Fleming had hit the floor first.

THE SICK AND THE WELL

BY GABRIEL HART

Benjamin Turner thought it was adorable, for a second, the way his wife kept lifting her shoulders, whisper-smiling the name of that new planned community out loud. One of those cozy-cute thinking about autumn kind of shrugs; like giving herself a fun little chill thinking about early onset holiday season, imagining what Thanksgiving or Christmas might look like in that "little village" everyone was talking about. It appeared like something out of a story book – only, no one bothered to ponder exactly what story was being told.

Instead, Renee Turner read the ad to her husband over breakfast.

THE NESTLES *"Once you're here, you're home forever!"*

"Located just one short hour from Las Vegas, The Nestles offers a safe yet vibrant residential sanctuary for the modern American family looking into the future by nodding to the past. The master-planned community is a smart update to the quaint Euro-style village – from its meticulous cobblestone gated entrance, your path graduates seamlessly into more traditional blacktop suburban streets, every road leading to a new neighbor guaranteed to become an old friend. With each unit in "snuggly" proximity, The Nestles "new village" sheds the outdated cookie-cutter grid blueprint of your current neighborhood for a sprawling circuit of winding mountain-adjacent roads, playfully curling between each unique property. Each home a charming stone cottage made of locally sourced material from Nestles Mountain into which The Nestles is thoughtfully ensconced."

"A self-sufficient, forward-thinking community built atop a deep, vast mountain spring, The Nestles thrives independent of the drying municipal water systems, where residents can cultivate their lawns, shower regularly without ration, hydrate to their heart's content –

"And Ben, it says here no money down—we'd be foolish not to do this..."

Benjamin raised his eyebrows to his wife; a neutral, uncommitted response of suspicion, presence, and *it's too early in the morning to be entertaining life-changing events like this.*

"Hmmm... sounds, uh, interesting. Where would Kayden go to school? We can't drive him back and forth to Henderson..."

"No, of course not! It says right here: Nestles Public School located just five minutes from the gate, grades K-12." She paused. "And Ben? Water. Did you hear the part about water? I don't know about you, but I don't like this whole showering every other day shit... Especially knowing Vegas gets to use as much as it wants."

Benjamin scoured his mind for any reason to negate Renee's big idea. Since he was a retired microbiologist and she worked from home, their professional lives weren't anchored to location. Yet, Benjamin felt they were still just getting settled into life in Henderson, one of the suburban tentacles sprawling from Sin City. But he admitted: after a year, it still didn't quite feel like home. It was hazy to get to the heart of this matter – Renee was the type who wanted a vacation from a vacation the day after they went somewhere to get away.

"What if we just took a drive out there this weekend, you know, just to get away?" asked Renee.

Benjamin did the eyebrow thing. "Sure. Just to get away. Why not." Being agreeable often bought him points with Renee, and lately he had fallen far behind.

*

It would be an impromptu family trip for the Turners. Their moody son Kayden, with brown bangs permanently covering his twelve-year old dagger eyes, brooded in the backseat at the thought of moving again, so fixated on his phone to make himself invisible. They drove along a newly paved two-lane highway that had recently replaced an old service road. Renee nodded excitedly when Benjamin pointed at what must have been it, though she couldn't clap or speak while she was on the phone with their representative.

"Okay, looks like we see it now... should be, what do you think Ben, five minutes?"

Benjamin raised his eyebrows, this time accompanied by his shoulders. It was difficult to tell distance with the mountain distracting his view out the windshield; no matter how close they approached, it remained an unmoving, imposing presence. One like they'd never seen before, so iconoclastic it started a mild argument: Renee insisted it looked like a scene out of an intricately designed snowglobe. "What snowglobes have you been staring into, Renee? This is the desert, for one, and that looks like a broken molar with bits of bacteria decaying the cavity!"

She stopped talking, crossed her arms, then did his eyebrow thing to see how he liked it.

"I'm sorry, Renee. I promise to keep an open mind, honey. I'm just curious what this mountain might have looked like before it was... well, whatever happened to it."

"Water, Ben! They have water."

Renee couldn't conceive why Benjamin was looking *past* The Nestles as if the adorable village was transparent. Glazed, his eyes instead pierced the mountain; the surrounding, compromised monolith, while his inner dialogue was also clashing within itself, conflicted by the view's undeniable majesty. It did, in fact, appear a city of the future – a practical, post-modern solution to the forever problem of draught and urban blight. Out of necessity, The Nestles would be a pioneering development, where real estate moguls were beginning to favor the proverbial divining rod over their usual exploitation of vulnerable demographics; at least, in order to water those latter seeds.

"Here, maybe your favorite song will help," said Renee, as she shuffled around for "Hymne" by Vangelis, the cascading synth instrumental most known for its appearance that one 80s wine commercial. The nostalgic song always calmed Ben, always awoke him from the malaise his scientific brain imprisoned his heart in. He often found himself on the cold, nihilist end of his studies, every breakthrough he made confirmed humans behave like a selfish virus—to deny it, he felt, was absolute cognitive dissonance.

But for the moment, Ben's favorite song steadily re-wired him as they drew nearer to the majesty of The Nestles, and his lower lip dropped in astonishment. Towering against the otherwise flatlined wasteland of the desert, it was an oasis for the eyes.

Once their tires hit the subtle bumps of the cobblestones, it was a new pleasant sensation that welcomed them to the gates. They parked where the rep instructed over the phone, then a woman appeared.

"You must be Renee?" she said, offering her hand. "I'm Jeanine, I'll be your guide and, hopefully, your dealmaker to your new home at The Nestles."

"I am! And this is my husband, Benjamin," she said. "And our son, Kayden." The boy gave a half-hearted salute with an attempt to smirk.

"Lovely. Well, so nice to meet you all," she said, adjusting the wide brim of her black Stetson La Roux.

"Oh my God, I love your hat," said Renee.

Jeanine giggled, blushing. "Oh, thank you! I swear, these days, it seems like I never take it off..."

"Well, I wouldn't either if I wore it that well."

"Aw, thank you. Listen, would you mind terribly if I just hopped in the car with you all to show you around, I can maybe navigate in the passenger seat? I'm having trouble with my contacts lately so I just walked down here to meet you..."

"Oh my God, not at all," insisted Renee. "I'll drive. Ben, you don't mind, do you?

"Of course not. Here, let me get the door for you, Jeanine..."

Jeanine horseshoed around their hood with a humble grin, obliging Ben's accommodating gesture. As she helped herself in, Ben noted her headwear's tight, constricting fit; no hair fell from the inside of the hat. He spotted a large blood-colored blemish he assumed covered her whole neck had it not been for a black scarf she wore. As she sat down, she adjusted it, stretching it taller up her throat. Ben knew she must have felt his eyes on her. She scrambled into her purse, "Oh, I bear gifts," she said, taking out three bottles of water for the Turners. "This is our community's own natural spring water, bottled at the source."

They were parched; everyone back in Henderson was always thirsty from rationing; no one ever knew how much conservation was recommended for what day, the protocols seemed to change by the hour. The Turners nearly embarrassed themselves from how fast they grabbed the bottles out of Jeanine's hands.

She giggled. "Don't worry, I remember what it was like to be thirsty. Just know there's plenty more where that came from. Oh, hang a right here, Renee—what we call 'The Well' will be your first left."

It was the only architectural anomaly in The Nestles. Its water facility was too large an operation to disguise as quaint, yet it was the heart of the community; all its piping as valves, its silos as aortas. Every inch of it painted blue as the ocean depicted in exotic vintage postcards.

"Here at The Well, we pump water up from the spring, distributing right into the municipal water supply. You can even drink it right from the tap."

Renee peered at Ben and Kayden. Ben smiled sincerely, Kayden did the eyebrow thing.

"Now, let's see the unit I want to show you—your near-future forever home, in other words. Take a right here, Renee?"

It was just like the ad pitch claimed, but better: Each cottage they drove past radiated fairytale enchantment; predominantly stone with wood roof and trim, exterior walls shrouded in overgrown ivy, the rear of each home built into the mountain itself.

"The developers of The Nestles teamed up with an engineering company that deals exclusively in sustainable, repurposed materials, which is why each of these homes you see has an ancient feel – this was all part of Nestles Mountain, before…"

"Before what, exactly?" said Ben.

"You know, before it became what you see here," she said. Matter of fact yet bereft of evidence. "Oh, turn right, the unit is right here…"

When the home came into view, Ben did the eyebrow thing but also nodded his head. Renee knew those tandem gestures signaled his approval—a good thing, considering she had already made up her mind. "Oh my. Isn't it adorable, you guys?" She looked to Kayden. "I see you wanting to smile so bad, kiddo. Don't be shy."

Jeanine led them in. "As you can see, it's similar to the others—hardwood floors, all the interior the same idea – but it has its exclusive shape. This particular one is three bedrooms, though which one can be used for an office…"

"Oh, I just love it – love it, love it, love it!" exclaimed Renee. "Ben?" She repeated his name, devolving into a more discrete, yet firm whisper. *"Ben? Would you stop looking at her neck? She probably has psoriasis…or eczema. Just stop, please…"*

He snapped out of it, sufficiently embarrassed. "So sorry, sorry." He caught Kayden staring at her as well, focusing on her hands where the red blotches peeked from under her sleeves. "Kayden, what do you think?" he said, repossessing his attention.

"Oh, uh… its cool. I guess I could live here."

"Ben?" Renee asked for final judgement.

"I think it's wonderful."

"Jeanine, we are ready to sign!" she beamed, clasping her hands in prayer.

*

They learned quickly there were different rules at The Nestles. What should have been a month-long nail-biting escrow for such desirable property was cinched up in less than an hour, much like buying a car. All Jeanine needed was their good credit score after her fast, auctioneer-cadence listing terms and details they "didn't need to worry about, this is all just legal jargon I'm obligated to orally recite to you."

Not a moment later she smiled, sure to make eye contact with each of them. "Congratulations on your new home,"—the real, tangible words the Turners were waiting for, snapping their daydreams into fruition.

Renee clapped her hands into another genuflected freeze-frame, bringing her fingers to her lips as she surrendered to Benjamin's embrace. "Great! Can we give you a ride back down the hill, Jeanine?" he asked.

"Well, you better!" said Jeanine. "How else would you enjoy your new home?" They all laughed except Kayden, who wondered what was funny.

As they drove though the winding roads back to the gate, Jeanine explained more, now that they were official Nestles Homeowners.

"So, one thing is that all us homeowners are encouraged to keep the Nestles at 100% capacity. It's in our best interest, a built-in incentive with property value to appreciate..."

"Oh, so you work for The Nestles, or you're just a homeowner?" said Ben.

"Well, in a way, once you become a homeowner, you sort of straddle both distinctions. So again, we can't have any vacancies here, and right now we are only at 98%."

"Oh? How many units are here?" asked Renee.

"There's exactly a hundred homes, so two are still vacant," said Jeanine. "We just can't really afford to not be at full capacity, you know... run risk of anyone wondering why someone wouldn't want to live here."

"What do you mean by 'afford' it?"

"Property values fluctuating and such. A vacant home just sticks out like a sore thumb, the residents begin to wonder why it can't be filled. We keep the Nestles HOA running like a tight ship..."

Her exposition remained inexplicable—a cliffhanger, in fact, when all four of their heads turned to the right at a man with no clothes stumbling into the path of their vehicle.

"Oh my God—today he's goddamned *naked?*" Jeanine lost her composure, surrendering to her own outburst. "I'll take care of this..." she mumbled, dialing her cell.

"Don't do it!" screamed the naked man. He wasn't addressing Jeanine who was calling the authorities — he was alerting the Turners, who were giving him their full terrified attention. Under his long, thinning grey hair he was covered in red blemishes of varying size from head to toe. "Don't sign anything! Look what happened to me..."

Benjamin white-knuckled the steering wheel as he slammed on the brakes on the one-man barricade banging on his hood. "What, what do I do?"

Renee screamed, and Kayden's mouth opened but nothing came out.

"Drive! Just drive, plow into him!" said Jeanine. "They're on their way to get him, just go!"

"You don't want this!" the man continued, punctuating each word with another punch to their hood. In a blur of both fight and flight, Ben slammed on the gas, knocking the man's exposed body to the left, revealing more expansive discoloration on his backside. The vehicle clipped him on the headlight, spinning him off into relative safety, at least from properly being run over.

On cue, red flashing lights from a municipal van came into view, screeching to a halt at the shocked man in compromised fetal pose on the hot asphalt. Two men in helmets and batons jumped out the back, bludgeoning him into submission before grabbing his wrists and ankles, forcing him into the back of the van.

Ben's gas leg was shaking uncontrollably, causing their dramatic peel out to retard to decelerating jerks, polyrhythmic under his hyperventilating.

"Ugh, thank God," said Jeanine. "I'm so sorry you folks had to see that, but at least you saw how swiftly the Nestles Neighborhood Watchmen show up when trouble is brewing."

They pulled up to her car at the gate. "Listen, I just want to congratulate you one more time for joining us here at The Nestles," she said, clapping her hands three times. "If you have any questions, anything at all, I'm just a phone call away." The Turners had questions, right then and there, but their adrenaline rendered them paralytic. "I... I... Okay, thank you," was all they could exhale, manners over matter.

*

After the odd welcome on their breakneck speed closing day, it took a couple weeks for the Turner's to settle confidently into their picturesque Nestles cottage, leaving their imperfect life back in Henderson a distant memory.

They unfurled into their daily routines — Renee on the computer, Benjamin taking the occasional consulting call when he wasn't working on his memoirs; an idea he got the first week as a Nestles resident, once he really came to appreciate the serenity. "It's time," he told Renee. "Who knows what a lifetime of accumulated knowledge might reveal once I really reflect?"

The memoir was peeling back memories and emotions he wasn't prepared for, but he encountered them head-on. When thinking about his own father, a nuclear engineer, he was gracious how attentive he was to Ben growing up, despite his long busy hours. In contrast, Ben felt as though he had been falling short with Kayden—even this memoir project was further testament that he was busying himself to avoid interaction with his own son.

"Kayden, have we ever told you much about your grandpa?"

The boy pursed his lips, shaking his head no in the glow of his phone.

"Well, wait here. If I can find it, I've got just the thing – something that can tell a lot about him." Benjamin kept a large box of his father's belongings in the attic, sentimental items he planned to pass down to Kayden one day.

Benjamin returned with a metal yellow box, with what Kayden thought looked like a compass or a vintage car speedometer built into it. "Do you know what this is?"

Kayden shrugged.

"This was your grandfather's Geiger counter, from the 70s. They call it a Cold War model, a CDV-700. He used it for projects to measure the amount of radioactivity."

Kayden's interest was vaguely awoken, enough to lower the phone from his face. "Huh, that's cool. What would you do with it now?"

"I just think it's super cool... and to me, represents your grandpa's career as a nuclear engineer. I played around with it when I was your age, got me interested in cellular activity." He paced around the house. "I wonder what we can test it out on...here, come with me outside to the well."

Ben looked over his shoulder, pleased with Kayden leaving his phone behind as he rose to follow. When they arrived at their personal well—each cottage came with an old-fashioned stone-enclosed cylindrical water-reserve—Benjamin placed the brightly colored CDV-700 on the brim. "So, watch, you turn it on like this..." he said, barely flipping the switch before he heard the sound of screeching brakes.

"Sir, what are you doing?" said the driver as he exited the van with two others, all in blue helmets and batons.

"I'm... I'm just..."

"Stay right where you are, don't you move one inch!" said the driver, restraining his arms to cuff his wrists as another grabbed the Geiger.

"What?"

"Sir, this water is still property of The Nestles. We do all its testing at the Nestles Well. When you closed on your home, you signed a clause which forbids Our Homeowners to test the water beyond our methods."

"Where are you taking me?"

"We're taking you to in, Sir. Your wife will have to re-negotiate the deed on your home after we book you. Jeanine will be in touch soon."

"Renee! Kayden, go get your mother!" was all he could utter before the van door slammed.

Kayden stood motionless at the well, in shock from what just violently transpired. Though Benjamin hadn't the chance to show him how it worked, Kayden saw the Geiger counter come alive before they grabbed it. Any reasonably intelligent twelve-year old would know what a needle bouncing all the way to the right could mean.

*

With no window to the front seats or out the back, Benjamin couldn't express his cold sweat. The Nestles Neighborhood Watchmen van backed in carefully to a loading dock, underneath the Nestles Well where it was painted the same shade of cerulean, so one couldn't tell it was the portal to The Nestles

Residential Holding Facility; a "gentle" jail you wouldn't know about unless you were a guest there.

The van door opened. "Not to worry. Mr. Turner. We've already spoken to Jeanine and she is on her way to speak to your wife about re-financial negotiating. As long as you do as your told, you shouldn't be here long."

Despite its immaculate continuity, Ben found the endless sameness of the blue painted decor disorienting, finding himself leaning into their lead, a loss of confidence and overall depth perception "As you can see, we have everything in blue for calming effect," they told him. "We don't want you to feel like a prisoner here, just a temporary guest until we get your future here at The Nestles sorted out. It's just one room but you're not going to be alone. But first, we have to get you into this jumpsuit here, just standard procedure to tell who's who," said the guard, unlocking his cuffs, pointing to a changing stall.

He was re-cuffed when he re-emerged, then led down another blue hallway.

He wouldn't have known there was a door there on the right if it wasn't for its merciful window. The guard unlocked the simple knob, opening the door. Inside were four cots, each flush against a blue wall, one of them occupied by a bald-headed man. At first, he was startled from his gaze. But when Ben walked in, and the door shut behind him, the man started laughing.

"You don't remember me, do you?" he said.

"What? What do you mean?"

"You were looking right in my eyes when you hit me with your car, Sir."

It all came crashing down on Ben, and something about the submissive – or what is sarcastic? – address of 'sir" somehow made it worse.

"I... I'm so sorry. Truly, I am." Ben felt a bad rush to his head, a dizziness, his mind a roulette wheel spinning round every unnamed emotion. "What is your...can I ask you your name?"

"Name's Remy," he said with a nod.

"Remy, I'm Benjamin. What happened to your long grey hair, did they shave your head?"

"Don't worry, it's gonna happen to you too," said Remy, rubbing the top of his bare skull.

"Can you... maybe tell me why we're here?"

"Oh, I see how this works — you want something from me now after you almost killed me with your car? I was trying to help you, you know."

"Help me? You weren't wearing any clothes, I'd say you were the one that needed help..."

"What, are you saying I'm crazy?"

"Well, I'm not a doctor, but I say you *were* a naked guy who was punching my car and screaming at the top of his lungs."

"It was the only way, Ben. You know how many other ways I've tried to warn people?

"Warn people what?"

"Not to move to The Nestles."

"Why? I mean, don't *you* live in The Nestles?"

"They forced me to live here, Ben, and even so, I haven't been home since that day you clipped me two weeks ago. That was my third strike, they said. And the thing is, if I tell you what this is all about, you might not ever leave here," said Remy, pointing to the blue floor. He paused, then lifted his finger to Ben's face. "If I tell you what I know, then *you're* gonna be a crazy guy too."

Ben had to admit: he no longer felt sane.

"Please, go ahead. I'm listening."

Remy stood up from his perfectly made bed, self-consciously rubbing his hands over his hairless head, still unaccustomed to it being gone. He mentioned he communicated better when he paced around a room, or even a street like their first encounter. "See, I'm used to wide open spaces...I lived alone down on the desert floor, a homestead I built myself about 10-15 miles from the mountain. They had no idea there was someone living where they were testing."

"Testing?"

"This was bomb testing territory, man." Remy said, lowering his voice to a growling whisper. "How do you think this cute little chunk got taken out of the mountain?"

Benjamin lifted his chin, then lowered it slowly, a drawn-out knowing nod.

"Water. Let me guess — they found a mountain spring?"

"Bingo," said Remy, pointing his finger. "Well, they corked that shit, made a deal with guess who to take care of it, keep it hush while they all made a buck? Don't answer, I'll just show you..."

Remy grabbed a pen, wrote out NESTLES in all caps on his left hand, then crossed out the last S.

"Nestle? Oh, Nest-lee"

"Bingo!" said Remy. "It's so obvious its... arrogant. Insane. But that's how these megacorps are — so out of touch, they don't realize how naked their corruption is. And it rarely occurs to most people because it's all so out in the open, so exposed...one feels crazy just for entertaining the thought."

Benjamin *did* feel crazy for entertaining the thought, as Remy's explanation seemed swerving into eco-terrorist paranoid schizophrenia.

"Yeah, I mean that sounds a little too...convenient, Remy," he said, a teetering critique.

"What, don't believe me? Well, I bet your thirsty." Remy tossed a 12 oz. plastic bottle of water at him. "Look at the label, real small on the back."

Ben flinched. The bottle hit his elbow and bounced onto the blue cement floor. Reluctantly, he picked it up, turning it to the back. He read out loud:

SOURCE: DEEP PROTECTED WELLS, NESTLES MOUNTAIN, NV. BOTTLED BY NESTLE-PURELIFE. US.

Well, shit," said Ben, humbled eye contact to Remy.

"You're right, the well *is* shit," said Remy. "It was likely fine before the military bombed the mountain, before the whole side collapsed." He unzipped the front of his blue jumpsuit, revealing his unsightly red blemishes. "How do I know? Because I was fine before I started drinking that water."

"I'm so sorry, Remy." Then, Ben said something he immediately wished he didn't. "You know though, there are varying levels of uranium that occur naturally in ground water..."

"Man, who's side are you on?" shouted Remy, throwing his finger. "Sounds like you're already nice and comfy in the denial they want you to be in..."

Ben stared at the ground, bracing the avalanche of reason versus comfort versus unfolding fact. In the same moment he decided there was a difference between a theory of conspiracy and a conspiracy theory, he remembered what he brushed off as Jeanine's psoriasis; when he was scolded not to stare, then scolded Kayden for the same natural impulse. All the while, Remy risked his freedom—then almost his life when Ben hit him—to show them, openly, what could happen to them, just as he was doing again, now.

"When was the last time you examined your body, Ben?"

"There is nothing wrong with my body..."

Remy laughed. "Maybe not where you can see. If you're so convinced you're fine, unzip your suit and show me your back, just real quick."

Solemnly, Ben pulled the zipper down, slipped the jump suit from his shoulders, and slowly turned around. He couldn't see Remy shake his head, sadly.

"Sir, I'm sorry to be the one to tell you this, but there's a red area if inflamed skin about the size of a dinner plate there on your lower spine. That's where it started with me too."

Ben launched into a panic, clawing behind his waist to feel it. "What? How can I know..."

"Well, if you aren't gonna take my word for it, Acuate Radiation Sickness will spread. Eventually. you'll see it in other spots that'll be easier to see. How's your hair? Tug on your hair."

Ben already had both hands on his head – the default pose of stress – so all it took was make two fists and pull. He uprooted two large tufts of hair, easy as pulling weeds after a hard rain. He opened his hands in front of his eyes, releasing the strands; they fell slowly, but surely, to the blue floor.

There was an uncomfortable silence. What more was there to say?

Ben wanted to hear everything now, every detail that led Remy to The Nestles: How the military found out he saw the explosion from his homestead, how they likely would have just bombed him out in kneejerk response; but he took to the hills and hid out for days until they found him, just like a terrorist overseas they were testing the strength and radius of bomb for.

They held him at a Federal Prison Camp at Nellis Air Force Base for "well, I'm not sure how long exactly, long enough for them to ship me off back to what they were now calling Nestles Mountain—never even had a name before." While they gave him a new home there, free in exchange for his silence, he felt he was just going from one prison to another. "When you can't speak freely, you're not free," he said. "They likely just knew it'd be just a matter of time before I'd be first to get sick from the water, so I was basically just a write-off for them, Nestle, and whatever convenient real-estate behemoth got involved here..."

Ben's fist hit his own thigh. "Our fucking dream home..."

"A hospice," finished Remy.

*

Renee hadn't been feeling well that day; no matter how much water she drank, it wasn't enough. Yet, as her stomach swelled from the water, she couldn't help feeling nauseated. Then came the frequent urination. Was she pregnant? *Maybe I should lay down*, she thought

She awoke rudely to Kayden shaking her. "They took Dad, they fucking took Dad just like that!"

Her mouth was so dry she couldn't speak. Nothing a glass of water couldn't help until the doorbell rang.

MISCARRIAGE

BY ALEC CIZAK

Bob Cork had been adjusting information on a report about a gas station robbery. Captain ordered him to hustle over to the Korean War memorial. Bob finished typing corrected times on liquid paper and drove to the church across the street from the bronze statue of a charging soldier. A small crowd followed two people matriculating down Lincoln. He left his car behind a marked Lake County vehicle. A uniformed deputy kept the gawkers at bay. Bob joined the deputy to observe the main act:

A slim blonde, all legs, pockmarked skin, wearing denim shorts and a tie-dyed WLS T-shirt had duct taped her hand to the grip of a silver revolver. The barrel of the gun rested inside the mouth of a taller man in a burgundy suit and tie. Duct tape held the barrel in place as well. The woman inched the man backward. Bob recognized her, though he couldn't recall from where.

He had no trouble identifying the man. Dan Rutter. Attorney at Baker and Barrett, a firm on 9th Avenue, sliding rich folks through cracks in the code.

When Bob worked sex crimes, he endured a trial designed to lock up a serial pedophile. The DA worked seven months to build the case. Dan Rutter and his cohorts grifted the jury with a boohoo about abuse the toucher suffered as a child. Didn't make sense to Bob how everyone else in the world managed their demons without hurting others. A reporter at channel five called him and the prosecutor heartless for casting a victim as a monster.

Brad Porter, the deputy, kept the minor crowd from the woman and the lawyer. Not even thirty, his skin had grayed and his hair had thinned to strands jutting in lonely clumps from under his hat. Bob knew his father, police veteran and sharp-shooter Butch Porter. Unlike his father, Brad Porter never put in for detective. Must have been content answering domestic calls and writing tickets. Like he knew advancing in the department would make the rest of his hair fall out. He beckoned Bob closer. "She abducted him at his office," he said. That's all anyone had at that point. Bob thanked him, told him to say hello to his father. "Pa'll be glad to know you're still kicking."

Bob fished a pack of Wrigley's spearmint gum from his pants pocket, unwrapped a piece and shoved it in his mouth. A poor substitute for the unfiltered Camels he'd forced himself to eighty-six a month earlier. He approached the lawyer and the woman. He held his hands where the woman could see they were empty. He let his shoulders slump, his belly sag over his waist. If he looked like a chump, maybe the woman wouldn't find him threatening. She sneered at him. "You don't want this turd's brains on that nice tweed jacket of yours, I suggest you skedaddle."

"Afraid I can't do that." With caution, he removed his badge from his inside breast pocket. "I'm a detective, ma'am. Just want to know what's going on."

The lawyer tried to speak. Muffled. Gibberish. "Hush," the woman said to him. To Bob, she said, "I'm taking this slime for a stroll. Folks need to know what he done to me and my daughter." The lawyer shook his head. The woman kicked him in his shin. "My finger slips, you sleazy son of a bitch, your skull's an instant jigsaw puzzle." She laughed, said he'd have a closed-casket funeral. "No different from my little girl's." More muted protests from the lawyer. Must have been tough for him, unable to spit ten-cent bullshit, worm his way out of the situation. The woman turned to Bob. "This jaggoff's going to apologize, publicly, on television." Bob asked how so. "It's happening already." Her hand taped to the gun twitched, prompting an unearthly squeal from the lawyer, a sound Bob heard in a science fiction movie about giant rats. "You jaggoff cops are going to get channel five to bring one of their fancy cameras and we're going to listen to this prick sing." She nodded at the lawyer, as though Bob might not fathom which prick she meant.

"I'm happy to discuss this with you," said Bob. "But you insult folks, it's going to be difficult."

"Get on your little walkie-talkie, officer. Until I see a camera and microphone in this shitbag's face, this parade keeps on."

A regional barb cast Haggard, Indiana, as a suburb of Chicago. A stupid joke, for sure, considering forty miles separated them. Sometimes, however, Bob wished he had Windy City resources. A tactical team would have been nice.

Position units on the roof of the Art movie theater and have a deadeye incapacitate the woman. He didn't want to bring in the media, appease her. Every lunatic in town would take hostages to snag their fifteen minutes. "Ma'am," he said, "why don't you tell me your name?"

"Got nothing to say till I see that fancy news van."

"I need more information," he said. "Make it a lot easier for me to convince my captain to put in the call, get a camera here, like you want."

She stopped. "You don't know who I am?" She didn't wait for his response. "How long you been a pig?" How flattering. As though Bob Cork sold used cars for two decades and decided to become a cop after a midlife inquisition. "You never heard of Lita Lynn May?"

Bob almost extended a hand. "Lita? Good to meet you." He smiled. "I'm Bob C..."

"Lita's my daughter, shit-for-brains." She swallowed and continued. " *Was* my daughter." She yanked the lawyer's head. "This tub of bile twisted shit every which way in court, got the demon who killed her off the hook without even probation."

Ah, yes. Now he remembered. One of several parents anxious to see Chad Bullock thrown over the wall. Son of senator Ward Bullock, Chad spent time at IU Northwest before determining himself too smart for school. One of the few kids under the age of thirty who, in this year of our Lord, 1978, kept his hair short, his collars clean. He'd been accused of abusing women every which way. As in, the boy had issues with his mother and wouldn't rest until the women of

Indiana understood his Oedipal rage. Could it even be called Oedipal? Didn't Oedipus love his mother? Chad Bullock beat a girl from Crown Point with an iron wedge. A piece of plastic would hold the girl's skull together for the rest of her life. He'd burnt the skin off two hookers from Lublin. And he'd stabbed Lita Lynn May in the face with a pair of sewing scissors. Ninety-nine times, according to the examiner. Bob knew the detectives who'd interviewed him. Every moment they spent in the tank with the little shit confirmed his guilt. Then Dan Rutter weaved his spell. Convinced the jury Chad Bullock's childhood, growing up in a castle near South Bend, left him scarred. Jury wanted the spoiled brat locked away in the Crossroads mental health facility in Gary. Rutter and his crew spoke with the judge, got the boy a vacation in Switzerland where, apparently, hanging out in the Alps cured psychotic tendencies. Poor Heidi. Poor Swiss. Bob wondered how many of their women would be mutilated before they put the animal in a cage, where he fucking belonged.

Or maybe they'd gone all gooey on villains, the way Americans had for the last ten years. The woman had every right to hold the lawyer accountable. She led Dan Rutter into the street. Looked like she intended on heading toward Haggard Elementary, a one-story red-bricked building full of children. More gawkers gathered. Bob said to Brad Porter, "Let's get these sheep out of here."

"Might take more than me."

"You got my say so," said Bob. "Tell roll call what you need."

As the scene travelled, tiny step by tiny, cautious step, additional uniforms arrived. They dispersed the audience and played goalie any time an idiot wandered too close to the action. The woman said, "The hell you getting rid of the witnesses for?"

"Can't let anything happen to civilians," said Bob.

"What does that make me?" The woman's body jerked toward him. The lawyer produced a guttural squelch.

"I don't want anyone to get hurt," said Bob. "Least of all you. I know you've had it tough…"

"You ever lost a child?"

Not like her, he hadn't. His wife Judith miscarried in the early part of the decade. She'd blamed it on Nixon, the excitement of Watergate. Said Tricky Dick made her blood boil so bad her uterus evicted the baby. Bob went to see a doctor on his own. Learned his sperm didn't swim with vigor, enthusiasm. Doctor blamed the cigarettes. Bob kept the news to himself. Let Judith think, for the last four years, the failure had been hers.

He said to the woman, "No ma'am."

"Don't pretend you know my pain for a single moment's second."

"Yes, ma'am." He held his hands up again, as though she'd pointed the revolver at him.

She nudged the lawyer. He scraped his shoes on the pavement behind him, maybe feeling for impediments, rocks, potholes, things that might make him stumble, tug on the woman's arm. The woman kept her gaze on the world beyond the lawyer's bean-shaped head. She said, "Get me my camera, pig. This don't end until this here shitbag apologizes on television. I got to keep repeating myself, I might get tired and trip, you dig?"

Again with the sweet talk. Calling him a pig, expecting a favor. One he didn't believe he could fulfill. Captain would probably take a chunk of his ass, he caved to the woman's demands. The woman interrupted his thinking, said, "I don't see you on your little walkie-talkie, officer."

He excused himself and returned to his cruiser. He called dispatch over the radio. "Put me through to the captain."

Upon hearing the details, the captain said, "The longer this goes on, the more sympathy she stacks." Bob agreed, asked for advice. "Can we run a reverse on her?" said the captain.

"I'm a basketball fan," said Bob.

"Trick her." The captain spoke in a soft voice, as though he believed Bob dumb enough to chat with him in front of the woman. "Diversion, Cork. Bullshit her. We let Rutter take a bullet, no telling what those weasels at B&B will put us through. In court *and* the filthy press."

Worried about the department's image. Great. Bob said, "Can we get a van from channel five?" They'd need a familiar reporter to go along with the grift. Camera. Mic. Everything had to appear on the level, convince the woman they respected her grief. He told the captain to put an armed officer behind the lens. A marksman.

"Dammit, Cork," said the captain, his voice still low. Bob informed him the procession had traveled a block south. The woman could not hear them. "Last thing we need is some sad-sack broad eating a county bullet."

"She's angling for Haggard Elementary," said Bob.

The captain tossed the hot potato to him. "You decide, Cork. Consequences will be on your desk, not mine."

The uniforms diverted a herd of young folks, maybe students from Valpo. Shaggy hair, bell-bottoms. Reeked of marijuana. Three of them in May the Force Be with You T-shirts. Fucking clones. Bob straightened his tie. He got back on the radio and instructed dispatch. "Yes," he said, "captain's okay'd it." He caught up with the woman and the lawyer.

The woman didn't face him when she spoke. "What's the story, officer?"

"Channel five's on the way."

Sweat dripped in and out of pockmarks on the woman's cheeks. Had her face reflected the shitty cards life dealt her before her daughter died? So many Indiana women looked the same—including Bob's wife. Following the miscarriage, she stayed up late, forcing herself to laugh with Johnny Carson and other Hollywood phonies. The tiny black and white television in their bedroom hummed long after the national anthem played and the station dropped to static. On Fridays, nights they'd previously reserved for baby-making, she insisted on watching Graveyard Joe host cheap, scratchy horror movies on channel nine. Bob resorted to wearing a blinder and wrapping his pillow around his ears. Not long into this routine, Judith's skin deteriorated. He couldn't shake the hunch that his refusal to confess blame for the miscarriage contributed to her rapid

aging.

Tammy Lynn must have been psychic, must have wanted to prod his

conscience. She said, "What's on your mind, officer?"

He nodded down 9th Street. "Here comes your camera, ma'am."

She steered herself and Dan Rutter in a straight line for Haggard

Elementary's playground. Children laughed and screamed, ran around in that

bizarre way children did, finding joy in mindless movement. Several played

kickball in the corner by a break in the high fence surrounding the blacktop. A

group of girls and a boy skipped rope near the entrance to the school. On the

opposite side of the kickball diamond, half a dozen boys played with plastic toy

soldiers in a sandbox, mostly throwing sand at each other and laughing when one

of them took some in the eyes.

"Ma'am," said Bob, "can I ask you to veer to the right?"

She turned her head. Must have seen the school. "Sure thing." She

continued backing toward the opening in the fence.

"I thought I asked you to veer to the right?"

"You asked. That don't mean I got to comply."

"Ma'am, the children."

She stopped. Her smile lightened her weathered cheeks. "Yes?" she said.

"The children?" She glanced at the playground. She snapped Dan Rutter's

terrified face forward. "Nobody gave a shit about *my* child."

The news van parked across the street. Bob told the woman he needed to make sure channel five had followed his directions. The driver opened the sliding door. Inside, Cathy Moon, slender, raven-haired, former Notre Dame cheerleader, sat near a control panel, compact mirror in her hand, grooming her eyelashes. She glared at Bob. "Well, well. If it isn't the Salem witch hunter." He refrained from explaining a pedophile and someone wrongly accused of witchcraft in Puritanical America could not be equated. The other passenger in the van stepped out in jeans, cowboy boots, and a button-down shirt held together at the neck by a bolo tie. Time and experience had carved ravines in Butch Porter's face, turned it into a roadmap. He grinned and offered Bob his hand.

"Been a while," he said. "Detective, I hear?"

"That's right, Butch." He shook his hand and helped him pick up a camera and battery pack. Combined, they must have weighed seventy pounds. "You got instructions, right?"

He showed his right palm, revealed he'd worn a ring concealing the tiniest single-shot .22 Bob had ever seen. "Got this here rascal in Ko-rea."

Bob scratched his scalp. "You only going to need one bullet?"

"Impression I got from roll call," said Butch, "one is all it'll take."

The woman and the lawyer stood a few feet from the entrance to the playground. Teachers hustled students back inside the building. "She steps on school property," said Bob, "I'm going to need you to fire that shot."

Butch leaned around the front of the van. He gnawed on his lower lip as he stared at the target. "Tricky. Captain insisted nothing happens to the shyster."

Bob spit out his gum. His fingers ached to cradle an unfiltered Camel. He removed a fresh stick of Wrigley's and popped it into his mouth. As he chewed, he raised his eyebrows and shrugged. "Something happens to the woman," he said, "I don't see how the lawyer's not going to be affected."

After telling Butch and Cathy Moon to hold on a second, Bob weaved through meandering traffic, cars filled with rubbernecks, cars the uniforms should have redirected.

Scars on the woman's face appeared to have dug deeper, gathered more sweat. "That the bimbo from channel five?"

"She's won several awards, far as I know," said Bob. "I'm not mistaken, she's headed to Chicago in a few months. Earned a spot on the channel nine news."

"She's a dingbat," said the woman. "They put her on TV to get men to pay attention. She wears short skirts on assignment, always has perfect, straight black hair. Like a small-town Morticia Addams, but without the kinky wit."

"She's what we got." Bob tried to arc around her, stand between her and the playground.

The woman jerked the lawyer to the left, obstructing Bob's path.

"Now, ma'am..." He held his hands up for a third time. Felt silly doing so.

"Hey, pig," said the woman. "You told me you ain't lost a child like I did. I figure you're implying something."

"Don't you want to talk to the camera?"

"I see." She smirked. "You got yourself a dirty little secret, don't you? You chew gum to keep from spilling the beans?"

"Ma'am," said Bob, "all I ask is you stay off school grounds."

"I'll go where I damn well please."

Cathy Moon's narrow heels smacked the pavement until she stood next to Bob. He gave her room and loitered to the side of the sharpshooter. A cord attached to the battery pack slung over Butch Porter's shoulder snaked along the ground, up into the bottom of a microphone in Cathy Moon's hand. She looked at the camera and nodded. The reporter spoke into the microphone: "I'm standing outside Haggard Elementary where grieving mother..."

"You think I'm stupid?" Tammy pointed at the camera. "The little red light there, it ain't even on." She shoved the lawyer through the break in the fence and followed him onto the blacktop.

The pop from the gun wrapped around Butch Porter's ring-finger sounded before the camera hit the ground. Bob closed his eyes, chomped twice on his latest stick of gum. He heard the second shot, competing with the echo of the first, two minor thunderclaps dancing on the walls of the school. When he opened his eyes, he stopped chewing. The sharpshooter had scraped a bullet across the woman's throat. She must have squeezed her revolver's trigger. The right side of the lawyer's face decorated the fence. The rest of him lay atop the woman. They convulsed in mingling puddles of blood.

"Jesus, Bob, I apologize," said Butch Porter. "I went for her hand. Guess I ain't got it like I used to." His son, the deputy, rushed over, placed his hand on his father's back to comfort him.

Children on the playground shrieked and sobbed. Bob stared at the woman's fluttering eyes. She'd made a mistake. He knew *exactly* how she felt about losing her daughter. He returned to his car. He spoke into his radio, called for the necessary vehicles and personnel to clean the mess. He ducked away from the scene, walked toward a liquor store down the street. As he stepped into a phone booth at the edge of the liquor store's parking lot, he spit out his gum and dug through his pockets for a dime. The phone at his house rang three times before his wife answered. He said to her, "Listen, honey, we need to have a talk."

DALHART

BY JAMES WHELPLEY

ONE

Erik Collins woke to the sound of his children screaming. He lumbered into the living room in his t-shirt and boxers just in time to see them disappear, book bags strapped to their little backs. Larissa stood in the doorway until they were safely on the bus, then waved to the driver.

When she turned around, her husband asked, "They do know I'm in the other room trying to sleep, right?"

"Please, all they know about they daddy is he asleep in the other room! What do you expect, Erik? You work while they're asleep, you sleep while they're awake. Two thirds of the year, they barely see you." A couple months ago she would've joked that the children didn't know they had a father. But they'd talked about that.

"Six months and I'll be back on days," Erik said.

"In six months, they see you for four months, then have to wait eight months to see you again. There are prisons that don't ask their guards to rotate like this."

"That's not how Dalhart do things. Besides, we need the differential."

Larissa stepped close and wrapped her arms around her husband's waist. Her head didn't reach the middle of his chest. She was used to hearing her voice rumble in his belly like hunger. "Your appointment today?"

"Yeah."

"What the doctor gonna say?"

"Same thing he always say."

She squeezed him tight. He was big and warm and she loved the way he smelled. "I wish you'd take some time off?" She listen to him groan. "We could find a cabin somewhere. Wouldn't that be nice?"

He put his arms around her. He thumbed the clasp of her bra through her shirt. "You wanna rent a cabin just to watch me fish?"

"Beats watching you sleep," she said.

He stooped to kiss her. She had to leave, said she'd be late for work. She told him the invoice for the repairs to her car was pinned to the fridge. It came to more than the estimate. It always did.

Erik Collins remained standing until he was in the examination room. He'd broken a lobby chair during his first appointment and didn't wish to repeat the incident. At 6'7" and 306 pounds, he exceeded the maximum weight for plastic chairs.

"Blood work looks the same," said Dr. Saenz.

"Meds aren't helping?" Erik asked.

"You're still alive, they're doing something."

"What now? Different drugs?"

"There are no different drugs, Erik. You take these until you have a heart attack, then we operate."

"Nobody operating."

"Okay, then I'm going to tell you the same thing I always tell you. You need to change your eating habits, get some exercise, find some way to reduce stress."

"Right," Erik smirked.

Dr. Saenz stopped writing in the file and looked Erik in the eye. "It might be time to consider another line of work."

The Dalhart Correctional facility is the most far-flung prison in the state of Texas. At the tip of the panhandle, it's eighty-six miles north of Amarillo, but only twenty-five miles from the borders of Oklahoma, Colorado, and New Mexico. Two-hundred and sixty-eight guards and forty-five non-security personal are daily responsible for fifteen-hundred inmates on fifteen-hundred acres. Erik Collins had just opened his locker when officer Borchers sat next to him, facing the other direction.

"You're still having problems with Ortiz?"

"Ain't no problem," Erik said.

"He's talking about your wife."

"They went to school together, that's all."

"That's what he says to you everyday? He walks up and tells you he went to school with your wife?"

"He can't do shit," Erik said. "He in here, she out there."

"Not forever. You can't let him talk to you like that – you gotta slap him down. A student gets outta line, you slap him down. They don't respect one of us, job's harder for all of us." Brent Borchers was what the public imagined all corrections officers looked like. He wore a flat top despite never being in the military. He'd failed the exam to become a cop, and the Army didn't want him. He had cow bones covered in baby fat and smooth, red cheeks. The inmates, or "students" as they were called, hated him because he was good at his job, and didn't care what they thought of him.

"Say I slap him down, then what? He get out. Am I supposed to slap him down on the outside?"

"No," Borchers said. "We fuckin' bury him on the outside."

Officers on the second shift relieve those overseeing the inmates in their various literacy programs, including CHANGES, the course for inmates scheduled for release. Half the population attended these programs in the morning, the other half in the afternoon. Those that aren't in class receive instruction in career and technology programs – their choice of construction carpentry or pipes and plumbing. Then it's two hours in the TV room before dinner.

"Wife need that money." Henry Buckson stood next to officer Collins and folded his arms over his barrel chest. Buckson was fifty, bald as granite, and a three-time loser. Three times convicted of opening cash-registers at gun-point. Three times turned-in by whatever woman he was staying with – after he'd had too much to drink, and they'd gone a couple of rounds. Buckson had done worse, but armed robbery and battery were what put him in Dalhart.

"She'll have five-thousand at the end of the month," Collins told him. "In six months, another five – that was the arrangement."

"Arrangement's changed," Buckson said. He craned his neck to look at Collins. "Call it inflation."

"You mean leverage," Collins said without returning the look. "Maybe I call it off."

No inmate in Dalhart was close to officer Collins' size, but Buckson was as hard as any man there – and as dangerous. "Call it what you want," he told the guard.

Erik Collins wasn't on the floor at dinner time. It was his turn on the catwalk, looking down over the inmates at the cafeteria tables – the same tables they had at his children's school, he thought. The carbine rifle looked like a toy in his hands. It was loaded but he would never fire it. Collins was a lousy shot. He was sure he'd failed qualification more than once, but that's not what his record would reflect. That wouldn't fly on a city police force but this was the Department of Corrections.

Tonight's dinner consisted of the marble-sized meat pellets the inmates called "donkey balls," smothered in a gray gravy. It was the only protein ever left on the divided cafeteria trays. Collins was thankful not to be on the floor. The floor was where Ortiz would talk to him. Manuel Ortiz had gone to high school with Larissa in Dumas. His wife told him they had dated. Ortiz had been in the habit of branding his girlfriends. Larissa was light-skinned and the bite marks on her neck turned to welts she couldn't hide from her father – which resulted in welts of their own. A bite on her chest healed with a keloid scar and was a source of embarrassment whenever she wore a swimsuit.

Ortiz repeatedly asked Collins how long he'd be on nights, reminded him daily that he would be out in a matter of months, and asked if Larissa ever mentioned the Lucky Eagle – a hotel and Casino just across the border in Oklahoma. Erik Collins never asked Larissa about its significance and never would.

Ortiz stared up at him from the dining room floor. He showed Collins his open mouth filled with donkey balls. He slapped the air as if it were Larissa's behind. The men around him laughed. Borchers looked at Collins from across the catwalk and shook his head. The men sitting with Ortiz were hardly menacing. They weren't gang members, just Mexicans who'd been pulled over with too much *mota* for a judge to want to consider it paraphernalia. They didn't ask Ortiz if he was crazy, or why he'd chosen the biggest guard in Dalhart to fuck with. They didn't have to. Unlike Borchers, officer Collins wasn't the kind of guard who took inmates out of their cells in the middle of the night to fall down a flight of stairs.

"10-52," the call went out over his radio while Collins was in the restroom. "I've got a 10-52 in Adam-two. Open two." It was thirty minutes until the end of his shift. Erik was already mentally preparing for the hour drive on the unlit highway, already wondering what Larissa had made for dinner. 10-52 was the code for a medical emergency. It wasn't a fight, and Erik wasn't CPR certified, so he didn't hurry.

When he reached Adam block, several guards were already standing outside a cell door. Inside, a small, thin man with dark, stringy hair sat on the far end of the lower bunk, still wearing his State-issued blues. Blood covered his nose and mouth. On the floor of the cell was a larger man in his undershirt and shorts – stone dead.

Borchers whispered his explanation of the scene to Collins without being asked. "Ole Stanz was right in the middle of breaking in his new *cellie* when he kicked the bucket. They think it was his heart." Frank Stanz was pushing fifty, potbellied, and prematurely gray. His eyes and mouth were open, his face frozen in a rictus.

"We have a new student?" Collins asked.

"Transfer. His first night and this shit happens. Welcome to Dalhart," Borchers smiled. Collins recognized the smile from hunting photos taped inside Borchers' locker. "Last one here means you take *the guppy* to the infirmary."

Vincent Samardzija was doing six months for Assault on a Minor, which was a max sentence. He had allegedly bitten a child while in line at the meat counter of a Food King in Lubbock. He was nicknamed *the guppy* by the guards because of his slight build, and because guppies ate their young.

"What kind of name is Samardzija?" Collins asked as the two men walked the narrow hall toward the infirmary.

"Serbian. My grandparents emigrated after the war."

"Which war was that?" Collins asked.

Vincent was slow in answering, "I don't remember."

Dr. Clete Haskins was waiting in the infirmary. The good doctor had retired twice, but found the complacency didn't suit him. He'd marched with Dr. King in Dallas and kept a framed photo of that day on the wall where his patients could see it.

The doctor cleaned the blood from Samardzija's nose and mouth with gauze that pulled and snagged on the gaunt man's unshaven face. He asked Vincent if he was in any pain, Vincent said he wasn't. "Eyes are dilated, you on drugs?" Vincent shook his head. His eyes looked black until Haskins passed his pen light over them. Collins saw that they were brown, with large black pupils that failed to react to the light. "Might be a concussion," the doctor ruminated.

"Does that mean I have to stay up all night?" Vincent asked.

Collins wondered who the lucky dog on the 11-7 would be, who would spend his entire shift in the infirmary, watching the guppy lie on a cot. The doctor asked Vincent if he had a headache. Vincent said he didn't.

"You keeping him overnight, Doc?" Collins asked.

Haskins looked at Samardzija like a bowl of cold soup. "You can take him back. There's nothing wrong with this man."

Collins escorted Samardzija back to Adam block. "Did you really try to eat a baby?" Collins asked, his curiosity finally getting the better of him. Guards were instructed not to ask an inmate what he'd done. Their cases had been tried and their punishments handed down. Besides, no accurate judgment about a man's character could be made from what he might say.

"She wasn't a baby," Vincent said. "She was sixteen years old. And she was a big girl!" Samardzija intimated that the girl was fat.

"Why you bite her? It a sex thing?"

"It wasn't a sex thing," Vincent shook his head. "Her mother was taking too long at the counter."

That made Collins laugh. "How'd you get the max?" he asked. "Family couldn't afford a lawyer?"

"I don't know that I have a family," Vincent said.

"What you mean you don't know?"

"If they're alive, I don't remember their names or where they are. I know who I am, but when I try to remember more than that, it all vanishes – like trying to recall a dream when you're awake."

Collins smiled. "Don't waste that on me, man. Should'a told that to the judge. It's too late, you here now." He pushed the button on his radio, "Open Adam one." The lock banged in the door to the cell block and the two men stepped through. "Open two." A smaller bang came from the cell door and Collins slid it open. Parker's body had been removed. Samardzija would have the six by eight to himself, at least for the night.

Collins placed the inmate back in his cell. "Close two," he said into his radio. The door closed and the lock banged. "Don't change that record," he said to Samardzija. "You keep on forgetting. Rest of us gotta live with the shit we do."

TWO

The kids were already out the door when Larissa revisited the idea of Erik taking time off. She'd found a cabin for rent. It was on a lake reported to be teeming with perch, carp, and *sunnies.* Erik thought it was probably just a stock pond. He asked his wife where it was. She told him half an hour from the Lucky Eagle Casino. Erik didn't ask her how she'd found it.

The first Thursday of every month, a local barbecue pit catered lunch and dinner for the guards at Dalhart. Brisket, chicken, pork and beef ribs, smoked sausage, barbecued beans, tater salad, and cole slaw. The leftovers would clog the break room fridge until Saturday night when everything was thrown away. The men consumed no less than two sagging disposable plates of food in a sitting, heavy gun belts unbuckled across the seat of their chairs. They complained of the gout that made their toes stiff and painful, of high blood pressure, and higher cholesterol. They blamed their medications for the symptoms of the diseases they took them for. Except for the men with gout, they were the same medications Erik was taking.

Collins and Borchers were on the floor for dinner. Tonight was boiled haddock. With two plates of barbecue sitting his stomach, Erik thought the fish smelled especially foul. It was served with an individual loaf of corn bread and green beans that looked and tasted like they'd been boiled in the same pot as the haddock.

The inmates had taken it upon themselves to segregate the dining hall. Half the prison population was African-American, despite making up less than twelve percent of the surrounding population. They occupied the east side of the dining hall, while the whites and Mexicans unhappily divided the west. The division helped the guards head off trouble, immediately discerning when an inmate wandered someplace he shouldn't.

Collins always took the east side. This didn't prevent Borchers from reminding his partner to avoid Ortiz. The inmates on the east side were wary of Borchers and traded the opinion that his pappy was a klansman. Borchers wasn't liked any better on the west side. Ortiz sat at the end of a row of tables and each time Borchers passed, the guard stopped in front of him. Ortiz would say something in Spanish and the table would laugh. Borchers, having grown up Catholic in Midland, had been called *puta, pendejo, and maricón* all his life. He appreciated a novel slur and would ask what it meant, which usually cut the laughter.

"Siddown Buckson, you haven't been dismissed." The shout came from the catwalk. Borchers and Collins turned to see Henry Buckson on his feet in the center aisle. Buckson grabbed Ortiz by the back of his head and slammed his face into the table in front of him. He slammed his head again before anyone made a move to stop him. With a man on each arm, Buckson still managed to slam Ortiz's head a third and forth time. Inmates crossed the aisle to watch the fight, others took the opportunity to settle scores of their own. A guard on the catwalk called it in over his radio, the other fired non-lethal baton rounds into the crowd. Collins and Borchers drew their nightsticks and pushed through the crowd.

Buckson was swinging wildly at the inmates who'd pulled him from the table. Ortiz stumbled to his feet. Bits of food were stuck in the dark, syrupy blood that coated the right side of his head. Collins broke through the crowd just in in time to see Buckson lift Ortiz into the air and slam the smaller man down across the cafeteria seats.

"Hit him!" Borchers yelled.

Buckson turned. Collins towered over him, his baton raised. One swing and Collins wouldn't owe this man a dime. All debts would be forgotten. He could hear Borchers yelling to hit him – but his voice sounded as if it were coming from miles away. Collins was frozen. Buckson's grin was full of large square teeth that cut his neck in half. Borchers pushed Collins out of the way and cracked Buckson in the head with his nightstick.

Officers flooded the dining hall to restore order. Four inmates lay prone, their fingers laced behind their heads. Henry Buckson was in handcuffs. Blood trickled into his ear from the top of his bald head. The crowd had formed around Ortiz. His head hung from his shoulders, his arms spread out wide. The cafeteria table's plastic seat had broken and impaled Ortiz on the metal shaft beneath.

The water in the bathroom sink was tepid and reeked of the lead in the pipes. Erik Collins splashed it on his face and the back of his neck. The pain in his chest was excruciating – as if someone were pulling his ribs toward his spine from the inside. His hands had always been too large to open pill bottles and blister packs, so Larissa made sure there were loose pills in his pants pockets alongside his car keys. He swallowed the nitroglycerin tablet without water. He could hear Borchers somewhere outside the door regaling the other officers with his account of the melee. Collins went into a stall, sat down, and prayed not to die on the toilet.

In response to the fight, the inmates were returned to their cells without TV time. It was not a night for one of the more popular programs, which was why Buckson had chosen tonight go after Ortiz.

"How long will I have the cell to myself?" Samardzija asked Collins through the bars.

"We'll get another bus first of the week, if not from the courthouse, from another facility. We have room, they don't."

"You can't put anyone in here with me," Vincent said.

"Not my call. Need the room."

"If you do, I'll hurt them," the inmate threatened.

Collins smiled. Vincent Samardzija was 5'6" tall and 115 pounds if you pulled him out of the lake fully clothed. "You just had a bad night. Most the guys get along with they cellie. Stretch hard enough, don't need nothing make it harder. Don't bite no one, you be fine."

Samardzija ignored him. "If I stop eating, maybe I'll die," he said.

"You stop eating, you get an IV," Collins told him. "That don't work, we force-feed you. Took two hours to get a can of spaghetti down last guy tried to pull that. Half of it probably still in his lungs."

Samardzija still wasn't listening. "I tried before, but the neighbors called 911. I woke up in the ER hooked to a bag of plasma." Vincent grabbed the cell bars. "You can't put anyone in here," he pleaded.

Samardzija's eyes were black holes. They expanded until his image seemed to split into two. Four dark orbs began circling Collins like planets. Erik felt lightheaded. He reached in his pocket for another nitroglycerin tablet. Dr. Saenz had warned him about the dosing, but Erik was twice the size of an average man and had always taken more than instructed. The image of Samardzija overlapped, folding onto itself until one black eye stared at him from the middle of a narrow face. The darkness at the edge of his vision was encroaching. Erik knew he was about to pass out. He stopped feeling in his pocket for a nitro tab and reached for his radio. He mumbled something he couldn't understand into the receiver before everything went dark.

When he opened his eyes, he expected to see the fluorescent lights overhead and the mocking, worried faces of his fellow guards surrounding him. But he was still on his feet. His large arms extended into the cell like tree branches that had grown between the bars, creeping from one side to the other, where Vincent Samardzija held him firmly by the wrists.

"Your pulse is bounding," Vincent said.

"What that mean?" Erik asked.

"It means you have a bad heart."

THREE

Erik Collins was still in bed when the school bus pulled away from the stop. Larissa was dressed and ready for work. She sat on the bed next to her husband and stroked his back like she would one of her children if they had taken sick. He told her there was no money for a vacation, that there would be no cabin, and that she wasn't to bring it up again.

Haskins had gotten the medical examiner's report back on Stanz. Cardiac arrest triggered by hypovolemic shock. Haskins reasoned the inmate had been sick with cancer. His body destroying itself from the inside was the only explanation for the apparent blood loss. The only injury noted on the report was broken skin around Frank Stanz's left wrist, where his new cellmate had fought to pry the dying man's hand from his throat.

"10-52 in Adam two, inmate unresponsive," the call went out over the radio. When Collins arrived at Samardzija's cell, Borchers was already there. It was his voice on the radio. "I don't know what's wrong with him," said Borchers. "He won't answer me."

"Threatened to stop eating," Collins told him.

"When?"

"Last night."

"You see him at dinner?"

Collins shook his head. There were too many men to notice whether one man had touched his food.

"Hey, Guppy." Borchers' baton tolled on the cell bars like a railroad crossing. "When was the last time you ate?"

Vincent didn't answer. He lay curled on his bunk with his face to the wall. He moved enough to let the guards know he was alive.

"Wait here," Borchers ordered. "If Doc's already left, I'll see if we can get him back. Open one," Borchers said into his radio.

When Borchers had gone, Samardzija rolled over and let Collins see his face. "You have to help me," he said. "Don't let them feed me."

"I tol' you what happens you don't eat."

"And I'm telling you what will happen if I do. Don't put anyone in here with me. You gotta let me die."

"Can't do that. Inmate die, the State ask questions. Got twenty-five-to-lifers doing so much time they can't see the end. But you – you only got six months."

"No one will ask questions," Samardzija insisted. "They'll just send me somewhere else. That's what they did at Roach and again at Mechler. Please, you gotta help me."

"Why? Why I gotta help you?" Collins asked.

"Because I can't help myself," said Samardzija.

Erik Collins didn't speak. He looked at the scrawny man telling him he'd rather starve to death than finish his time in Dalhart. Samardzija lay on his bunk, clutching his insides like he had a belly full of razors. He stared at Collins, his eyes a black coal fire.

"Why you really bite that girl?" Collins asked.

"I told you," said Samardzija.

"Tell me again."

"Her mother was taking too long."

"Where?"

"The meat counter."

"What you in line for?" Erik asked.

"Wuh?"

"The meat counter. What you there to buy?"

"I don't know."

"You don't know, or you don't remember?"

"I dunno," Samardzija repeated. "Ground beef."

"Bullshit," Collins told him. "You wasn't standing in line for no ground beef."

The inmate sat up on his bunk and placed his feet on the floor. He looked at Collins through the bars. "Blood sausage," he said, his voice no longer a tinny whine. "They make it there. Only place in more than three-hundred miles."

Collins stepped back from the bars. "Blood on your face the other night. I take you to Haskins, he don't find so much as a fat lip. No marks on Stanz's hands from hitting on you, only scratches on his wrist. They from you, but why?"

"You gotta help me," said Samardzija.

"I ain't gotta do shit," Collins told him.

Officer Erik Collins walked down the line of cells in Adam block. It was well past lights-out. Those who could, were asleep on their bunks. Those who weren't looked out at him with white, blinking eyes like nocturnal animals. Collins stopped outside a cell door and looked at the men sleeping inside. He clicked his radio. "Got a disturbance. Open fourteen."

"What's this shit?" asked Henry Buckson from his bunk.

"Need backup?" a disembodied voice called.

"Negative," Collins answered. "Transporting one to an empty."

All Buckson could see from his bunk was the shape of the giant guard.

"We have an empty?" the voice called.

Collins didn't answer. "Get up," he told Buckson.

The inmate did as he was told. He stepped onto the gangway next to the guard.

"Close fourteen," Collins said.

Buckson lifted his chin as high as he could. He was ten inches shorter than the guard and gave up more than fifty pounds. He was like a child standing next to his father. He'd never been afraid of the larger man – no one was. To everyone at Dalhart, Erik Collins seemed docile and lumbering. But that wasn't how he looked now, under the auxiliary lights of the cell block.

"Wasn't no disturbance," Buckson said. "Don't need no doctor. Ain't going down no stairwell with you."

"We ain't leaving the block," Collins assured him. The two men started back the other way. "Open two," Collins said into his radio.

"You putting him in with the guppy?" the radio squawked.

"Only empty," Collins reported. "Just be for the night."

Buckson peered into the cell and saw the reed of a man sitting on the edge of his bunk. He smiled at Collins. "This on yo' tab?"

"Just for the night," Collins repeated. He nodded at Buckson and the inmate stepped into the cell. "Close two," Collins said into the radio. The lock banged.

Samardzija was on his feet, pacing the rear wall of the cell like a cornered animal. "Don't do this! Please don't do this. I don't want to."

The big guard turned his back. It was late. His shift was almost over. "Open one," he said. The lock banged in the door to Adam block. The next shift would be coming on soon. The door closed behind him. He waited for the sound of the lock.

No one on Adam block even heard Buckson scream.

SCATTERSHOT
BY
NEVADA MCPHERSON

They called me Scattershot when I was a kid because I was hyperactive and had a hard time staying focused. Nothing focuses the mind like the stark fact of survival, however, so after my mom walked out and my older sister joined some Christian cult, I focused on avoiding my daddy's fists and belt. One night as he was lying prostrate on the floor with a single gunshot wound to the head from his own pistol, I focused my mind on getting the hell out of Georgia, heading west, intending to take that famous left turn at Albuquerque, and that's when I met her.

I'd stopped at a bar outside Shreveport for a beer before finding some cheap place to stay for the night. They had a special event going on in a big shed out back: 'female oil wrestling,' the banner said out front and there was a crowd to see the spectacle. Men, mostly, some with women leaning on their arms holding a cigarette or a beer or both if they were real dexterous. I walked past one bleary-eyed redneck princess who was smiling at something the goon beside her said, and as she glanced my way I could see the expression on her face as a thought crossed her mind like a cloud passing over a cow pasture. She was giving me the eye, but when she got a better look at me her interest turned to puzzlement, flirty little smile went lopsided and I just kept walking. I'm used to that look that says "Wait--what *are* you?"

As I neared the ring, through the cheers and jeers to the sound of writhing, female flesh slapping and the occasional grunt, I could see where the grunts were coming from: some beefy butch powerhouse with a crew-cut and a bunch of bruises being set upon by a slender, muscular force of nature in a white bikini, bronze skin glistening with sweat and Wesson oil, her black, wiry hair caught up in two puffs on either side of her head like an African goddess masquerading as a Swiss Miss, giving that white bitch twice her size what-fucking-for. Yeah, the beefy bitch was able to get grip on her a couple of times but not for long, and a few minutes later the African goddess rose as the winner, the ref raising her arm as she smiled, not for the crowd but for herself, claiming a hard-won victory.

She must've known the jeers would turn ugly because she was ready for it, sneering back at them. I got the impression she wanted to flip off the booing bastards but I also heard voices from the back, calling "Go home, nigger!" It wasn't that she was scared to flip them off, I could tell that by the way she looked in the direction of the loudest assholes, smiling. It's enough that she won. She started out of the ring, taking her fifty-dollar prize with her.

When I got to the parking lot, I saw her wearing cut-off short-shorts and white go-go boots, denim jacket thrown on over that white bikini top, heading toward a beat-up motor scooter out by the fence. There was a posse of rednecks heading that way, too, looking to cut her off at the pass. She saw them, continued walking briskly but didn't run. She was clearly not the running kind, and though she wanted to get the hell out of there, they got in her way, cock-blocking her from her ride. "Get the fuck out my way," I heard her say.

I hurried over to my truck, got the shotgun out from behind the seat and started in that direction.

"I saw you cheat my sister out of that prize money when you bit her on the shoulder," one of the posse was saying. "Now give it up."

"You a goddamn liar," she told the pale, wormy-looking miscreant.

"No, *you* the goddamned liar," he said, reaching to grab her by the arm, a whole clutch of shitheads closing in around her. I racked the shotgun. They turned and looked me over like the slack-jawed bitches that had given me the eye before, seeing me as some freakish hybrid with the body of a girl and the face of a boy or vice versa.

"Let her go," I said, summoning steel into my voice.

"What's it to you?" the miscreant asked as I aimed the shotgun square at his crotch. The rest of the posse fell back and I took a step closer to that lead bastard who looked pissed but also might be shitting his pants because I'd just as soon blow his dick off as look at his pock-riddled face the color of watery oatmeal.

He released the African goddess and she stepped behind me, whispered, "Thanks." I started backing away as the pod of shitheads and their leader receded like the tide. One of them put away a knife and another slipped a .32 into the pocket of his ripped jeans as he turned to walk off. I'd figured at least some of them were armed but not with a match for what I was holding. I'd stolen it out of the back closet, carrying it with me as I stepped over my old man's corpse on the way out the door, leaving the .38 there with him, having wiped it clean and placed it in his hand well before rigor mortis set in. But this was all I needed to hustle me and her over to my truck. We hauled ass and I told her we could go back for her motor scooter after that place had shut down for the night or early in the morning and she said fuck it, wasn't worth a shit no way. She went to take a look at herself in the side mirror, and, finding none, moved to see herself in the middle one, but that was gone, too. "Hey, what happened to all your mirrors?" she asked.

"I got rid of 'em a couple nights ago when I was drunk," I answered. "I'm gonna unload this heap soon's I can anyway."

"How come you did that?"

"'Cause I ain't never looking back."

She seemed surprised, laughed a little then settled back, looking forward down the road. Turned out she was on the run, too, making money anywhere, anyhow she could to get to the West Coast. That's where she wanted to go and I did, too, so we decided to travel together.

*

And we've been together ever since. It's been a few months now and female oil wrestling contests don't come around that often. Anyway, never know when there might be a ringer brought in. Keisha's tough but she ain't big and some of them gals are bigger than me and Keisha put together. Me nor her like taking orders from anybody and we really don't like being stuck in one place for any length of time. I never say 'never' but neither one of us relishes the idea of turning tricks for travel money, so we had to find some other way, and we did.

Me and Keisha got to talking to this guy named Roy one night at a bar in Cheyenne. His daddy used to run a bail bond place in Laramie, but he'd keeled over during a weekly poker game and Roy took over the business. The more we talked, getting a buzz from the Michelob that was on special, the lower he sat back in his chair, stretching out those long legs like kicking back in his own living room, looking from one to the other of us. I wondered if he might be getting ideas about a threesome or something (*ain't gonna happen, buddy*), but turns out that wasn't what he was thinking. Long story short, Roy saw a lot of raw potential in us that night, and was willing to work with us, getting us ready to work with him.

I never even knew for sure what a bounty hunter was, exactly, but now I am one, and so is Keisha. It's been a while since I ditched that truck with no mirrors and got a black eight-cylinder Charger with a straight shift. I do the driving and she keeps the guns loaded. She can read maps like fucking Magellan and she's a good shot, too, getting better all the time. Besides Roy and his guys, we don't have any other men in our lives and don't need any; we got each other. Sometimes, in the shower together, when I'm down on my knees eating her pussy, I wonder what I ever did without her, which is why I'd kill anybody who threatens her, and if not kill, cripple or castrate. She'd do the same for me and when we go after one of those bail-jumpers, we're relentless.

Next on our list is a guy charged with domestic battery and since he's supposedly some blowhard drunk, I'm locked and loaded, waiting in the shadows by his travel-court cabin while Keisha's in the bar across the street softening him up and trying to get him outside, headed this way. She walks out by herself, though, hurrying out to the car. He's nowhere in sight. She looks kind of freaked out.

I get in on the driver's side, still keeping an eye on that rinky-dink dive, and she's double-checking her .38, spinning the chamber and snapping it shut.

"What happened?"

"That bastard didn't go for it; lucky I didn't get rolled. This ain't no friendly place for niggas."

My eyes sweep the parking lot and I realize she's right; we—I—made a gross misestimation. Keisha's so beautiful, most men fall at her feet, while me, all I get is dirty looks and disdainful gazes from these yahoos, maybe a sidelong glance from some of their misfit sisters, cousins and aunts. But this place is just as right-wing racist as the place I come from, maybe even more. A few leftie nuts, too: hippies that are more about pleasing themselves than the whole peace-love thing, and you can't let the long hair fool you. Look at that Manson bastard they finally busted who had that whole bunch of brain-dead bitches so cowed they slaughtered all those rich people just to please him. I'm not protective of rich people by a long shot but I also don't believe in killing unless you've got a damn good reason. I had a good reason when I did it, I keep telling myself because it's true. It was him or me that night, it really was. Anyway, I gotta double down on my racist bastard radar, which of course Keisha has turned up way higher frequency than I do. She has to. Matter of survival.

We sit in the car, trying to regroup, studying on how to catch him unawares when he comes out tipsy, or maybe jimmy his door and be waiting when he stumbles in. Just wouldn't want some nosy son of a bitch watching to go in the bar and tell him. Minutes later, this white and red El Camino drives up and two young guys get out and go inside. Momentarily they come out with the guy we're there for. He looks a little woozy but not drunk. We hear them talking.

"So, where'd they find the freak?" he asks.

"Nick heard him hucking it up at some bar. Talking about a festival he's heading to in California."

"He ain't gone make it that far. He, she, whatever."

"You got that right. More like a shim."

They laugh, get in the car and spin out. I crank up, put the car in gear. "Sounds like they're up to some sure-enough shit," Keisha comments.

"Sure does."

I followed for what felt like a safe distance to some other podunk town north of Laramie and they seemed to skirt the main drag. I only saw one traffic light in the next block. They kept going and the sky turned from dark blue to black and damn, they kept going.

"What the fuck are they up to?" Keisha asked. "We burning a shitload of gas following these motherfuckers."

True, gas is high as a cat's ass, but, we'd tailed 'em this far, seems like a waste to just turn around and go back. Even though I'd looked forward to bagging another bail jumper and going back to Chaparral Court, home sweet motel for the time being, I felt like we were close to nabbing this guy, but close to something else, too. Now that we were in alien territory like the dark side of a full moon, I found myself fighting a creeping feeling of dread instead of the usual nervous excitement in the pit of my stomach that precedes the slapping on of handcuffs and handover to Roy and company, a hot shower (or cool, depending on whether the thermostat is working in Suite 14) and then sliding between the coarse cotton sheets with Keisha in all her perfection and losing myself between her breasts, her legs, her lips, bringing her to climax before she returned the favor, and then falling asleep, our bodies intertwined.

Watch it, Scattershot. Realizing I was getting lost in what I really wanted, I had to shake those images out of my brain and tend to this sticky situation I only wanted to be over so we could get the money in our hot little hands. *Focus.* Damn this bastard for fucking up tonight's plans, for leading us on what could be a wild goose chase.to some redneck cowboy orgy or cracker-ass crank fest, where he could blend into the crowd and we'd be so outnumbered we'd have no choice but to turn back. I'm almost out of cigarettes. No coffee either because I never dreamed we'd be going this far.

"Damit, I gotta piss," Keisha announces. Yes, there's that, too.

Just as we followed the two red tail lights that looked like a demon gazing out at us, beckoning, I detected a faint glow up ahead and slowed up, realizing we're in such a deserted place, our Dodge, with its raging V-8 and bright headlights might call more attention to us than we wanted.

"What 're you doing?" she asked. "I ain't gotta pee that bad, yet."

I watched ahead as the two demon eyes disappeared and the car headlights swung onto another road. I slowed up even more. There were several cars out there where they were going, at least ten. One set of headlights revealed a gathering of people moving toward the source of light, and I could finally see the flames licking skyward, illuminating jagged tree limbs, and then I could make out the small grove of trees. There didn't seem to be a house anywhere around, just the group of cars, figures moving toward the glow.

Keisha watched, too. "What the fuck?" she breathed.

"I don't know. What do you think?"

She watched the scene for a moment, sizing it up. "Damn if I know either," she answers. "Don't just look just like no redneck throwdown."

I pulled off the edge of the dirt trail of a road.

"We shoulda called Roy." she says.

"I wouldn't know how to tell him where we are."

It was dawning on both of us how much we really did need back-up this time, that the red, demon-eyed tail lights had drawn us into something downright evil.

There was movement among the crowd and then a set of bright headlights made a crude stage of a flatbed truck sitting under one of the trees and a rope was thrown up, high in the air over one of the craggy arms of what looked in the flickering light like a misshapen oak. A noose dangled at the end and a murmur went up from those gathered.

A couple of young men, one in a baseball cap, the other in a cowboy hat pinched up too tight, climbed onto the flatbed using what must've been makeshift steps or a stool, and between the two guys was a slightly built young black man. At least it looked like a black man, but with feminine qualities, too. There was a dirty, blood-stained pillow case on his head. After all my experience of being both a strange object of strange desire and outright derision, looking at his torn blouse and leather mini-skirt, I knew he must inflame anyone whose narrow little view of life just couldn't abide difference. No live and let-live here. These people were always up for killing anything, from deer to ducks to anybody who looked at them cock-eyed, much less a black man soon to become a black woman who'd wandered across their path either by mistake or design, so I knew we had to get him out of there before they had their way and fast.

Keisha turned to me. "I don't think we can take 'em all at once, even with that cannon of yours in the back seat. What do you think?"

Even if I could get a fix on that rope and shoot him down like Blondie freed Tuco at the end of *The Good, the Bad, and the Ugly*, he'd still be in the midst of an angry mob before we could get to him, so it looked like our only hope would be to create a diversion. "Is there still that bottle of whiskey in the back floorboard?" I asked. "And that red kerchief you wore yesterday?"

She turned, stretched to get both and then took out her lighter, already down with the program. "What's the target?" she asked.

I looked around. We'd have to get closer than this and time was of the essence. Hard to see too much without swinging the headlight beam around but it looked like we could tear around the periphery and get close to that flatbed if we could lure those bastards enough out of the way nobody'd have a clear shot at us. No doubt some of them had firearms close to hand, though they probably figured that poor kid was easy pickin's without having to waste a bullet. Just pull that truck up a couple of yards and watch him swing, choking to death while they slap each other on the back and celebrate their cruelty.

I didn't want to draw their attention too soon but I started easing the car forward. "When I get up to that third tree," I said, "Light it and toss it at the closest car right past that. I'll pull up to the other side of that truck."

"Then you want me to shoot that goddamned rope?" she asked, cocking the pistol. "I can do it if we get close enough?"

"You sure?"

"Damn sure."

"Think you can grab him and get him in here before the horde descends?"

She looked at me like *what other option is there?* "I sure as hell ain't giving 'em three lynchings for the price of one."

I drove forward, then gunned it, drawing the gaze of the crowd. I felt a slight pull in the tires and realized we'd hit a patch of mud. We fishtailed for a second, then got on more solid ground and then one, two, three; Keisha lit the kerchief stuffed in the bottle of whiskey and tossed the whole works at the shiny, sleek El Camino with the demon-eyed tail lights. The initial blaze surprised, then fully shocked with the spectacular explosion that followed when the heat hit the gas tank. The rag-tag crowd turned to look, along with the cowboy hangman who stepped to back of the truck, gazing in awe, and a couple of guys busted a move after us but before I rolled to a skidding stop just long enough to get the kid off the back of that truck, Keisha was leaning out the window, aiming high. She fired a shot and the two figures running our way, paused. The rope was still hanging by a thread but one more shot and it fell to the flatbed. Pinch-Hat lunged just as Keisha leapt up, taking him totally by surprised and even more when she kicked him hard in the balls. While he was doubled over, she fucking swept that leather-skirted kid off the back of truck like she was a bodyguard protecting him from rabid fans at a Detroit rock concert. Hugging the kid like an over-sized baby, she got in and with him on her lap, we took off and I took pleasure bumping off a couple of drunk red-necks stupid enough to think I'd slow down just because they stepped in my path, yelling. I gunned the engine and started back to the main road while some of those bastards loaded up to come after us. I pretended that once again, no mirrors, no looking back.

"Keisha, get the cannon," I yelled, over the wailing of the kid who was still so in shock, he hadn't even made an effort to take the pillowcase off his head. I plowed forward headlong and realized too late I'd somehow veered onto a pig-trail dirt road that wasn't taking us back to the main road but towards what looked in the dark like a field. The headlights hinted at a tree-line in the distance, so I swung right.

"What are you doing?" Keisha screamed, over the softening wails.

"I don't know," I screamed back, in no mood to explain, just to put distance between us and them.

Seeing the trees ahead at the edge of the field, Keisha cried out. "You're gonna get us trapped!"

Like hell I will, I thought, flying along the edge of the field, through brush and tall grass, cutting a swath through the darkness. I realized then that even though we'd somehow gotten off the beaten trail, those bastards could see us, and I could see a fairly straight path ahead so I killed the headlights, without slowing down.

"I give up," Keisha said, in a pissed off voice. "You're crazy!"

"Yep," I responded, squinting at what looked like a break in the tree line up ahead to the right. Wringing what moonlight there was from the sky to guide me, I took a deep breath, making a beeline for the break, turned on the lights and floored it. The kid having just removed the bloody pillowcase from his head screamed, glimpsing a low wall of dirt ahead, clinging to Keisha as I gripped the wheel, praying that I was right in thinking—hoping—that the piled-up dirt was excavation from a drainage ditch beyond. I was glad I was going so crazy fast, only wishing it were faster but turned out it was enough. The dirt acted as a ramp and we became airborne for a couple seconds and landed KA-PUMP without getting stuck. I couldn't look back but Keisha must've seen some pinpoints of light behind us and cried "Hurry!" which I didn't need to hear, too busy doing it, speeding through a strip of seedlings, weeds and PA-PUMP, back onto a two lane road, shitty, but still, asphalt, and I floored it again. Seeing that it was a straightaway, near's I could tell, I killed the lights, sped ahead, and then turned the lights back on.

And we kept driving, twisting and turning wherever we could, to throw 'em off.

When daylight broke, the three of us were sitting in the back booth of some diner. We'd managed to wash up in a gas station bathroom. The kid's name was Avery, and she (not much longer to go before 'she' would be what people would call her. More 'she' than me, practically, just going by looks) held a coffee mug in trembling hands to trembling lips, a cut from a sock to the mouth from one of her captors still evident, but not bleeding for the time being. "I don't know what to say," she said, in a soft voice. "Ya'll saved my life."

"You don't have to say nothin,'" I told her. Keisha smiled at me with sleepy eyes. "Where you headed? California?"

"Yeah." More coffee. "Where ya'll headed? How'd you find me out there?"

"We were looking for somebody. Some asshole. Out priorities got rearranged when we saw you. We'll still catch him, though. One of these days."

"Catch him? Ya'll ain't cops, are you?"

"No. Not cops. There's a bounty on one of them bastards. Maybe more than one, but one in particular we were after."

She nods. "I see." She set down her coffee, shivering in the early morning air conditioning. "I'm sure you'll get your man. Ya'll got it going on, that's for sure."

Keisha took out a cigarette. "Well, when times are bad, we good, and—"

"When times are good, we bad," I finished, thinking 'bout our stuff back at that motel. We ain't got that much stuff. Worth going back for? Decide after breakfast.

"You gone call Roy?" Keisha asked. "Tell him what happened?"

"Yeah . . . We'll decide everything after breakfast."

"Decide?"

"How you getting the rest of the way to Cali?" I asked Avery. She shrugged. "Decide after breakfast."

"Right," I said, starting to feel a little better. Coffee kicking in. Remembering California was where we were headed, too, when this trip started. I saw the waitress loading up a tray with what looked to be our order, and realized just how hungry I was. The place was getting more crowded, and there was that warm, cozy smell of breakfast food and more fresh coffee. And that highway out there. The big, bright open highway going west.

No looking back.

LUCK

BY E. B. HUNTER

"So, what do you say?" The stranger leaned closer to me, the mixture of whiskey sours and clove cigarettes on his breath nearly made me gag. "Would you rather be lucky, or good?"

"This is a ridiculous question," I slurred and motioned for another glass. The tender gave me a sideways look and kept polishing the bar.

"Ridiculous or not, you said you would answer my question if I bought you a round. Are you a liar as well as a drunk?"

I looked at the stranger with one eye closed (a little trick I had for keeping the world from spinning). His ears were puckered with scar tissue like he'd seen a few fights. The red stubble on his square jaw and the dark circles under his eyes told me he was out of patience, and I didn't much feel like pressing my luck with him.

"Alright, alright." I said, raising my hands, "I think I'd rather be lucky."

He rubbed his chin, his calloused hands sounded like wood being sanded on his rough face. "Why?"

"That's what it's about, isn't it?" I took a cigarette from my pocket and tapped the butt on the bar before lighting it. "The way I see it, that's all I really do now. I press my luck."

The stranger lifted an eyebrow and I exhaled into his face. He waved it away and I continued, "I've never been good at a damn thing in my life, but lucky? Sure. I could try and be good. I've tried before, and look where it got me." I waved a hand across the seedy bar filled with others like me. Drunks with no one to go home to. Staying until after last call. "Even if you're the best, you can fail. Look at Tony over there." I pointed to a balding man who was crying into a gin. "He was the manager of the Golden Bird Casino. Best in the biz. Six months ago, there's a gas leak and half his staff drop dead."

The bartender finally brought my drink, setting it hard on the bar and slopping sticky brown sauce onto the gleaming wood. I raised it in thanks. "Slainte." I took a drink and the stranger's eyebrow sat arched as he watched.

"I don't follow." he said.

"Wouldn't have happened to a lucky man." I said, giving him a wink and finishing the glass.

I set the glass down on the bar and watched it multiply before my eyes. The world spun, even with one eye closed and the glass slid away and smashed on the floor as I slumped forward.

"Jesus Christ, Pete!" the bartender shouted. I'm ashamed he knows my name. I have no clue who he is.

"No problem, Nicky." The stranger said. "I'll take care of it."

I felt his hands on my back, then the world went dark.

*

A pounding sound formed in the darkness accompanied by a rattling chain. I opened one eye as the motel manager pounded on the door again.

"If you don't open this door, Halladay, I swear to God I'm gonna break it down!"

"Hold on!" I shouted and took a deep breath. The mildew in the carpet filled my lungs, and despite the stench, I didn't feel much like getting off it. I sat there with my forehead pressed to the grungy carpet, my nose squished flat, and wondered what the hell happened.

"You die in there or somethin'?" Another bang.

I pressed my hands flat on the floor and pushed myself up. The room spun and I closed my left eye, shuffling to the door. I opened it, keeping the chain in place and gave Saul the evil eye.

"What the hell do you want, Saul? Can't a guy get any damned sleep in this fleapit?"

"Sleep? You want sleep?" He came closer to the gap. "Then pay me my Goddamn money, Halladay!" he shouted.

"I'm up to date. I don't gotta pay until the fourteenth."

"Yeah, and that was two days ago, asshole. Now pay up."

"What?" I retreated into my room, walking across the mungy carpet and through dust motes to a duffle in the closet.

"It's the sixteenth, wiseguy." Saul barked.

I squatted down and pulled out an envelope labeled 'Saul's bucks' and went back to the door.

"How the hell is it the sixteenth? Last I checked, it was only the seventh." the envelope was snatched from my hand the second it cleared the door jam and Saul shoved a newspaper back at me.

"Look for yourself," he said, "and clean up your shit, Halladay. You're starting to smell the place up."

"Here? No! Say it ain't so, Saul!" I looked at the paper, and sure enough, March sixteenth. I shoved the paper back, but Saul had gone. The stairs to the left of the door rattled as he made his descent, and I thought for certain they would collapse under his weight.

The door shut and I collapsed onto the bed. *How did I lose nine days?*

My head pounded, and my stomach growled. *It certainly feels like I haven't eaten in nine days, but that can't be.* I got up and stumbled to the bathroom, the room still spinning slightly. Before me stood a pale, long faced man with short black stubble and cropped black hair. The blue eyes that stared back at me were mine, but the gauntness of my cheeks was new, and the sickly grey of my skin was startling. I clutched the sink and leaned into the mirror.

"What the fuck happened to me?" My head throbbed and a memory shook loose. A stranger at *McGinty's* who asked questions. If I was going to find an answer, that's where it'd be.

I grabbed my jacket off the back of the chair and headed out.

The sun was beating down. I looked around, keeping my left eye closed as a migraine started to pulse through my skull. I pulled a smoke from my jacket pocket then slung it over my shoulder.

I walked past Saul, watching an old black and white Western, and flipped him the bird. He turned as my shadow crossed him and I waved and gave him a big 'fuck off' grin.

The sun was scorching, and I was sweating out the alcohol from my current binge. *Nine days. Nine fucking days! How could I have lost nine days?*

The sound of an alarm blasted me in my grey matter as I rounded the corner. I scrunched my left eye and covered my ears. I stepped back, and as I did, a man came sprinting from the alley. He caught my foot and landed in a heap, nearly taking me with him as he crashed to the ground.

"Jesus Christ, buddy! Are you alright?" I shouted.

He turned onto his back, lifting his arm and pointing a nickel plated pistol at my forehead. Footsteps thundered down the alley, in hot pursuit of the man with the gun (and a bag of cash I had previously failed to notice).

I put up my hands, my full attention on the little black hole staring me in the face. The alarm cut out and I opened my eye, the pain easing enough for me to face my doom head on.

The gun went off, exploding into a thousand pieces of shrapnel in the thief's hand. Something hit my chest as I hit the deck, hoping no follow up shots came from the guards behind me in the alley.

The thief screamed as the others walked up, holstering their weapons and staring with wide eyes.

"What the hell'd you do to him?" the short one asked.

"Nothing!" I said, climbing to my feet and dusting my knees off. "The gun just went off." I shrugged and the tall one looked me in the eyes.

"What's wrong with your eye?"

"Nothing. What's wrong with your eye?"

He pointed at my left eye and said, "You one of those weirdos with contacts or something?"

I looked around, thinking I'd lost my mind. "Are you talking to me?" I put a thumb to my chest. "I just looked at my eye, and it was the same as always."

The short one peered up at me. "You best go check again buddy, cause there's nothing natural about that shit."

"Can someone drive me to the fucking hospital?" the thief said, groaning and rocking on the ground.

"Shut the fuck up, man." the tall one kicked him in the shin, "Lucky we don't finish what this guy started."

"You probably should take him in." I said, looking at the bits of fingers and blood scattered across the sidewalk.

"Yeah, yeah." The short one said. He stepped forward and hauled the thief to his feet, helping him walk back to the bank (but not before slapping him in cuffs). "You got some, uh–" he said, pointing at my chest as he walked by.

I looked down and there was a streak of red on my shirt roughly the size of a finger. *What the fuck is happening today? I need to get back to McGinty's and find out what happened that night.*

A sunbeam caught me in the face and I squinted my left eye. The eye that the security guards agreed looked fucked up. A pain jolted my cerebellum and I closed my other eye, fumbling for a cigarette with blind fingers. I got it lit (pro like me doesn't need to see) and as I inhaled, the tension left my body and the pain dimmed. It was still there, a rhino throwing a tantrum in my cranium, only now the rhino was in a tutu and only miffed.

McGinty's was empty, not even a tender in sight. I took a seat on the worn burgundy stool, my ass filling the dents perfectly, and put my feet up on the worn brass tubes running along the bottom.

I took my lighter out of my pocket, flipping it open and closing it. The metallic *slink-clack, slink-clack* echoed through the empty space. The silence was creeping into my skull and the pounding was coming back. I wanted another cigarette, but I had just put out my last one. *What am I watching my health?* I reached in my coat and grabbed another as Nick appeared from the back.

"What do you want, Halladay?"

"Jesus," I exhaled, "No, 'hello'? No, 'how's it going Pete'?"

"Fuck you. How's that?"

"Well, now we're getting somewhere." I laughed. "Can I get a whiskey?"

"Can't serve you until after eleven."

I looked around and said, "who's gonna know?"

"What do you want?" He pulled out a dirty glass and filled it to the brim with pale amber goodness. The whiskey slopped over the side, muddying the lipstick on the rim into a red blur.

The glass was sticky in my hand, but I lifted it to my lips and took a swallow. "I was in here last night– or I guess it was last week."

"Yeah, I remember." Nick smiled as I took another drink.

"That big fella I was with, the ugly one with the carrot top–"

"You mean the one who paid for your drinks and stopped me from throwing your ass to the curb?"

"Yeah, that's the one. You know him?"

"Nope." He slung his rag over his shoulder and crossed his arms. The classic bartender wall of silence.

"You sure? He'd never been in here before?"

"Look, I don't know him, but he was talking to your pal Rudy before he came and talked to you."

I nodded and flicked ash onto the floor. "You seen the guy since that night?"

"Nope."

"You seen me since that night?" I took another swallow.

"Get the fuck outta here already. I'm sick of looking at you and that creepy ass eye."

I downed the rest of the drink and slammed a tenner on the bar. "Keep the change," I said and muttered "you fuckin' asswipe." as I turned away. I headed for the door, but turned before I reached it to see Nick bent over the taps. I cut to the right and went into the mens room.

I turn on the light and the fluorescents flicker, filling the tiled room with sickly light. The mirror above the trough sink shows my long pale face and stubbled chin, the same as the one in my room did, but my eye...it's changed.

The right eye is still the handsome baby blue that got me all the girls when I was a youngin', but the left twinkles back at me with an emerald intensity I'd never seen before.

"What the fuck?" I said and leaned closer, drawing my skin back to get a better look. My iris was an iridescent green, changing colour slightly as I moved side to side. It reflected the light, flashing like a high vis sticker you'd see on the side of a cop car. *No wonder those guys said it was creepy. I'm one spooky bastard.*

I left the bathroom, and Nick had left his place behind the bar. The man with the red hair stared out at me, the jagged scar on the side of his face crinkling as he smiled.

"Fancy another?" He said, raising a pint glass. He didn't wait for an answer and pulled the tap, letting near black ale run into the crystal cup.

"What's happened to my eye?" I asked him as I walked back and took my seat.

He stopped pouring, leaving the perfect amount of foam. He looked down his nose at me, his eyes quizzical as he set the drink on the bar.

"So you've used it already?" he said.

"Used what?" I took a sip, the foam tickling my lip.

"The luck, Pete. The luck."

"Who the hell are you, anyway?" I pointed at him, doing my best to give him the evil eye. "You come round here and ask a bunch of questions, the next thing I know, I wake up *nine* days later with a headache and a mismatched eye."

He smiled and leaned on the bar, placing his enormous mitts on the polished wood. The smell of cloves rolled over me as he laughed. "You're sharper than I thought you'd be. You were nearly a vegetable last we spoke. You remember all that?"

"I do." another sip "Well, I mostly do. Except those nine days."

"Well, that's my doin'." he said. "Speaking of, we best be moving along. I reckon that prick Chester won't be too far behind now."

"Say what now?"

"There he is now."

I spun in my chair and a man walked into the bar. No, seriously, and he was six feet somethin' of muscle under the most ridiculous turtleneck I'd ever seen. He zeroed in on us, his right eye the same glimmering green as my left.

"Who's this dildo then?" I said and took a deep pull from my beer.

"Chester. He's your opponent."

"What the hell are you talking about?" I put the empty glass down with a bang and rounded on the stranger. "And who the hell are you anyway?"

"Yeah, you're right. You don't know enough." He shook his head. "Best come with me."

He went through the swinging doors behind the bar and I looked back as Chester pulled a revolver out of his black coat (black coat, black turtleneck, black pants and neck stompin' boots. This guy looked like a complete prick).

I scrambled over the bar as the air rippled above me, alive with leaden death. I landed in a heap but scrambled to my feet and through the swinging doors.

The floor went out from under me and I landed on my hands and knees in the sand. The ocean crashed beside me and a crab scuttled nearby as the salty air filled my lungs.

"Should be safe for a moment."

My stomach rolled and the Guinness found itself deposited on the beach as I retched it up. "What the *fuck* was that?"

"Just a portal. Nothing too crazy." He shrugged. "I'm not allowed to interfere with the game, but the game isn't technically started until you know the rules."

I stood up on shaky legs, the afternoon sun scorching my pale skin. "What fuckin' game?"

He looked around, but no one was within a mile. "Let's find some shade first. Boys like us don't do well in this sun, eh?" He chucked my shoulder and walked toward the boardwalk.

What the fuck have I gotten into this time? I rubbed my aching eyes as I followed.

I sat myself down in the cool, wet sand under the shabby wooden walkway and looked up at the red headed stranger towering over me.

"Right. To start off, my name's Lugh."

"That's awful."

"What? No it's not."

"Your name sounds like you have a loogie stuck in your throat. Lugh. Yuck is more like it. "

"Shut it, we don't have much time." Lugh said, and I ran my fingers along my lips, firmly zipping them. "I've had a bad go of it the last few games, so we want to try and give you an edge here before Chester finds you."

"Who the hell is Chester, and what the hell's the game?"

Lugh stared at me with his fierce blue eyes and I raised my hands in apologies.

"The game," he said "started centuries ago. Two people are chosen, one by me and one by that bastard Ecne."

I raised my eyebrow.

"We had a tiff a long time ago. He reckons it's best to have skill, and that natural born talent and well polished skill will win against luck every time."

"You mean that stupid question you asked me at the bar?"

"That's part of it." He nodded, "You're my contestant. You play for the side of luck."

"The hell I do." I stood up and kicked some sand his way, "You can't just kidnap someone and force them to compete in a game. And what's this 'it's just a portal' bullshit? You literally teleported us miles away!"

He shrugged again, "I'm a God, it's not that big a deal."

I looked him dead in the eye and I felt my jaw go slack (I might have peed a little). "You're a God? Capital G?"

He gave a mock bow. "Lugh, Irish God of Luck, at your service."

"Fuck." I ran my fingers through my hair as pain flared behind my eye and I scrunched it closed. The throbbing ripped through my skull like a bullet and little flashes of light started to pop across my vision.

A voice came from behind me and I nearly jumped out of my skin.

"What are you doing?" it purred, "You know you can't interfere with the match, Lugh."

"Piss off, Ecne. You know damn well we changed that rule after the match in 1218, don't be an arse." Lugh shook his head and I turned to take in the man who had appeared next to me. He was medium height and his slim body was accentuated by his billowing white shirt under a pencil thin vest. With his tight black pants, knee high boots and oiled black hair, I wondered if he was in costume of some kind, or if he always dressed like a douchey pirate.

"You only have five more minutes to explain the rules," Ecne said, pulling a silver pocket watch from his vest, "best make it fast." His pale skin drew tight on his skull as he smiled at Lugh, his eyes glinting and feverish.

"What the fuck is happening." I said and rubbed my eyes. The pressure helped the pain a bit, but I had a feeling whatever Yuck was going to tell me was going to make it worse. I sat down on the damp, cold sand doing my best to not scream.

"Are you listening?"

"What?"

"I said, 'are you listening', Pete?" Lugh snapped his fingers and Ecne stared down at me with his crazed smile still plastered on. "We're running out of time."

I looked up at him. My head was pounding and I just wanted a drink or seven to make it stop.

"You and Chester are to fight to the death."

"What the fuck?"

Ecne laughed and I wanted to punch his slim nose into his brain, Bruce Lee style.

"If you win, you keep the luck."

"What 'luck'?" I jabbed a finger at him, "I'm under a shitty boardwalk being told I'm to fight some maniac with a gun to the death. What fuckin' luck?"

Lugh smiled at me and I caught a family resemblance with the creepy pale fuck beside us.

"I don't know what, but you did something to activate it already." he pointed at my throbbing, green, mutant eye. "Once it does that, then the game is on, and I can't help ya."

"Precisely," Ecne said, "so I will be calling Chester now and telling him where you are. He produced a Nokia from nowhere and held it away from his ear as it rang, as though the trilling was too boorish for him to handle. "I refuse to sink to your level, Lugh. I will tell him the proper way and not break rules by transporting him here." he put his ear to the phone as a tiny voice squawked on the other end. "Yes, Chester. This is Ecne. Please come to the boardwalk right away. We're near a 'Joe's Crab Shack'. You know it? Delightful, see you soon."

I looked at Lugh, and that impish smile was still there. "How many times has your guy won?" I asked.

"Twelve times. Not bad, if you ask me."

"How many times have you played?"

Ecne let out a bark of a laugh and Lugh waved him off. "Don't worry about that right now. Worry about Chester. You've only got a few minutes." A screech in the parking lot behind us was followed by the slam of a car door. "Maybe less."

I blinked and the Gods had vanished, leaving the smell of cloves and apples to mingle with the sea air.

"Motherfuckers." I said and turned to peak out from behind the boardwalk.

Chester walked toward me, his turtleneck looking even more ridiculous in full daylight.

"Come out, Lucky!" he shouted at me. "I want to show you what I can do."

"I'd rather not." I said, "I don't fight guys who go around dressing like Shaft." I poked my head around the corner again and the buzz of a bullet zipped past my ear. The sand behind me puffed up and I sat down quickly as three more popped into the sand. *Some lucky beachcomber will find that someday...along with my corpse.*

"You're a dead man, Lucky, so you might as well face me. I'll make it quick."

"What did they promise you for this? For killing me?" I said, frantically looking for something I could use for a weapon.

"Same thing they promised you, I'm guessing."

"Nope. Can't be what I'm getting." I found a broken bottle and pulled it out of the sand by the neck. Its jagged edges gleamed and I shifted it around, testing the balance like I knew what I was doing. "They promised me luck."

"Luck? What a goddamned waste to die for a bit of luck." Chester said, closer now.

"So you must have gotten the same question then. Luck or skill. And you picked skill."

I could hear my heart pounding in my chest. I heard his footsteps now, thumping closer in the sand. *I'm only going to have one shot at this.*

He stopped just outside the boardwalk, his shadow cast long and distorted along the beach. I stared at it and my head started to hurt. My ears were ringing and my left eye's vision was blurring to the point I couldn't see. I scrunched it closed and rubbed at it with my free hand.

"I didn't choose skill. I *am* skill." Chester chuckled.

A high-pitched ringing filled my head alongside the pain that was driving away my vision. I could barely think, but I never did much of that anyway. The shadow took a step and I opened my left eye and sprang from under the boardwalk, throwing all I had into a viscous downward slash with the bottle.

The gun popped off, clipping my shirt as the bottle struck home. The jagged end slipped across Chester's face, shredding the skin off his still human eye and slicing down the side of his nose.

He stumbled back and I pressed the advantage, tripping on my feet and bowling into him. I fell on top of him then rolled to the side and covered my head, expecting a barrage of bullets to rip through me. But Chester didn't pull the trigger. He lay on the ground, twitching as blood from his face poured through his nearly severed nose and into his throat. He gurgled and twitched, dying with his ruined lidless eye staring up at the sky.

I laid on my stomach, looking at Chester's stupid turtleneck as it became dark with blood and his green eye flickered back to its dull brown.

"Well. That was a quick one." Lugh said beside me.

"What the fuck happened?" I said.

Lugh walked over to the corpse and bent down. "Well, you killed him."

Ecne appeared at Chester's head. He wrinkled his nose as he pushed Chester's head to the side with his boot. "That's a new one. Death by seashell."

I got to my hands sand knees and crawled close enough to see a seashell embedded at the base of Chester's skull.

"Look at that," Lugh said, "must have severed his spine."

"Ugh, he's soiled himself." Ecne said. He waved his hand and Chester disappeared. "Enough of that." He looked at Lugh and wrinkled his nose, pulling his lip up into a sneer. "You win this point, but that makes him number thirteen. Don't you 'luck' types hate that number?"

A searing hot iron pressed itself inside my head and I shut my eyes. I rubbed them and when I managed to crack open my right one, I stood there alone with Lugh.

"What a prick." he said, and I nodded my agreement.

"Can't say I like you much either though."

"I don't blame yeah for that." He said, "But you're gonna like me even less after I tell you what I need to tell you."

I opened both eyes and looked into his. There was steel there that wasn't there before.

"What're you talking about?" I said.

"I chose you for a reason."

"And that is?"

"You're sick, Pete."

Another flash in my head and the world tilts. "What do you mean?"

"A tumor." He pointed to my eye, "Right behind there."

"What are you talking about? I don't have a tumor."

He shrugs, and suddenly the headaches and the blinding pain in my eye made sense. It had been happening for a while...but I thought it was just from all the booze and the pills and living my fucked up life. I didn't think I would ever live long enough to die from something like a tumor.

"How do you know?" I said.

He cocked his head to the side, like I asked a stupid question, and said, "I'm a God. I know."

"Alright." I rubbed the back of my head. "Fine, Mr. Smartypants. How do I fix it?"

"I don't think you can."

"Then why did you choose me?" I grabbed his coat and pulled him down to my height. "Why me?"

He looked away, "Because you're a loser, Pete. I've lost the last three hundred years. I couldn't put any more good men through the ringer."

I let go and stumbled back, walking over the dark splotches of blood in the sand where Chester had died moments before. Now him and his stupid turtleneck were gone. Scrubbed from their douchey existence by squabbling, childish Gods.

"You picked me because I was disposable? Some piece of shit that could be used in your game." I nodded. "Nobody to come looking for Ol' Pete the drunk, hey?" I thought of Malorie going about the rest of her life without knowing I had died. Without being able to tell her how sorry I was…how much I loved her and missed her. *Not yet.*

I turned from Lugh and started walking off the beach to the parking lot.

"Where are you going?" Lugh called after me.

"You gave me some luck," I said heading for the maroon Porsche that screamed 'my owner wears turtlenecks'. "I'm going to go use it."

I opened the door and the keys sat in the ignition, glinting in the sun. I turned the key and the engine roared to life as sweet, citrus scented air conditioning blew my hair back. I shifted into gear.

"Time to see what this loser can do."

THE DAMN FOOLS

BY 'DOC' CLANCY

"Hey Willy!" came the voice, low but audible from the edge of the rise. It was dusk now, and Johnny had been watching through the binoculars for hours.

"Sergeant to you, boy." Will didn't like being called "Willy", but he fought it just enough to make it stick. "And get your fool head down."

"Begging your pardon, sir," Pvt. Jenson said mockingly from behind them. "Some of us aren't used to calling a negro 'sir' yet, sir." His voice hardened. "And we sure aren't used to one calling us 'boy'." Jenson liked to wave his Southern aristocracy like a rebel flag. Sometimes Will had to make a point with him. Today he made a point by letting it go.

"I still don't see anything, er, Sarge." Johnny said looking back out over the rise at the dilapidated village below.

Will crawled through the dirt and thin brush alongside him. "Certainly nothing that could wipe out a whole company," he agreed. In fact, two whole companies as well as a few smaller depleted units – nearly 300 men in total – had tried to march past this nameless, shabby village and had never been heard from again.

"Still no activity?" Capt. Thompson asked from their small camp a few yards back.

"No sir," the sergeant said backing away from the lip of the hill before standing and handing the worn pair of binoculars to his CO, who took them tensely and awkwardly made his way on his hands and knees and then on his belly to stop alongside Johnny.

"How long since last movement, Pvt. Harris?"

"I thought I saw something this morning, but even when I do see people they barely move between the huts. It's like they're sick or something."

"Could it be an outbreak of some kind?" the captain asked, raising the binoculars to his eyes.

"I don't think so," Will said. "If our boys had picked something up, they would have radioed for help. And those things usually burn themselves out quickly. Troops have been disappearing here for months."

The platoon froze stiff as they heard tires approaching, all of them turning back to look beyond the camp. The tension abated slowly, even after they saw it was an army jeep. A man who was probably almost thirty but who had a very youthful face jumped down and returned the driver's salute before the jeep sped away.

The man approached, a lieutenant by the bar on his helmet. Will stepped in his way as he approached. "Here are my orders, sergeant," he said brusquely. "Where is your commanding officer?"

"Over there, sir," Will said, but stepped more firmly into the lieutenant's path.

"Can I help you, sergeant?"

"No sir," he said, shifting the toothpick in his mouth from one side to other. "Just keep low after that line in the dirt. We lost Hanson there."

The lieutenant nodded and began to step forward, though by this time, the captain had come over to meet him. "Capt. Thompson," he said, presenting his orders and saluting tautly.

"Lieutenant." The captain returned the salute as an afterthought as he tore open the sealed orders.

"News from Tokyo?"

"Yes sir. And from Charleston."

The captain froze, and Will saw him notice the pin that the lieutenant war over his name on his fatigues: A curiously curved sword. It was just like the one the captain wore.

"*Abhara*," the captain said softly.

"*Cad abhara*, sir," the lieutenant responded with a narrow grin as the captain scrutinized the orders.

"Sergeant," Capt. Thompson began as he folded the orders and put them in his shirt pocket. "Lt. Ford is here on special orders to investigate possible supranormal enemy activity in this village. You will afford him any assistance."

"Supranormal?" Will asked.

"In this sense," the lieutenant condescended, "it means things out of the ordinary scope of warfare."

"I understand the word," Will said, with some heat in his voice before adding "sir." He rubbed his chin where the stubble was getting thick enough to hurt his skin. "Not much normal about war to begin with, sir. Are we talking about experimental weapons? Germs? Brainwashing?"

"Can these men be trusted?" Ford asked the captain. Will felt a flash of impatience at the question but it was asked with such earnestness, especially in comparison to Ford's manner so far, that Will felt his curiosity piqued more than his ire. Johnny looked back over his shoulder from the rise. Curt Song, Jack Donahue, and the other privates drew closer.

"I have trusted and do trust these men with my life," Capt. Thompson said with conviction, "though none of them have been trusted with the secrets of our brotherhood."

Ford nodded at the captain and then squinted at Will. "What's your name, Sergeant."

"Freedman, sir."

"No," Ford shook his head, "Your full name."

"William Freedman, sir."

Ford looked as if he were adding sums in his head. "No middle name?"

"I don't like to say, sir. I have enough trouble with these white-bread boys of mine."

"It might be important, sergeant."

Will shifted on his feet. "Shakespeare, sir. It's a family name."

"Shakespeare!" Donahue exclaimed, pausing the nervous shuffling of his deck of cards between his hands and turning to his buddy Song. His Brooklyn accent always made him sound like he was cracking wise, and he usually was. "No wonder he lets us call him 'Willy'." Jenson, meanwhile, scraped the ground with his boots and spat in the dirt.

Ford smiled, but not at Will's expense. "The numerology of your name is strong, Sergeant." He stepped just up to the line drawn in the dirt. "You said you lost Hanson here?"

"Yes sir."

"Did you find a bullet?"

Will looked at the lieutenant with skepticism. "His head was almost blown clean off, sir."

"Did you hear a shot, then?"

The men looked at each other. Song ventured: "It happened awful fast, but we must of, right?"

Ford smiled. "Unless it was magic that killed him."

"Gee whiz," Donahue snorted. "This guy's been in Korea too long."

"Whether you like what I'm saying or not, private, you will follow the military code of conduct when addressing an officer." Ford paused to make sure Donahue and anyone who had snickered were properly cowed. "Gentlemen, your captain and I belong to an ancient order charged with protecting the world from just such malicious magic." He looked around at their confused and wary faces. "Oh, it's quite true. Surely you've seem the sabre that Capt. Thompson wears on his uniform and that I wear as well. That sacred symbol signifies that we both served on the Occult Front during the big one: W-W-Two."

"Lieutenant," Will began, "I'll admit that Hanson's death was hard to figure. But Joker Platoon here has seen a lot of strange things. That's what we do. We take the jobs that nobody else can handle –~ and that's why they call us 'the Damn Fools'. But We've never seen anything like what you're talking about."

"What's that around your neck, sergeant?"

Will felt around his neck to the silver chain that sat close to his throat. "It's a crucifix and a St. Michael's medal, sir. My mother gave them to me when I shipped out."

"Why?"

Will was embarrassed. He knew where this line of thinking was going. "She said it would protect me, sir."

"And that's not magic?"

"Respectfully, I don't think it's the same thing, sir."

"But you," Ford said with a smirk, "or your mother, at least, believes that they'll protect you right?"

Will was silent, squinting one eye at the lieutenant while he shifted the toothpick to the other corner of his mouth with his tongue.

"Alright," Ford said, clapping his hands and rubbing them together like he was readying for a meal. "We'll know for sure what's going on very soon. Captain, will you share our new orders with the men, sir, or shall I?"

"I'll do it, lieutenant," Capt. Thompson said, looking haggard. "Break camp. We're marching into that village immediately."

"Sir!" Will exclaimed. "We're down to twelve men, we still don't know‑"

"What's left of Company C is retreating this way with the whole damn red army behind them," the captain interrupted heatedly. "I understand how you feel about your men, Freedman," he said, softening his voice. "I understand you're still feeling the death of Hanson. And I know that's why you still have twelve men following you into whatever's down there. But I *have* seen the kind of things Lt. Ford is talking about. Right now there's wounded men coming this way with nowhere else to go, and this is the only defensible position for miles in this part of the mountains. So we're taking this village or we're not coming back."

"Yes, sir," Will said heavily as the captain and Ford turned away to discuss their plan of attack. Will didn't like the look of that lieutenant's face as he turned away. He flicked his toothpick into the dirt at his feet. He wouldn't have long to make sure the men were ready.

Johnny crawled back over the line and stood next to Will with his binoculars still around his neck. The captain and Ford were out of earshot, so he asked: "Is this guy one of us now, Sarge?"

Will scowled. "I think he wants this to be something bad." He shook his head. "Nah, he's not one of us. But he is a damn fool."

*

"You feel that, men?" Lt. Ford asked. "That thrill in the gut?"

Nobody answered. The line moved slowly down the path on the south side of the rise, men's flesh made the same by the cover of night and the wet dirt smeared over their faces. The village was quiet and still as they drew down closer to it. It seemed bigger from the ground and not just because it was nearer. They were used to looking down at it, but now those straw huts were tall enough to look down at them.

Tensely, the men looked around, their gun barrels locked to their line of sight as they pivoted their gaze to either side, smooth and calm like Donahue, jerking fearfully like Johnny, or straight ahead, loosely coiled like Will. They were about to enter the most dangerous part of this walk now: in the open between the shadow of the rise and the village itself. Despite the possibility of being full of people who wanted to kill them, the actually line of simple buildings that marked the edge of the village also marked relative safety. Will had already identified points of cover for his men, gesturing and pointing them out to each of them as they moved in the dark.

Will's foot hit the moonlight outside the mountain's shadow and he broke into a run, the officers and his men taking his cue and following him into the open. Lt. Ford sped up, passing Will in the dirt by a few paces before suddenly stopping.

Will didn't stop, neither did his men. They were better trained than that. But after a moment Will saw what Ford had seen. A beautiful woman, pointing at them, shouting and crying with a hate so pure that it needed no translator.

Will had just come around the corner of the first hut when it happened. For an instant, he swore he saw a shape, long and gaunt and pale at the other side of the village. It flickered across the dirt strip between the huts too fast for him to see clearly, but he felt a wave of icy terror run through his body in the hot Korean night air. And then the world turned to fire.

Will grabbed Johnny and dragged him to the ground as the hot wind of the explosion flew over them. The kid was screaming and a patch of blood covered the place where the left of his face should have been. The captain's back was on fire, but Will saw him drop and roll behind the nearest building. Donahue and Song had scrambled in opposite directions with a few other men in tow. Jenson and Filmore were in pieces in the open dirt. Parts of Jenson were still alive and he was screaming for his mama. Will ran to him, ducking as another wave of fire filled the air above him with heat and deafening noise. He dragged him back to the cover of the nearest hut, cautiously popping his head and his rifle barrel to the level of its rear window and finding it empty. He looked down at Jenson's spasming body. One arm and both legs had been blown off and not cleanly.

"Jesus..." Jenson just managed.

Will couldn't tell if it was a curse or a prayer. "He's got you," seemed appropriate.

Jenson looked up at him with a lolling eye. "None of your Catholic mumbo-jumbo please."

"Didn't you hear, Jenson?" Will asked. "Pope just announced that Heaven's segregated."

"Oh yeah?" Jenson responded, taking the bait sardonically like he always did.

"They finally added a section just for assholes."

Jenson chuckled, the laugh bringing blood to his lips. And then he died. Will hadn't liked him – Jenson had resented him, challenged him, made him be hard on him. But he was one of his, and he was glad he'd died with a laugh instead of in screaming horror like so many others.

The shouting and the flames had stopped. "You all right, Freedman?" the captain shouted.

"Yes sir." Will looked around at his platoon. Capt. Thompson stepped forward into the village. He turned back and nodded at the men. Will followed first with the others behind him, rifles still at the ready. The village appeared empty. Will looked back and saw that the ground where they had been ambushed was totally undisturbed. It hadn't been artillery and it hadn't been mines. Cautiously moving forward, he spotted Lt. Ford. He was standing feet apart, braced as if ready to fire a weapon, but his rifle was on his back and his service revolver was still in its holster. Instead he held his hands before him in some kind of arcane sign.

"If you come closer, do it slowly," he said without taking his eyes off whatever was in front of him. The captain took a few steps and stopped, putting his hands into the same shape as Ford's. Will held his rifle up as he moved in, coming around the front of a row of huts, and he saw it, hiding in the deep darkness between. The beautiful woman was there, her skin pale as the moon. Her eyes were rolled back so far that they could see only the whites, but behind her, its mouth against her neck, was the creature Will thought he had seen. It was shaped like a man in a worn and dirty robe, but the fingers it held to the woman's throat were too long, the bones of its arms too thin. Its hair was straight and black and hung over its bone-white and hollow face. Its eyes were a deep and shining black and seemed to take no notice of any of them. Will crept closer and its eyes twitched up to look at him. Instinctively, he raised his hand, his mind reeling with a cold fear at the unearthly, ungodly thing. The being looked at his hand, still stained red by Jenson's blood and flew backwards silently into the trees beyond the village, like it had been caught by a sudden wind. The woman collapsed to the ground.

"Do you believe me now, sergeant?" Ford asked snidely.

The Fools snapped into readiness again as shapes emerged from around the village. The people were haggard and defeated, and they were all very old.

*

They had placed the young woman in a bed in one of the huts. Ford and the captain were standing outside trying to keep the crowd of elderly villagers from getting any closer, though they continued to press in slowly as the dawn rose yellow in the sky.

"This is a waste of time, captain," Ford said, confidant in the villagers' inability to understand his callous words. "These people are our enemy. And we have every reason to believe that this woman set that creature on us."

"These are noncombatants, lieutenant," Capt. Thompson said pointedly. "Sgt. Freedman has learned a good deal of field medicine in his time under me, and since he's already patched up our own wounded, I intend to allow him to continue offering humanitarian aid, regardless of the recipient."

Inside, Will could hear the conversation, and hoped that Ford was properly put in place by the captain's comments. He had tried to clean and drain the woman's wound – a hideous round ring of punctures on her neck, with several similar scars nearby – but he had been through many towels before it finally stopped bleeding. The flow had been slow but very steady, and he had feared her to be beyond his help as she tossed and shook between consciousness and feverish sleep. He looked down at his hands. The dark skin on the backs of them was covered in dry, ashy lines that made them looked cracked. He had just gotten Jenson's blood off them, and Johnny's, and Kemper's, and Wilde's, and now they were covered in somebody else's that he didn't even know. Not a good day.

He stepped out into the open. The faces of the people were dull despite their insistence on waiting outside. "Somebody tell them that she'll live, I think."

"Pvt. Song," the captain began. "You speak Korean, yes?"

"Not very well, sir," Song began. "My parents wanted me to be a nice American boy."

"If it's as bad as his English we're in trouble," Donahue ventured.

"Enough of that, private," the captain said testily. "You've more than the rest of us, son."

Despite a few false starts, Song managed to communicate the condition of the injured woman to the villagers. The very thin old man who seemed to be their leader seemed relieved, becoming more animated, his large, thick eyebrows moving up and down over his small, twinkling eyes.

"Hey Song," Will said from the doorway. "Ask them about the thing that did this."

Song searched for the right words, and after a moment the conversation became rapid and agitated. "He says that it lives out beyond the village and that it feeds on the hatreds and conflicts of men."

The old man continued. It sounded to Will like Song was repeating some of what was said, trying to make sure he was understanding it correctly.

"Uh," Song began hesitatingly. "Some American soldiers came through here once, captain, after the men of the village, including Mi-Ja's-" he repeated the name to the old man, who said it back again. "-the girl in there, Mi-Ja, her husband was killed in the war, sir."

"Go on, private," the captain insisted.

"I don't want to sir," Song said. "It makes me kind of sick. But they roughed up the whole village sir, and Mi-Ja there, well, she got the worst of it."

"I think I understand, private, but where does this thing that's killing our troops figure into it?"

"He keeps saying 'Yaosagma', sir. It's not a word, I don't think, but part of it sounds a little like 'sorcerer' or 'evil spirit'. Might be the thing's name." The old man continued speaking. "He says it lived in the forest for centuries, but after what happened, Mi-Ja called it, invited it in." The old man made a last firm statement and pulled down the front of his shirt, all the other villagers around him doing the same. Each had a series of round scars on their necks like the ones on Mi-Ja. Song took a deep breath. "He says that they all agreed."

*

"You realize that this is probably a trap, captain," Ford said.

"These people are afraid, captain, and they're tired," Will countered. "This thing is killing them as sure as it's killing us, just slower."

"Prepare the men to move out," the captain said, refusing eye contact with either of them. The lieutenant began to object, but Capt. Thompson silenced him with a gesture and a cold stare. "My decision is final. We have no option but to resolve this situation or die trying."

"Hey, Shakespeare," Donahue said, rushing onto the scene. "The girl's awake."

Will stifled his objection to the new nickname and ran to the hut where Mi-Ja was resting. As soon as he entered a ceramic bowl flew towards him, and he ducked behind his hands as it crashed into the bamboo frame of the doorway. Mi-Ja was definitely awake, her cheeks were hot pink with rage, and her thin, wide eyes flashed fire as she unleashed a torrent of what he could only assume was the most vile obscenity at him. He backed out of the hut and nearly into Song.

"Sorry, sir," Song said. "I should have warned you. She half talked to me, until she saw the ol' stars and stripes on my uniform. Somebody else wants to talk to you though, sir." Song indicated an old woman with a kind but desperately sad face. "This is Mi-Ja's mother, sir. She wanted to thank you for helping her daughter." The woman bowed profusely to Will, her hands cupped in front of her face. "She told me that Yaosagma's been taking more and more from her daughter lately and probably would have killed her this time." The woman looked at him, with a smile that filled all the wrinkles around her face. "They don't know what it is about you sir, but they seem to think you're on the side of the buddhas, so to speak."

The old woman tottered forward and pulled Will's arm towards her with her still cupped hands, dropping a necklace of sandalwood beads into his palms. He rolled over the small, wooden pendant with his thumb and found it carved with a seated Buddha on the other side. "Thank her for me," he said, finding himself sincerely moved. Song translated but hadn't needed to. She had heard his tone of voice and smiled before Song explained the words.

He put the necklace on in front of her. His mother wouldn't have approved, but there the Buddha was, right between Jesus and St. Michael. The village elder had offered to take them to the place where this Yaosagma nested and he'd be leading his men there soon. He could use all the help he could get.

*

They were down to eight men, not counting himself or the captain and definitely not counting Ford. "Are you good with that arm, Wilde," the captain asked.

"Yes sir," Wilde said, stretching his left arm in its sling. "It's not the arm I use for shooting."

"At least not shooting his gun, that is." Donahue said, provoking laughter from his comrades. "Anyway, it's Johnny I feel bad for. I mean how are the girls gonna look at him now when he gets home?"

Johnny laughed nervously, but not because of the joke about his torn up and bandaged face. "If I get home, you mean."

"None of that talk, son," Will said. "Whether it's with your face or your libido, you've got plenty of sturdy, gap-toothed Nebraska girls to terrorize yet." The men laughed, and Johnny smiled, despite the pain in his split lips.

"Will Kemper be alright, sergeant?" the captain asked.

"Practically had to strap him to the bed, sir," Will grinned. "Anybody'd think I was punishing him for missing a foot and three fingers by making him stay."

"Captain," Ford said, unamused by the proceedings. "If we're going to do this, we need to get started. And you and I should cast a ward first."

The captain nodded. "Yes, lieutenant." He produced a worn and bent volume from one of his pockets. The title was gilt on the cover, as was the emblem of an eye surrounded by five interlocking swords. "Men, the lieutenant and I are going to perform a ritual which is a part of our religion, but which nonetheless, in the view of certain sealed documents prepared by the Department of Defense, was found to have been efficacious in combat situations during the Second World War. The casting we are about to perform will be for the entire platoon, and it is not required that you participate or even believe in the efficacy of the ritual for it to be effective." The captain and lieutenant nodded at each other, and the captain began to recite from the book. Will was just good enough a Catholic to be uncomfortable with the rite and to recognize the language as Latin. "*Abhara*," the captain said at the end.

"*Cad abhara*," Ford responded, the same exchange of words as when they had met. A few of the men mumbled nonsense along with him, said "amen", or moved their lips silently out of habit. Will just watched silently. Whatever had just happened, he didn't feel any differently.

The men began to move out, Capt. Thompson, Ford, and Will taking the point behind the old man, who furrowed his thick eyebrows as he walked, almost completely obscuring his eyes as they looked down, watching his feet. He led them through the tangled brush and low hanging branches of the forest. "Almost there, men," Ford said, that hunger lighting his eyes again. But the men were tense, each limb that brushed them might have been the hand of the creature they stalked, each movement and sound in the dimly lit wood might be the same thing approaching. The old man at last stopped, holding the leafy knot of a tree's limb back and stepping aside. It was clear from his posture that he would go no further.

Will blinked in the light of day as he followed the officers into the open valley. It hadn't occurred to him to wonder what had become of the troops that had gone missing before – notuntil he saw their remains here. Machines of war, tanks, jeeps, artillery were stacked high on either side, moldering corpses in helmets and fatigues still inside. Broken and separated human bones littered the ground, along with melted pieces of firearms and equipment. Will tried not to step on them for his first few paces. After that it became unavoidable. The trappings of war appeared to get older and older as they walked deeper into the valley. They were in the shade of the mountainside now, and surrounded by the crumbling remains of imperial troops, Japanese first, then Chinese, their primitive artillery nearly overcome by the encroaching of nature.

At last they saw it. They had heard nothing of its approach. Yaosagma simply appeared at the mouth of the cave opening at the valley's far end, ringed as it was by the armor and the swords of invading samurai. Its face, a mockery of the human visage, bore an impossibly wide smile of jagged, yellow teeth, its brows were furrowed upward in a way that seemed to be mocking them and its black eyes, so large and round beneath their wide, angular lids, shown with a calm, unblinking, predatory stare.

Behind Will, the men fanned out as best as they could in the tight, debris-filled valley, rifles at the ready. "You ugly sonuvabitch," he heard Wilde mutter, balancing the barrel of his M1 over his slung and bandaged arm. But it was Johnny who shot first, three bullets right into the chest of the thing. The first two only produced small clouds of dust, the third resulted in the spilling of a thin line of black fluid down its old and dirty robes. The thing doubled forward, but only began to stand tall again, its smile open-jawed and leering as the rest of the troops opened fire. Yaosagma stretched up and forward, bending at the waist at an unnatural angle, and its mouth became a protruding ring of teeth shaped like the wounds Will had seen in the village. Fire spilled from that toothy maw, from its eyes and from its spidery, clawed hands.

Wilde screamed. The bullets left in his loaded clip had exploded, leaving his rifle a shredded mess in his bleeding hands. He was squinting tightly, streams of blood flowing down his face as he fell to his knees, tossing the gun away and clawing at his eyes. The ratt-att-att of gunfire continued to fill the valley, and Will felt the heat singe his eyelashes and the stubble on his chin as he dove to the littered dirt, the waves of flame cooking his back as they passed over him. Ford and the captain were moving to either side, trying to outflank the thing. They were shouting a complicated call and response in some dead language. The creature, so far oblivious to their approach, continued to send great tongues of flame in the direction of the men.

"Donahue!" Will shouted from behind the nearly petrified rubble of an old Chinese wagon. "Are you still with me?"

"Yes sir! But we're pinned down."

"Fall back!" Will shouted. "I'll draw its attention."

"But, sir-"

"That's an order, private! I'm not asking you to leave us, but this thing has the high ground. We need to draw it out."

It was a moment filled only with gunshots and cries of pain before Donahue acknowledged the order. Will waited for an opening. Finally, Yaosagma noticed the approach of the officers as they climbed through the last layer of debris and stood before him. It looked at each of them, its mouth returning to that wide, serrated smile. Will took this moment and stood up. He lifted the rifle to his eye line, aimed and fired in one motion. The thing's head snapped back so that it was staring at the heavens, but then slowly moved back down to look at him, a single drop of that black blood spilling down its face from a hole just barely right of the center of its forehead. Will, Thompson and Ford, all stood near the thing now, but it jerked its head up to watch Donahue and the painfully few men he was leading in retreat. The look on its face made it clear that it was enjoying itself too much to allow an easy kill to deprive it of more prey. It raised its hands, and streams of fire tore through the ground at its feet, past Will, and out into the valley were the men were withdrawing. The jets of fire rose in force and speed as they approached their position, tearing the earth away from that side of the valley, taking the men down in a rockslide full of the bones of men and vehicles.

Capt. Thompson lunged at the thing, a silver dagger glinting in his hand, but it seized him at the chest, its icy touch visibly startling the captain before he was pushed back into the rock wall behind him with such force that Will could hear his bones crack before he slumped to the ground. Then it turned to Ford. Will stepped back instinctively, unashamed at the freezing fear and animal revulsion he felt looking at the thing. It drew closer to Ford, who continued his mysterious chanting. The creature's smile faded, and it merely looked at him with those huge black eyes. Ford stood his ground, but his voice was rising in pitch. Will ducked behind cover again, his eyes wide, his heart racing and breath ragged. Ford let out a long scream and Will could hear the sound of him struggling. But Yaosagma remained completely silent. Will felt his hands shaking. He'd seen horrible things, but he didn't know a man could keep enough air in his lungs to scream like that. Then there was silence. Will steeled himself and peered over the wagon again, his whole body shivering. Ford was gasping and choking, his body spasming wildly. The creature's face was buried in his gut, but its eyes looked directly at Will, pools of black tranquility above the bloody bowl of Ford's open abdomen. It lifted its head when Ford stopped moving, its eyes still locked with Will's, the blood dripping languidly from its chin. It glided low over the ground towards him, its spindly arms before it, its robes trailing behind.

Will cried out, ducking down behind the wagon. "My Jesus mercy, my Jesus mercy, my Jesus-" his word descended into noise as his voice cracked and his breathing went wild. Something hot and wet rolled down his cheeks. He grunted, then again, then once more, trying to force control of breath. He blinked the tears out of his eyes. He wasn't going like this. He took hold of the pendants at his neck as he often had when he thought death was near. He had forgotten the Buddha that lay there with them now. He rubbed them with his thumb, calm now. Still. His blood was still pounding in his ears.

Yaosagma peered down at him from the top of the old wagon. Will looked up into the endless night of its eyes, but it was looking curiously at the Buddha pendant. It reached for it with one of those long-fingered hands, then suddenly cried out. Until then, he had not heard the creature make a sound, but this noise was like all the devastation he had seen it cause rolled into one agonized shout. The creature flew backwards over the wagon. Will stood up, just in time to see the creature standing, arms folded, in the mouth of the cave, rocks and dirt falling down over the entrance before its blank stare. The side of the mountain seemed totally closed now, like a wound that had healed without leaving a scar.

*

By the time the retreating C Company arrived at the village, they had gone several days with no sign of Yaosagma. One of the village huts had been repurposed for the wounded, who lay on blankets across the dirt floor. The survivors were being groomed by field medics to be moved along with their own wounded, and they were impressed with the care they'd received so far. "Tell whoever did this, sergeant, that some of these men wouldn't have survived without their efforts," one of the medics told Will as he interrupted Song and Donahue's game of cards to redress their bandages.

"I will, sir," Will said humbly, moving to check on Johnny, who still hadn't woken up.

"Sergeant," the captain said from where he lay. He was in the worst shape of all. He was sweating and swollen. Will thought his back was broken but couldn't be sure. He waved Will over. He'd been conscious a few times, but this was the first time he'd been coherent. "What happened?"

Will bowed his head. "I don't know, sir. The thing saw this Buddha pendant that one of the villagers had given me and it just... went away."

The captain smiled. "The old man said..." the captain was struggling to keep his breath. "...he said that it feeds off hatred. That's why... the gift was important."

"That's why I scared it with Jenson's blood on my hands too," Will realized. "The thing couldn't bear kindness between enemies."

"If that's true, that's probably why it made such short work... of Ford. My order likes to think of itself as enlightened, but some of us... got too used to war." The captain breathed deeply, letting out a troubled sigh. "You did good, Freedman." There was a moment of silence between them. Two soldiers came in and the captain groaned when they lifted him onto a stretcher.

"I suppose that's the end of the Fools then," Will said as the soldiers moved his CO out.

"No," Capt. Thompson winked. "There's still work to be done. You'll have some leave coming when we get back behind our lines, but... I'll be calling you soon." The soldiers loaded the captain onto the back of a truck and went back for the rest.

Will walked out into the center of the village, passing Kemper on a crude crutch one of the villagers had made for him. "Sergeant," Kemper nodded as he passed, and Will moved on to the old woman who stood, smiling near her hut. He knelt down by her and she put an old and gnarled hand on his head. Will stood, and turned to go. As he walked, Mi-Ja emerged from her home, disheveled and staring, her beautiful eyes marred by crying. She ran to Will shouting, and began to pound on his chest with her fists. Will stood still, his hands at his sides. It struck him that in the purity of her anger, she was baring herself to him in a way that people seldom shared outside of the deepest intimacy. They were close enough to share their breath. She glared at him with her thin, wide eyes aflame, confused, lip quivering with sobbing rage, hitting him harder until she ran out of strength and sank to her knees, shaking with impotent wrath and sorrow.

"Why'd you let her do that?" Kemper asked as Will walked up beside him.

"Maybe she needed that. Maybe she can heal now," Will said. "Of course," he continued, his eyes twinkling, "I might just be a damn fool."

THE GENTLEMAN AND THE BRAT
BY ERIC ESQUIVEL

Deep below the Earth, in an underground bunker designed to safeguard the German military's most precious asset from the combined might of the allied armed forces, a young guard named "Hans" snorted yet another line of crushed-up methamphetamines off of the barrel of his Luger and tried like Hell to ignore the deep ache in his belly that came with the utter certainty that his country was going to lose the war—and he, personally, was going to be hung for crimes against humanity.

A strange, startling sound emerged from the shadows. It sounded like someone clearing their throat. But it couldn't be. The bunker was buried sixty yards under the earth, and the only living souls that were down there with him were on the other side of a heavy, locked door that he was (rudely) not given the key to.

Hans used the tip of his thumb to wipe the remaining residue off of his nostril, and quickly massaged it into his top gums, creating a welcome numbness in his mouth. He straightened his uniform, and mentally prepared himself to face the source of the sound-- ninety nine percent sure that there was nothing there, and that whatever noise he imagined hearing was actually an auditory hallucination, brought on by both war-time-stress and the "medicine" that his superior officers gave him to help him stay awake so that he could perform his (mostly ceremonial) duty.

Hans pivoted around on his left heel to face the darkness. But, instead, he found himself looking down the barrel of a Welrod pistol, held by an aggressively handsome Englishman in a three-piece suit and Zorro-style face mask.

"Terribly sorry," Warren Patrick Morrison --codename "The Gentleman"-- said as he pulled the trigger twice, and splattered the german sentry's brains against the cavern walls.

Ruth O'Brien--codename "The Brat"-- rolled her eyes.

"Why do you always do that?" she asked.

"It's rude to shoot a man in the back," The Gentleman replied. And the sound of his voice--even with the charming English accent-- made it clear that he was annoyed he had to say something so obvious out loud.

The Brat crossed her arms. The Gentleman knew her well enough that, even though she was wearing a domino mask that gave her eyes the effect of appearing pure white, she was glaring at him.

"He's a friggin' Nazi, Gent..." she sighed. And when The Gentleman winced, she wasn't sure if it was a result of her use of vulgarity, or her thick Boston accent (which suddenly became twenty percent thicker, whenever she wanted to annoy him).

"He was," The Gentleman agreed. "The absolute worst kind of human. Lowest of the low."

The Gentleman turned to The Brat. He spoke slowly and deliberately. "But I am an officer in Her Majesty's Secret Service . And, as such, I hold myself to a considerably higher standard."

The Gentleman nodded his head towards the heavy vault door.

"Now, let's bring our attention to the matter at hand. Have you got anything in that utility belt of yours that'll help us make it past this little roadblock? Perhaps some plastique explosive?"

The Gentleman and The Brat were, for lack of a better term, wartime superheroes. Their codenames, equipment, and costumes were created by their respective nations' dedicated Psy Ops divisions ("The Gentleman" hailed from The United Kingdom, and "The Brat" from The United States), but their missions were assigned and overseen by an international body dubbed, simply "The Alliance".

There used to be three of them. But the war had been long, and hard, and "The Velveteen Shadow"~ a Frenchman whose high-tech costume gave him the appearance of a living blob of ink, and negated friction in such a way that it allowed him to shrug off bullets as if they were mere suggestions~ had met his maker on the coast of Normandy, when the concussive blast of a German missile sent him soaring into the middle of the ocean, and he drowned to death.

For over a year now, it had just been the two of them. But, with any luck, they'd be out of each other's hair shortly...

"The door's got a lock on it," The Brat replied.

The Gentleman saw that it did. "Yes," he replied. "Indeed it does. But neither you nor I have the key. So I fail to see how that bit of trivia is particularly relevant."

"Door's got a lock," The Brat repeated herself. And she snapped a piece of bubblegum with her tongue to show how displeased she was to have to do so.

The Gentleman's left eye twitched.

She continued. "If the door's got a lock, then I can pick it. No explosives necessary. Which is lucky, because~and I don't know if you've noticed this~ it's pretty cozy down here. A C3 blast is likely to blow out our eardrums, blast off

our kneecaps, and bring ten tons of bedrock tumbling down on our friggin'
heads."

"I suppose I'll wait then," The Gentleman quipped as he leaned against
the wall.

The Brat wasn't given her title solely because of her abrasive demeanor.
Initially, it was because her superior officers were so impressed by her
intelligence and guile, especially relative to her young age. Sure, she was a bit
precocious for a junior officer~ but Ruth "The Brat" O'Brien had the walk to
back up her considerable talk. "Genius" wasn't quite the word for what she
is...but only because the word was too small. Ruth could glance at a piece of
sophisticated machinery and tell you exactly how it worked, and where every
nut and bolt went. She could take a sip of poison, break down its chemical
composition by taste, and jot down the formula for its antidote before the junk
hit her heart. Her hand-to-hand skills were nothing to write home about~ but
the allied forces compensated for that by loading her up with a thousand
overlapping utility belts. Each one contained about a dozen pouches, and within
them were every manner of gadget conceivable by the mind of man. The
Gentleman once joked that if The Fuhrer decided to unleash a swarm of blood-
thirty, antisemitic koala bears on them, he could rest assured~safe in the
knowledge that, somewhere within one of her pockets was an aerosol can of anti-
marsupial spray.

The Gentleman smirked. In the few seconds he took to think back on their past adventures together, The Brat had already picked the lock, and put away her tools.

"What are you smiling about, old man?" The Brat asked him. She popped her bubblegum with her tongue yet again. But, this time, The Gentleman didn't flinch. His reminiscing had put him in too good a mood.

"You," The Gentleman answered. "You are a walking miracle. In the course of this war, I have beheld countless horrors. Scenes that have caused my sanity to waiver at times. But I have also had the pleasure of watching you work. And your skills give me hope..."

"Hope for what?" The Brat asked. She could feel her cheeks getting red.

"Hope that God is on our side," The Gentlemen answered. Then he reached out and held the heavy iron door open for her.

"Ever the gentleman..." The Brat said, as she walked through.

"I try," The Gentleman replied.

On the other side of the door was a long hallway. At the end of that hallway was yet another door. If The Alliance's intel was correct, who The Gentleman and The Brat was searching for sat in the chamber that it led to. Waiting for death. Waiting for them.

In front of the door were two guards. They were both sprawled out on the floor. One of them held a flask. He was drunk. The other held smoking Howitzer pistol. He was dead.

The drunk gestured towards the dead guard.

"He pulled the trigger as soon as he heard you coming," The Drunk said.

"Smart idea," The Brat sneered. "Why didn't you?"

The Drunk reached out and grabbed a hold of the cavern wall to help steady himself as he rose to his feet.

"Too drunk to shoot straight," The Drunk answered. "I'd probably just blow off my ear and make everything worse."

The Brat took a micro-second to study The Drunk. She noticed pair of pips on his collar, denoting his rank ("Standartenführer"—the most senior field-grade position available in The Schutzstaffel). She noticed the small, shallow scars that hid beneath the coarse hair on his forearms, and the raised and rather nasty one that adorned his left cheek. She regarded the Glockenschläger that clattered at The Drunk's side as he stood. In the age of flamethrowers and mustard gas, the sword was a purely ceremonial affectation, a declaration of rank more than anything else. Most officers never even took their swords out of their scabbard. But there were telltale marks on The Drunk's that could only have been created by repeated drawing and replacing of the blade.

The Brat squinted at The Drunk. "You went to school in Freiberg, didn't you?"

The Drunk's eyes bulged. "How did you know that?" he asked.

The Gentleman folded his arms and looked at The Brat. He was curious as well.

"You Freiberg boys take fencing seriously there, don't you? It's baked into the culture. You have sword fighting clubs, the way American colleges have fraternities."

The Brat turned to The Gentleman.

"You see that whopper of a cut on his left cheek?" she asked him.

The Gentleman nodded.

"The Freiberg fellas, when they get cut, scurry home after the match and pack it with horse hair before they suture the wound. It ensures a gnarly scar."

"Why on Earth would they do that?" The Gentleman asked. And he made no effort to conceal his disgust as he did so.

"They think it makes them look tough," The Brat answered.

"Do they, now?" The Gentleman said. He looked into The Drunk's eyes as he issued a challenge: "Well... are you?"

"Prete!" The Drunk growled as he drew his saber from its sheathe.

"Allez!" The Gentleman shouted back, as he raised his fists

The Drunk charged at The Gentleman and lunged at him, attempting to bury the tip of his blade into the English hero's chest.

The Gentleman parried his German opponent's thrust with his naked forearm, creating a long, yet mercifully shallow wound across his skin.

"For Christ's sake, Gent..." The Brat yelled at him. "Just shoot the bastard!"

"Impossible," The Gentleman replied as he narrowly dodged a slash to the midsection. "He's unarmed."

"He's got a friggin' sword!" The Brat protested. "And he's about to skewer you with it, you limey goon!"

"Is he?" The Gentleman asked, as he kicked his fascist opponent square in the elbow-- causing The Drunk to drop his rapier.

The Gentleman caught the sword before it hit the ground. In the span of one exhale, The Gentleman flicked his wrist six times, carving a Star Of David dead-center into the chest of his Nazi officer uniform.

The Gentleman paused for a moment. Just to let The Drunk realize the shape of the scar he was going to die with. And then he drove the sword through the Nazi's eye with such tremendous force, it pinned the German officer to the cavern wall, like a homicidally racist butterfly in some nerdy child's insect collection.

"Whoa," The Brat whispered. With all of The Gentleman's perfect grammar, and fondness for social etiquette, she sometimes forgot her partner's capacity for violence. But he always reminded her eventually.

"Let's see you pack a fistful of horse hair into that..." The Gentleman quipped, as he jiggled the rapier to ensure that it properly scrambled his opponent's brains.

The Gentleman pulled a roll of self-adhesive gauze from inside his breast pocket, and quickly wrapped it around the bleeding wound on his left forearm. He brushed the dust from his shoulders, and cleared his throat. Then he gestured towards the final door.

"Shall we?" he asked.

The Brat, mocking him, curtsied.

She inspected the lock. It wasn't fastened. Whoever was behind that door clearly didn't expect anyone to make it this far.

The Brat turned the doorknob, and opened the door. But The Gentleman was the first to step through. Inside, he found a small and frightened little man. He had the absolute worst haircut The Gentleman had ever seen, and an embarrassing little square mustache to match.

"Oh, Thank Odin~" Adolf Hitler said. "It's The Gentleman, and his little fraulein sidekick. I was worried that The Allies had sent real soldiers, instead of their ridiculous 'super heroes'."

Hitler bounced out of his chair. Remarkably cheerful for a man who had caused the death of millions, cost his country the war, and had spent the last few hours sitting in the same room as his deceased (by suicide) love, waiting for his own death to arrive. He raised his arms in surrender.

"As you can see, I am unarmed. And I fully acknowledge my defeat. I surrender, and I await the judgement of your courts."

Hitler offered his wrists to The Brat, anticipating her production of a pair of handcuffs.

"...During which time, I will use the publicity afforded to me to address the world community and expose your nations' lies and hypocrisy to an audience larger than any I have ever known."

Hitler shooks his wrists at The Brat. "Do it," he said. "Bring me in. My war is far from over. It was never going to be decided on a battlefield, anyway. My war is for the very hearts and minds on the human race. Soon, you will all cede to my superiority. Soon, you will all~"

Before Hitler could finish his little speech, The Gentleman removed a loose brick from the bunker's wall and bludgeoned him to death with it. He hit him so many times, the little would-be-world-conqueror's head turned into a Rorschach test of gore and bone fragments.

There was a long pause after The Gentleman had stopped swinging. Then, to break the silence, The Brat said "What happened to the whole 'Man Of Manners' act?" she asked. "Doesn't rendering a prisoner of war into a fine pink mist with a hunk of concrete violate your personal code of honor?"

"Come now," The Gentleman replied. "This is Adolf Hitler you're talking about. Certainly an exceptions can be made."

He paused for a moment though, considering what The Brat had said.

"Althought, if anyone asks..."

"He killed himself," The Brat answered. "I saw it my own eyes. Dead before we even got here."

"Good girl," The Gentleman smiled.

"Pleasure serving with you, Morrison," The Brat said.

"The pleasure was all mine, miss O'Brien," The Gentleman replied.

CRACKS IN THE SIDEWALK
BY NOLAN KNIGHT

If it wasn't for Roy Combo dragging my sister to New York City, I never would've left Los Angeles. The day she decided to leave with him, I couldn't have cared less. Have my own battles. A wife that left with a kid who I don't really know. Chronic unemployment. But, back to my sister—Liz. She is an adult, so I looked the other way when she took up with Roy, one of my childhood buds in Long Beach. We played Little League together, had sleepovers, shared Playboys, you know? Growing up on the outskirts of Cambodia Town had its perils, but so does this place, the East Village. Way I see it, Roy traded L.A. for this mess because he couldn't hack it out west, the tattoo scene being what it was. The guy can draw, I'll give him that. Tattoo? Who knows? I'll never understand why he thought it'd be easier for him to make a name out here, but that's a tale for Roy to tell—probably one that involves drugs, or him running from some misdeed, if I were to take a guess. But he won't get the chance to tell anyone if I see him. Might never talk again. With Roy it's *on site*.

My mother hasn't heard from Liz in eight months, a complete wreck, taking care of my ailing father, watching her own mother wither before her eyes. Hell, our grandfather died three months ago, and my sister doesn't even know Pop Pop is gone. Needless to say, Liz missing is the last thing mom needs, and so I'm here, stuck to a barstool on St. Marks Place. The Holiday Cocktail Lounge ain't so bad though, a small room draped in X-mas bulbs with a c-shaped bar. Got a dog in here that runs the joint. Oscar, a dachshund. Well, his owner runs the joint— least she thinks she does, calves like whole pastrami from standing behind this rainbow bar for a decade; when folks come inside, they all bend the knee to scratch Oscar before acknowledging her. I tap an empty Narragansett on the wood, sparking the barkeep to crack another, sliding it beside my tumbler of rye. I hadn't taken a sip for two months before Liz went missing. Two whole months—an eternity for a guy like me. Even attended one a them meetings during my stint, you know? God fearing drunks. No good stories though, like they say. Just sadness and stale coffee. I didn't let them listen to any of mine either, sad ballads, slow and steady—drip, drip, drip. Anyway, that window is far behind me now.

The whiskey burns just right, the beer a cool breeze. I'd heard Combo comes here on occasion—sometimes they'd spot him food on the arm. It's been three weeks and I ain't seen one lousy new face except mine whenever I piss and it's staring back at me in the mirror right this second. *Fucking loser.* I splash water on my cheeks, remembering why I'm stuck here again. It isn't like Liz to lose contact. Even blinded by love, if that was the case. Roy Combo, master of needles, good ones and bad. Surely, he has something to say about Liz's whereabouts, and I'm going to beat it out of him.

The room explodes into debate the moment I re-enter. The topic at hand involves the use of mustard on dirty water dogs. Locals volley between best links to best buns to best mustards, regular or spicy—various shades of golden hues. Someone at the far corner brings up a Seattle dog with its cream cheese and lets me off the hook from having to discuss L.A.'s bacon-wrapped links sold in gutters by bacon-wrapped immigrants: the best (according to me). Rock music blasts about, transporting me to a better place; the band playing had their first gig a stone's throw from here, thanks to Andy Warhol. The New York Dolls romped here too. Monk, Bird and Mingus slayed here. GG Allin died here. I know a few things in this world, random trinkets from when I thought I was on track to become some great musician...

Such a loser.

I slurp the rest of my round, I pet Oscar, pay the tab and bail.

*

Outside it's pouring rain, not quite the spring season I'd anticipated. Not like I own a raincoat, but I would've packed more than denim. Back home I'd be in shorts while blooming jacarandas wept their violet puddles at the sight of my sandals. Here, I am ignored by rats in heaps of trash outside sanguine four-story walk-ups, their windows lit up like televisions, all broadcasting worlds more splendid than any I'll ever know. Maybe not, but you get the picture. I huddle under an awning, bracing my knees for the flights up to my fleabag apartment (which mom pays for), feeling every ache of forty-six.

My next-door neighbor hears the keys rattling when I arrive and opens her door. Marnie, a bit older than me, always in disarray, doesn't get out much since the pandemic and all. Who can blame her? Folks like us have been social distancing our whole damn lives. Why ruin a good thing, right? I invite her inside for a beer.

*

Marnie sips her lager the way my mother has her tea. My unit is a studio, big enough for me—two people is a stretch. She makes herself comfortable on a foldout chair.

"Anything today, Bix?"

I take a drag off my suds and shake my head no.

"Well, you're closer to finding your sis today than all the others."

"Is that right?"

"It ain't right, but it's somethin'."

"Yeah, I guess."

"This Combo guy, you really think he's still hangin' around here?"

"That's what I'm hearing."

"From who?"

"This tattoo parlor out in Brooklyn. Apparently, he had an apprenticeship lined up there before they left L.A. Was the first place I went when I got here. Old school shop with flash on the walls a hundred years old: screaming eagles, hula girls, Kewpie dolls—a pretty nice spot. One of the artists knew of Combo, but said nothing good. Hated his guts for reasons I can imagine. Anyway, dude texts me whenever he hears anything. Got the feeling Roy owes him some money, or stole some goods from him. I'm not the only fucker on the hunt."

"A real piece a work, this guy. Roy Combo his real name? Seems made up."

"That's 'cause it is. His birth name is Leroy Jenkins."

"Tell me what he looks like again."

I hold up a finger, fish through my clothes sack for a photo and hand it over.

Marnie slurps her lager, eyeing the pic with intensity. "Black guy?"

"Part."

"What else?"

"Honey, out west, no one really knows. I'm Irish, German, English and Mexican. We're a scrambled bunch. A *human* race."

"This your sister with him?"

I nod, not wanting to see Liz with Roy's arm around her.

"She don't look much like you, Bix."

"Like I said, scrambled eggs. —Hey, you *positive* you don't have any pals in town that might know a dude like Combo?"

Marnie adjusts her sweatshirt, stains running down Lisa Simpson at its front; the question has her perturbed. She huffs and says, "There's this guy that peddles watches in Washington Square Park. Usually sets up at the south side of the fountain. Me and him used to go together, so don't bring my name up, okay? If this Combo is the scumbag you say he is, sure thing Slippery Tom's heard of him."

"Slippery Tom?"

"That's just what *I* call the bastard."

"Why have you never said anything about him before, Marn?"

"Don't get me started."

"I see."

We clank cans and take in April showers out the window.

*

Sunshine breaks through the blinds, burning my eyelids—ears thumping from the sound of clanging church bells, then wails out an East Village dove. I'm sweating because the radiator is on overdrive, scorching the entire building to hell; a ceiling fan brings small relief. I passed out before taking off my clothes again. Marnie must've let herself out. Cracking a window, I stop to watch white petals fall from a Callery Pear, wind surging them up 9th Street like migrating butterflies. The only reason I know the name of the tree is because I overheard this Ukrainian couple talking about them over borscht in a joint across the street. I don't care for borscht, but can eat pierogis all day: One thing I've learned since being stuck out here.

I take my time walking down 2nd Avenue, black coffee in my hands to warm the bones. I pan streets for any sign of Roy, but after weeks, I fear I'm cutting corners. Today I walk the Bowery again, reading now familiar plaques of bygone debauchery—prostitution, saloons, Suicide Hall—all in attempt to mask my analyzing of every sleeping vagrant, every waking body that slithers up the street. Washington Square Park isn't far, so I cut down 4th through NYU. Students catapult across campus in expensive shoes, waiting in line at designer food trucks, tapping mommy's credit card with their phones: a new breed, coming-of-age story. Steam pours out a manhole, it's milky cloud the frankincense to my morning Mass. I drink it in with my eyes closed, imagining far off galaxies, an afterlife of painless possibilities.

One thing I noticed out here is that all the sidewalks are in decent shape. Back home, a person has to look out for cracks in the sidewalk. I tripped over a big one when I was a kid, running after Liz when she'd stolen my He-Man. Had to get eight stitches under my chin. Ever since, I always watch out for them. In my teens, high out my gourd, I'd pretend I could slip down them, busted concrete time warps into parallel dimensions—forbidden zones that I'd never known. A place that was mine and all mine—safe from the perils of bullies and teachers and family distortion. A boy can dream, right? And boys always dream best on drugs. Hell, ask Roy Combo.

Entering Washington Square, I am met by a legion of large tulips—orange and yellow—the health of which look suspect, plastic, Wonka-esque; I want to pluck one and chomp its milky petal. Sunshine breaks through the clouds, but only for a spell. A saxophone trio provide a soundtrack to nannies pushing strollers and skateboarders taking their licks. There are several slippery folks around the fountain, but which one is Tom? I shield myself from fountain spray and walk the gauntlet, fold-out tables featuring weed paraphernalia, faux designer purses and foreign candies. To get my bearings, I gaze at the arch, knowing it's at the north end of the park; I spin to see the back of a shrimpy man in a porkpie, seated at the other end of the fountain before a table of time pieces. *Slippery Tom.*

I make like I'm in a hurry, but while walking by, one of his watches catches my eye. I pull up and admire the works, all fake, not even trying to be authentic.

"Like anything you see, guy?"

"I dunno yet." I pick up a Folex, admiring rose gold, when my hand begins to shake.

The guy notices: "Hey, I got all kinds a watches, guy. Special ones for every occasion." He pulls two vintage pocket watches from under the table, surveys the park, then clicks them open.

There are no clocks within them, just tiny baggies holding pills, crystals or powder. I make like I'd been here before, his bold move not shaking me. "How do you know I ain't a cop, Tom?"

Tom begins to tremble, slamming the watches deep inside his coat. "What the fuck, pal? I know you?"

"No, but I know you."

"How so?"

"One of your associates. Roy Combo."

"Combo?"

"Big dude from Los Angeles. You know him."

"Tattoo guy?"

"Thinks he is."

"Yeah, I know *of* him. So what?"

"I'm lookin' for him is all."

"Yeah, well take a number. Fucker owes me cash. Landed him a quick gig with this chick I know from the record store. He tattooed crossbones on her neck, never gave me my cut."

"Which record store?"

Tom points. "Generation—few blocks that-a-way."

"When's the last time you saw Roy?"

"Right before. Say, a week and a half ago. You gonna buy somethin', or what?"

"I'm thinking about it, Tommy. Roy cop from you?"

"You know he does. Used to at least. I hooked him up with that gig figuring a small piece of the action, plus the rest of the cash he made would eventually land in my pocket, right?"

"But he bailed."

"Apparently." Tom scoffs, "Or he got sober."

"Listen, I got no use for a tin watch, but when I find Roy, I might be able to get your money back."

"What are you proposing?"

"Give me the name of this girl at the record store, and I'll see what I can do."

"Raven. Usually on the cash register. Can't miss her."

"Atta boy, Tom. I'll see you 'round."

"Hey, I didn't get your name."

"That's right." I turn to leave, then spin back. "Is it true this whole park used to be a cemetery?"

"The fuck should I know?"

I nod, walk around an ice cream stand and out the park, into the heart of Greenwich Village.

*

Generation Records looks like my kind of place, back when I was a touring drummer—punk posters plastered everywhere, sweaty rock icons drooling above miles of vinyl. Smells like the back of an old Dodge Econoline. I take in the tune blaring while perusing merchandise: It's Roky Erickson's "Don't Shake Me, Lucifer"—but not the original recording, no, this was from his comeback tour in 2007, a bootleg from a Swedish gig, I believe.... My brain clicks back. At the register, a twentysomething girl is dressed like Johnny Thunders, snapping a gumball; there's no tat on her neck. I walk over.

"Excuse me. Could you check on an LP for me?"

She fights to put down her cell phone: "What is it?"

"*Double Nickels on the Dime* by the Minutemen."

"Did you check our clearance bins downstairs?"

"This would be up there." I point to a wall of rare hanging records, imports mostly. "Goes for around two to three hundred."

"Oh, then no. We don't have it."

"I called the other day, and Raven said you did…"

"Yeah, well you'd, like, have to ask her and today's her day off. So…"

"You know when she'll be back in?"

"New schedule ain't out yet, but she works nights at Prince Street Pizza."

"Thanks."

The cashier returns to her phone, and I hit the streets.

*

Curbside, I check the time: barely past noon, and the sky is like billowing ash. My hand trembles, reminding me of Happy Hour. I find a bodega, buy a tall boy, snickers and short dog of Fireball. The owner insists they'll have a full liquor license soon, but for now, this'll have to do. He thinks someday I'll actually come back in here as he slides my beer into a paper bag.

Outside there is a drizzle, but I don't mind. I walk back toward home down Bleeker, just so I can cruise past The Bitter End and dream about smokey nights filled with wild tunes from Dylan to Mitchell and Diddley to Mayfield. I trudge onward, sipping my road soda, cutting north at Bowery, not even looking at the spot that once held CBGB, now a retail slut with no sense of history. *Place should be a fucking museum.* By the time I finally hit St. Marks, the juice has me buzzing as I step down into the Holiday, greeted by Oscar's wagging tail.

*

Patrons about the rainbow bar are clamoring where to get the best egg cream since Gem Spa has closed, victim of the pandemic. I don't have a pony in this race (a malt man, myself) so I sidle the far corner. The barkeep gets me suited, Dee Dee counts to four out a speaker and I'm off: a rat in the wall, marinating in a rollicking juke, hard booze and inebriated exchanges. The whiskey burns just right, beer a cool breeze...

I'll bet you fifty bucks, man—there's no way Bill Murray ever played Hunter Thompson...

Listen, honey—here's what's wrong with America these days, and I don't even have to bring up that Insurrection bullshit...

I don't give a fuck if they're free, mark my words, you will never see me wearing Birkenstocks. That's a fact, Jack...

The Finger Lakes—up north. Good fishing from what I'm told, but we're just going to pound beer and drop acid...

Yeah, fourteen since the first of the year. In this neighborhood alone. Narcan saved most of 'em though. Bad strains into mean veins, my friend. Welcome to hell...

So, he did play Hunter Thompson? No shit! Where the Buffalo Roam? Never fucking heard of it. Gimme a sec... No, no, a bet's a bet...

First off, don't call me honey. I ain't your sidepiece. Secondly, you're talking about a buncha greedy assholes now. What about people like John Lewis, huh? What about real patriots and shit...?

Well, see, slides are a different beast all together—they're not leather for fucking starters, and, shit, I like to wear 'em around the apartment...

"Shrooms too, maybe. Heck, I dunno. No coke though. Not like last time. Jesus. It's gonna be a helluva Memorial Day...

I heard there are good strains out here too though. Some shit called Hulk, another called Rambo. Know where a kid can cop 'round here...?

*

The day drags into night, cup after cup—drip, drip, drip. When I start to see double of Oscar, I know it's time to leave. I make it up two of the three flights to my room and have to take a seat. I can hear a tenant watching the news in their unit, something about Roe vs. Wade. Soon as my heart slows, I trudge back up. For some reason the key will not punch into my deadbolt; I place my forehead against the door, praying for an asteroid to smack Manhattan at this very second. Marnie's door opens; she takes the keys from me, opens the door and walks in toward the fridge.

I act like a gentleman, letting her drink my last beer. Lord knows, I don't need it. What I need is food, but my fridge only holds condiments.

"You got anythin' to eat in your apartment, Marn?"

She wipes her mouth with a sleeve. "Nope."

"Pizza sound good?"

"Always."

"When was the last time you went out for a hot slice?"

"Eighteen months."

"Well, tonight's the night. Go put on some shoes. I know a place."

Marnie begins to protest, then thinks better of warm gooey cheese. "Alright, fuck it."

*

Marnie takes my arm as we walk down 2nd Avenue, one-part chivalry, one-part her not letting me crash into anything. It begins to drizzle, but we don't mind. I'm in that perfect groove of being stewed: still happy and hungry with good grub in my future. I step into the street to cut across Houston, when Marnie pulls me back, saved from being smashed by a team of food delivery bikes. We laugh it off.

"You never told me the meaning of your name, Bix?"

"There is no meaning, that's why."

"You're telling me a woman waited nine months to bear a son and just named him Bix on the fly?"

"She liked to listen to this piano player all the time, Bix Beiderbecke—he was a cornetist and composer as well, but she never bought those records. Apparently, mom took a liking to the fella and named her only son after him. Didn't like Bix enough to find out that his real name was Bismark though, but, hey, it's all good."

"You would've been a Bismark."

"Sure as shit."

We share a laugh.

"You wanna know something' else fucked up about the guy, Marn?"

"Shoot."

"Beiderbecke was one of the greatest to play of his generation—he'd send every record he cut back home for his folks to hear over the years. He died young, the road taking its toll. Had what they called a mental break beforehand, was sent back home. It might've been a break, but really they said it was severe alcoholism, but anyway—when he got back home after years on the circuit, he opens a closet and finds all them records, sealed, just sitting there. You ask me, *that's* what really broke him. Sure, the alcohol had its due, but the guy's heart gave out first. Least, that's what I read somewhere. But who really knows anything about anybody?"

Marnie asks, "Hey, weren't you a musician?"

"Once upon a time."

"So, the name fits."

"Yeah, but I never had the balls to send any records back home."

Prince Street Pizza beams up ahead. The drizzle turns into a pour, so we rush inside.

*

A brick oven welcomes us with warmth as celebrity eyeballs leer from every wall. I'm in trance on a display holding greasy pepperoni pies. A female cashier with her head shaved and dyed like a snow cone lets us know we are standing in the pick-up line, not for orders. That's when I notice scabbed crossbones on her neck, jagged linework accentuated by a pink hue, possibly an infection. Marnie gives our order of four cheese and two Heineken, as I gaze on that tattoo as if it were a piece of Roy Combo—an extension directly to his whereabouts. I pay with my mom's credit card, point to Raven's neck and say, "Roy Combo?"

The girl could bite my head off.

"You a friend of Roy? Hope not. My boyfriend's got a crowbar with Combo's name on it."

"Funny, I got myself a hammer."

"He scratch you too?"

"He has information I need. Know where I can find him?"

"Yeah, but he ain't been home in a few days. Believe me, I know."

Marnie scoops the pie and grabs a table outside under an awning.

I pick up the beers. "If I find him, I'll be sure to leave part of him for your boyfriend."

Raven pulls a pen from behind an ear and scribbles an address on my receipt. I ask, "Where the fuck is Maspeth?"

Two of the pizza tossers shout, "Queens!"

*

Sunshine breaks through the blinds, burning my eyelids—ears thumping from the sound of clanging church bells, then violent shouts out an East Village vagrant. I'm sweaty again, the radiator a seething volcano; the ceiling fan whirls hypnotic as I rub crust from the eyes. Passed out partially clothed this time— boxers, shirt and one sock. I crack the window; white petals falling from the Callery Pear, flying up 9th Street like big beautiful—

Wait a second...

This isn't my apartment!

I spin to see Marnie making slow pour coffee in her PJs. She catches the shocked look on my face and cracks up.

"Don't worry, we didn't fuck," she says. "You are a goddamn animal though. Good lord."

"What do you mean?"

"We painted the town blood red, Bix."

Cobwebs form my brain. "We had pizza..."

"And a few beers. Then a few more. Told you about my favorite bar in Alphabet City—hadn't been there since before Covid—you seriously don't remember any of this?"

I shake my head no.

"Well, you insisted that we go to Sophie's, so we did. Had a few rounds, few shots. Played pool. You made a pass at me. I told you I'm done with men, only date women—*again*."

"Great."

"It's fine. You were loaded, just being wild. I had a goddamn blast. *Seriously*. Forgot how good it feels to be around good company. We hit Niagara and Lucy's on the way back."

"Lucy's?"

"Right next to Tompkins Square Park. We had to run from the cops because you chucked a bottle at their cruiser.... Anyway, you had a good time, believe me. I had a *great* time since you bought every round." She laughs. "I'm kidding. I paid for a couple."

I rub my temples, swish around rot in my gums. "I'ma go brush my teeth."

"Can't get into your unit, that's why I let you crash here. Got two bedrooms."

"Two bedrooms?" I crane to see her room. "What you do for a living again?"

"Nothing. My folks own the building."

"Why can't I get in my unit?"

"You broke the key in the lock last night. Total accident. A locksmith is coming in a few hours."

I use the bathroom, pissing for what feels like five minutes. I try to power through the hangover, but pain to the brain stops me cold.

Marnie pours a cup of coffee, sets it on the counter with a bottle of Advil. "Slam some of these and crash back out. I'll let you know when the locksmith's here. You got a big day planned, or don't you remember that too?"

I reach for my pants and retrieve the Prince Street receipt from a pocket. "Maspeth's in Queens. I remember."

"Rest up then. You got a score to settle."

I swallow four pills dry and lay back down, my brain on overdrive, conjuring triumphant scenarios where I clobber Roy Combo, he tells me through missing teeth where Liz is and I finally get back to warm L.A. sunshine.

*

I'm back in my apartment by noon, the locksmith a wizard for a hefty fee. Marnie's parents are going to take care of it, since the deadbolt was faulty. The aspirin and coffee did wonders for my head but not my anxiety, every nerve end buzzing with constant jolts. The showerhead beats my body with a million tiny punches, forcing me back into the living. The water is lukewarm. Having it too hot might zap all the strength I have left for Combo. Rage without muscle is a waking nightmare. Believe me. But I've thought ahead for this, reaching an arm out to the sink for a short dog of vodka. Water crushes my skull as I swill rotgut, liquor beading down my chin like fallen tears. I growl and snarl. I drink. I growl. I drink some more.

*

I can't tolerate learning which subway to take into Maspeth, so I schedule an Uber to pick me up out front of the Ukrainian restaurant across the street. The hooch has me feeling human again, whatever that means. The driver talks on speaker phone in a foreign tongue the whole drive. I take in the view from the Williamsburg Bridge, sunrays breaking through grim clouds, a beauty which I believed as a child was God herself. These days, I know better.

Tall apartment structures evaporate into shotgun houses, two stories each, like dominoes around mom-and-pop stores with tough names. Grey clouds permeate, casting this part of Queens in shadow. The car pulls up to a two-story home, like all the rest, only with brick accents. I stare at the address on my receipt and back at the residence before getting out the sedan. American flags flap all around me; the scent of a stoked chimney fills the block. I climb the stairs to the front door, only to see two sets of doorbells with no instruction or tenant names. I hit the first one and retreat down two steps. After thirty seconds, the door unlatches, revealing an elderly woman with cotton ball hair and a chrome cane.

"Yeah, whuddah you want, mista?"

"Hi, my name is Bix Coughlin. I was told my sister lives here."

"I look like ya sista? What's the angle, little man? You tryin' to sell an old lady insurance? An extended car warranty? snake oil? Beat it, ya brat!"

"No angle, ma'am." I pull out the picture of Liz and Roy. "I didn't get your name?"

"Phebe."

"Nice to meet you, Phebe. If you could just take a look at this picture. I wouldn't come all the way out here from the East Village if I didn't have good reason to believe she might be here."

"East Village is a dump. All of Manhattan is chaos these days—just like the old days! I hope you ain't lookin' no one in the eye ova there. You mind ya damn business, ya hear?"

"Promise."

"I'm serious. You're too soft for these parts! I can tell." She tries not to see the picture when she goes to close the door, but can't help herself. The door stops. "Ah, Christ. Yeah, I know them *deadbeats*. They owe me two months back rent. You here to pay that, busta?"

"I'm here to bring her home."

"And where's that?"

"Los Angeles."

"Los Angeles!" The woman's eyes cross before she laughs raspy notes. "I called it. Sweet baby Jesus, now it all makes sense. I knew they was trash people, but I rented the basement to 'em anyways. Unbelievable. *Los Angeles*! I deserve every bit a my grief ova them two louses."

"Are they here now?"

"Heard 'em come in early this mornin'." She finishes her chuckle before crushing the second buzzer and retreating back to her upstairs unit.

I wait for what seems like an hour, before hearing steps being climbed inside.

And there she is.

Liz gazes down on me through sleepy eyes, twenty pounds lighter than last I saw her; looks like she hasn't showered in days, her red hair thrown in a bun. My presence brings a jolt. Before she can slam the door on me, I wedge into its frame.

"Get the fuck outta here, Bix! Leave me alone!"

"I just want to talk—that's all. Listen, mom sent me."

"Yeah fuckin' right she did. Now, get the fuck off my porch."

"Just hear me out, and I'll go, alright? Look, I came all the way out here months ago. I promised her I'd find you..."

Pressure behind the door begins to recede. I exhale a deep breath.

She smells my breath and quips, "Still drunk, I see."

"You're wrong, girlie. I'm just a little hagged out."

"I bet."

"Just give me something to tell, mom. You're an adult, I get it—but, the woman thinks you're fucking dead, Liz."

"I bet she thinks Roy murdered me too, huh?"

"I dunno about that..."

"Fuck yes you do! That night before I took off—my fucking birthday party. Look at you. Don't even remember."

"Sure, I do."

"Yeah? You remember tellin' everyone at the party every fuck up I ever had? Tellin' my friends about that shoplifting case on my record. About me and Roy's miscarriage to mom? Everything I ever told you in confidence, you fucking asshole! You were my older brother. And all 'cause I said you should slow down on the booze that night."

"I don't really remem—"

"I don't care what you remember. And me an' Roy are married now, okay? So, whatever you think about my husband, you keep it to your damn self—"

"How the hell you think I found you, huh? That hubby a yours is leaving a trail around Lower Manhattan longer than the ones down your arms."

"We're getting clean out here, not like I need your approval, you fuck! We've been kicking for a long while, be straight in a day or two."

"I bet."

"Look at you, all self-righteous. How's Amy and the kid doing these days? On EBT last I checked, barely scraping by with guilt checks from mom. You fucking pig. Look at you, coming out here to give *me* some shit? After the party, next day we packed our bags and bolted—don't plan on ever going back either—so, you tell mom that, since she loves you so damn much. The woman never gave a fuck about me, and she knows it. And you, you fucking pig...you're dead to me. You and the whole Coughlin lot. Now, leave me the fuck alone and don't ever come back.

I scramble to keep her talking. "Pop Pop is dead."

The words stop her from closing the door, a trembling hand covers her mouth. She's about to break, but doesn't. Slowly, she composes herself and says, "Well, there's another dead Coughlin I ain't gotta worry about no more."

A shadow emerges from behind her: tall, stout and menacing.

On site.

I see red and lunge at Roy Combo, clawing his soiled tank top, accidentally knocking Liz to the floor.

My God, he's huge.

Roy holds me at bay with one beefy arm, track marks up it like ants on a log. For a junkie he's still crazy strong. I flurry to no avail as he walks me down the steps. That's when I remember why he chose the name Combo: Came in second place at the Golden Gloves when we were thirteen. I told you that, right? Anyway, he doesn't say a single word, marching me down. Soon as I'm winded, he throws a right cross that crushes my jaw, then an uppercut that turns Queens into a kaleidoscope of darkness, crumbling me to the sidewalk; there's a long crack and my body melts through it, deposited into an astral plain of nightmare dimensions...

*

I can hear a steady beat through the darkness. My arms convulse to it, leg pounding a kick drum. Through smokey haze I hear bass and a sax. I'm behind my old drum kit with two legends peering back at me. Bird. Mingus. The crowd roars me into a solo. Bap-ba-da. Bap-ba-da. I close my eyes to concentrate on the beat, but when I open them back up, the song has changed. Warhol and Lou look upon me as if I'm deranged. I squint as the scene morphs again. Johnny Thunders blasts beyond my beat, hair like a dead palm tree. The song becomes unfamiliar, speeding up, a jumbled mess—faster and faster. My drumsticks turn into liquor bottles; with each crash of the high hat, glass shards splash like streaking comets. I reach for another stick, but it's another bottle. This time it crashes over my head. I grab another, my skull the only skin being played. I close my eyes, pain jolting its own beat through my body. Crash! Bap-ba-da. Crash! Eyes open, D. Boon and Roky look at me in horror. More bottles, now blood, warm and unforgiving down my face. G.G. appears, growling in the nude, wiping my raining lifeforce across his undead corpse. The bottles are endless, my skull now soft, wet and pulverized. Rock 'n' Roll takes its toll, someone shouts as the crowd cheers me on for an encore. I live to bleed, fully embraced by the audience: my greatest professional performance—

*

My eyes open to the sight of the elderly woman...Phebe. I'm on my back, cold concrete at my spine; Phebe's knelt beside me, looking down. Her hair blends with the clouds. A row of onlookers, mostly neighborhood kids, flank all around. I cough blood, and they run away.

Phebe: "See! I told ya he ain't dead."

My brain throbs. Slowly, I sit up with Phebe's help.

"There someone I can call for ya, hun? And don't say the cops, 'cause they won't come here for a good beatdown."

I gaze around for my sister, but she and Combo are gone. I try to talk, but can't, my jaw busted, slackened ajar. I pull my cell and dial Marnie's number, handing it to Phebe before laying back down on cement, praying for that crack in the sidewalk to split open again and suck me down south. But it doesn't; just absorbs my blood seeping out—drip, drip, drip.

*

Four months later...

The whiskey no longer burns just right. I finally gave up hard liquor. One thing I learned on this sick, tragic quest.... *Tragic?* Stupid's more like it. One thing I learned was that when life intervenes, collapsing all around you, a person has no choice but to take it as a sign from the universe and, modestly speaking, when one's jaw gets wired for four weeks and you lose thirty pounds from only siphoning egg creams, I'd say that's a fucking sign to change things up in your life. I'm no dummy, dummy. So, fuck me, I did.

Never went back to Los Angeles.

Never told mom that I found Liz.

Said I was mugged when ma asked about the hospital stay and medical bills.

Now, here I am. A goddamn survivor...stuck to a barstool on St. Marks Place. The Holiday Cocktail Lounge ain't so bad though. Marnie comes in most nights, and we're still neighbors; her folks lowered the rent once they heard of my unfortunate bludgeoning. Been out here long enough that I even forget about that glorious sunshine back home, my spring sandals, the weepy jacarandas. All those absorbed punches in bunches from Roy Combo made sure of that, my brain swamped with endless fog. But that's okay. You can have L.A. Ain't mine no more. Not like Amy and the kid want me around either. So, I remain in the East Village because Oscar always needs a good scratch. His owner still runs the joint too, folks bending down to claw Oscar's ears before ever acknowledging her existence. Or *mine*, for that matter. Funny how in a world plump with chaos, fine folks (like myself) ultimately get put in their place. I tap an empty Narragansett on the wood, nod to the barkeep, get off my stool and go back to work.

I barback here six days a week now. The pay is shit, but that's okay. My grandma just passed, so I'll have some inheritance coming my way. The beers are free too (most the time). You didn't think I gave up all the sauce, did you? Don't worry. I'll be just fine. Somedays, I do get scared though...that Combo might walk in here. But last I heard from Phebe, he and my sister booked it to Florida, avoiding rent. She's suing them both; calls me often to see if I've heard from them. I tell her they must've went into rehab, but I know better. I think Phebe just likes talking to me, I dunno. She's one of the good ones. I'm sure Liz and Roy are fine too—like me, a heads-up penny, a cat with ten lives or whatever. Look at me now, cruel world—dunking high ball glasses and tumblers.... Dee Dee counts to four out a speaker and I'm off: a rat marinating in a rollicking juke, bad memories and inebriated exchanges. The whiskey may no longer burn, but the beer's a damn cool breeze. *Such a fucking loser.* Oh, you think so too? Take a look in the goddamn mirror, you dunce.

ABOUT THE AUTHORS

FRANK BILL is the author of the novel *Donnybrook* and the story collection *Crimes in Southern Indiana*, one of *GQ*'s favorite books of 2011 and a *Daily Beast* best debut of 2011, as well as *The Savage, The Ravaged* (with Norman Reedus) and *Back to the Dirt* (May 2023). He lives and writes in Southern Indiana.

MICHAEL BRACKEN (www.CrimeFictionWriter.com) Anthony-, Edgar-, and Shamus-nominated, Derringer-winning writer Michael Bracken is the author of more than 1,200 short stories, including crime fiction published in *The Best American Mystery Stories* and *The Best Mystery Stories of the Year*. Additionally, he is the editor of *Black Cat Mystery Magazine* and numerous anthologies.

ALEC CIZAK is a writer and filmmaker from Indiana.

'DOC' CLANCY Inspired by classic TV, b-movies, and the pulps, "Doc" Clancy's work has appeared in *Bachelor Pad*, *Gnarly Magazine*, *Pulp Modern*, and *Worlds of Strangeness*. He is the publisher of *CAVEMAN Magazine*, a modern attempt to capture the heady mix of gripping fiction, cartoons, and nudity that made vintage men's magazines great. He can be found online at DocClancy.com and @DocClancy on Instagram and Twitter.

ERIC ESQUIVEL is a writer based in Los Angeles, California. He has written for many different clients, in many mediums, but he enjoys hacking out pulp fiction the most.

GABRIEL HART is an author, poet, and journalist from California's high desert. His recent neo-pulp story collection "Fallout From Our Asphalt Hell" and poetry volumes "UNSONGS" and "Hymns From The Whipping Post" are out now from Close To The Bone (UK). Other works can be found in Red Dog Press's GONE anthology, Expat 5, and Hobart Pulp. He's a regular contributor to Lit Reactor, Los Angeles Review of Books, and The Last Estate.

E.B. HUNTER lives in a remote town in Northern Alberta, Canada with his wife and daughter, and spends his days working and his nights crafting stories for your (and let's face it, his own) entertainment. He has built characters and stories in his head since he was a teen, and with the recent diagnosis of ADHD, he now understands why there are so many ideas that race through his mind. He hopes that these stories portray people as they are, flawed humans who are capable of great and terrible things, and that you can see yourself within his stories. He strives for representation in his storytelling, and believes that everyone's story is worth being told.

NOLAN KNIGHT is the author of *The Neon Lights Are Veins* and *Beneath the Black Palms.* A fourth generation Angeleno and former staff writer for Los Angeles' Biggest Music Publication, the *L.A. Record.* His short fiction has been featured in various publications including *Akashic Books, Thuglit, Crimespree Magazine, Shotgun Honey, Tough* and *Needle.* His new novel, *Gallows Dome*, is set for publication on 6/12/23 via Down & Out Books. He lives in Long Beach.

VERONICA LEIGH has been published in numerous anthologies, journals, and magazines. She aspires to be the Jane Austen of her generation and she makes her home in Indiana. Her blog is: http://veronicaleighauthor.wordpress.com

NEVADA MCPHERSON lives in Milledgeville, Georgia: former home of Flannery O'Connor and site of Central State Hospital, once the world's largest "lunatic asylum." She is the author of Poser and Cracker, the first two books in the neonoir series, Eucalyptus Lane, from Outcast Press. A graduate of L.S.U.'s MFA Screenwriting Program, Nevada has also written several award-winning screenplays, as well as stage plays, non-fiction pieces, graphic novels, and countless to-do lists. More about her writing and artwork can be found at her web site, www.nevada-mcpherson.com.

DANIEL PYNE is a writer whose ten films include Pacific Heights, White Sands, The Manchurian Candidate and Fracture; his career writing and showrunning in television stretches from Miami Vice to Bosch; he is the author of five novels, including Catalina Eddy (2018), Water Memory (2021) and Vital Lies (2022), Pyne lives in Los Angeles.

BRIAN TOWNSLEY is an award-winning writer, as well as a podcaster and the Executive Editor at Starlite Pulp. He is the author of three collections of poetry, as well as the Sonny Haynes crime fiction books *A Trunk Full of Zeroes* and *Outlaw Ballads*. His short fiction has appeared in various publications, including *Mystery Tribune, Quarterly West, Black Mask, Berkeley Poetry Review, Connecticut Review, Frontier Tales*, and many others, and he had a Sonny Haynes story make the distinguished list in *Best American Mystery Stories, 2019*. He is a graduate of the Professional Writing program at USC and is also an alum of the mighty California Golden Bears. He lives in Southern California.

JAMES WHELPLEY is a detective noir writer from central Texas. The short story, The Boss's Daughter, was adapted for Starlite Pulp from his full-length debut novel, *Dancing in the Trap*. The second book in this series, *Tenerife*, was released in March 2022. Whelpley cites Raymond Chandler, Dashielle Hammett, and Ross MacDonald as his biggest influences, but also John Updike and Kurt Vonnegut Jr. Whelpley is a graduate of the University of Texas at San Antonio, where he studied Early Western American Literature as well as Greek and Roman classics. He likes hot jazz and cold drinks. But who doesn't?

J. WILTZ is a playwright and short story writer from Biloxi, MS. His flash fiction piece "Dol-Hareubang" received top honors at the 2019 H.P. Lovecraft Film Festival. His short play "Do Not Collect $200" has been performed across the US. J holds a bachelor's degree in English from the University of Mississippi and an MA in American literature from the University of New Orleans. He taught English in Seoul, South Korea, for nine years before moving home at the beginning of 2020. He currently teaches in Gulfport, MS. J's interests include books, movies, boxing, brunettes, tiki culture,

Chinese food, and Pomeranians. For a more elaborate bio, please visit him online at jwiltz.com.

Also from Starlite Pulp:

Starlite Pulp Review #1

Praise for the Review:

"Pulp fiction in all its glory."

"An excellent first Review!"

"Starlite Pulp is the most exciting new publisher on the block."

Outlaw Ballads by Brian Townsley
A Sonny Haynes collection

Praise for *Outlaw Ballads*:

"Sonny Haynes deserves a seat at the bar next to Marlowe and Spade."

"Townsley takes readers on a film noir-style tour to the early '50's in Palm Springs, California, that bears little resemblance to the Los Angeles many of us know so well. The Sonny Haynes series acts as a mental time machine, and is worth every minute of the trip."

"Sonny Haynes did what other men boasted of."

Visit **Starlitepulp.com** for your pulp books, hoodies, tees, decals, submission guidelines, & so much more!

(here's to the blank page)